Virtuous Deception

Virtuous Deception

Leiann B. Wrytes

www.urbanbooks.net

Urban Books, LLC
300 Farmingdale Road, NY-Route 109
Farmingdale, NY 11735

Virtuous Deception Copyright © 2018 Leiann B. Wrytes

ISBN 13: 978-1-945855-96-2
ISBN 10: 1-945855-96-7

First Trade Paperback Printing November 2018
Printed in the United States of America

10 9 8 7 6 5 4 3 2 1

This is a work of fiction. Any references or similarities to actual events, real people, living or dead, or to real locales are intended to give the novel a sense of reality. Any similarity in other names, characters, places, and incidents is entirely coincidental.

Distributed by Kensington Publishing Corp.
Submit Orders to:
Customer Service
400 Hahn Road
Westminster, MD 21157-4627
Phone: 1-800-733-3000
Fax: 1-800-659-2436

Virtuous Deception

by

Leiann B. Wrytes

Dedication

To those that taught me how to walk with no legs, my risen angels . . . To every courageous soul that dared to love me through the ugly, whose kisses made life beautiful . . . To the two pairs of beautiful brown eyes that depend on me . . . This moment is for you.

Acknowledgments

I cannot adequately express the feeling coursing through me as I write these words. This has been such an arduous journey, and I am deeply grateful to those of you who have traveled with me. I love you all, even though some of you were unruly witnesses. LOL. We have fought, cried, played, worked, and laughed together; survived, failed, and triumphed. We have *lived*. There are things I would have done differently, but I cannot say that I regret any of it because of the wisdom I gained in the interim. I have struggled to reconcile my present self with the self I had always envisioned that I would one day be. I suffered from the loss I felt, the overwhelming sense of inadequacy as I came to terms with the fact that the little girl whose dreams stretched beyond the universe would be hard-pressed to see those dreams even reach the height of the shortest blade of grass on a freshly manicured lawn. It was a bitter pill to swallow, and it took years to get the taste out of my mouth.

Time extended itself to me and was patient while I learned to appreciate it. I am certain that prayers and love sent from afar assisted with the transition, I, alone, had to make, which emboldened me to take ownership of my life and make the changes, the necessary shifts in my mind that ultimately enabled me to get to this point. To become this woman; finally, someone that I am unashamed to be. Thank you all for the lessons, the good wishes, and the prayers that the Most High always answers. I cannot thank you enough.

Acknowledgments

To my friends, my extended family, thank you. Shaniqua, I simply could not go without our daily convo. Your words and actions have comforted me during some of my most trying times. Your friendship is invaluable. Love you, girl. Baptiste, you are my cosmic brother and one of the most talented people on the planet. Thank you for your unwavering confidence in my ability to do this. I write with you in mind. Nick, we are survivors. I apologize for ever causing you to question the sincerity of my love. You have always been a true friend to me, and I hope that you can say the same for me. Sophie, there are many things I could say, but it can all be summarized with this: I admire you. I admire you: fierce, woman, warrior, and I love you unashamedly. Lamar, you're crazy, but I love you, man. LOL. I have always been able to count on you to have my back and speak the truth. The brashness you have to be yourself permitted me to do the same. Thank you. Millionaire, King, and Davrye (the McNamara Clan), love y'all!

To the family I was born into . . . I love you. To the two souls that parented me, Keithan and LaVida, I love you. We were not perfect, and I know you both gave your best. I could not have asked for more. To my sisters, Mayesha, Rochelle, and Raq, my baby bro, Nicholas Sean . . . You four are everything! I am so very proud of you! It is an honor to be your sister. Aunt Beda . . . Thank you for your faith and for serving as a creative muse. This story happened because of you. To Jaz, thanks for reading the rough drafts! Your excitement motivated me to keep going! Uncle Henry, I cannot tell you how important you are to me. Papa and Grandma Gloria, your *Wade* wrote a book. LOL. Thank you for filling my memory with encouraging words. I love you both so very much. Goodness, there are so many, I could not possibly name you all . . . that would be a *whole otha book* but *thank you!* Singing: *"We are family . . ."* I carry each of you with me into this new phase of my life. To the man that managed to love me more than himself, the father of my two children and the sole heir to my forever: Anthony, thank you for being my rock, my friend. I love you. And to everyone that participated directly or indirectly in my growth as a woman and as a writer . . . thank you.

There are many talented people in this space we call Earth, but not everyone is granted the opportunity to fully express their divine gifts in the capacity that I have. N'Tyse, you opened the door for me to step into a *new me*. For the 15 millionth time, thank you for being so open, giving, and honest. Thank you for offering this platform and sharing your energy. AMTP will always be *home*. Indie Love, you are the most awesome. Thank you for joining the WRYTES fan club. LOL. I appreciate your hard work, time, and effort you dedicate to my vision.

Last but not least, to you, my WRYTERS, thank you for investing in me! I promise always to give you my absolute best. I sincerely appreciate you taking this time to vacate your reality and enter the one I have fashioned for you. I hope you enjoy yourself in these pages. I love you with everything I have, and a little more.

Yours truly,
Leiann B. Wrytes

Chapter 1

Lisa inhaled deeply, the cold autumn air filling her aching lungs. This moment had been a long time coming. She wondered if the earth felt her vibration; if *he* knew how much she needed this. She rose to her feet, anxiously awaiting her turn. Lisa had not intended on sharing this moment with so many, but out of all the people present, his was the only familiar face. The soft ground was porous, its delicate constitution nearly mirroring her fragile state of mind. Even in her flats, it was difficult to keep her feet from sinking into the earth during the walk. The air felt different as she drew near to his side, each step speaking to the miracle of her living. Before long, it was time as she stood beside the man she had loved. She brazenly ran her fingers across his cold, full lips, and etched them along his square jawline. He was beautiful lying there.

As tears filled her eyes, she let them roam over his six-foot frame and drink in his chocolate features. It was certainly worth the wait. His wife had chosen well; his navy blue suit was impeccable. The brother was designed for Tom Ford. She stifled a moan as memories flooded her mind. She could still *feel* him. For a moment, she longed for more time before dismissing the thought as quickly as it came. As she turned to leave, she shot a quick glance at the weeping widow. The poor girl didn't know the man she married. She chuckled at the thought and raised her face to the peeking sun. The rays highlighted her caramel complexion. A smile found its way out as she departed the funeral grounds. She sighed with relief. The bastard was dead . . . and Lisa was free.

Three weeks earlier . . .

Lisa sat on the edge of the bed and fumbled with the zipper on her dark denim jeans. She had spent the better half of the last thirty minutes vainly trying to repair it. She looked out the window and admired the view from the penthouse suite. She was impressed. The soft white sand against the beautiful blue Caribbean Sea made for a truly breathtaking scene. Charlie caught her by surprise with this, but the trip was only prolonging the inevitable. Their getaways were becoming too commonplace, risky, but Lisa could never turn down a trip to Saint Maarten. She felt like the air wrapped itself around her there. She could only guess that was why Charlie suggested it.

Charlie began as a random Instagram snapshot, and it would've ended with their drunken dance beneath sheets had Lisa not received a special request every day for three weeks. Though she should have probably been alarmed by the persistent, nearly stalker vibe, she was turned on by it, instead. Giving up on zipping her jeans, Lisa walked out onto the balcony. There was something about the water that gave her peace. She lost her thoughts in the waves. Frank. She was missing Frank, her husband. For a second, she wondered how she had arrived at this intersection in her life, a point where no available direction seemed optimal.

Lisa hoped it was not too late to go back. Charlie might have had her singing a sweet melody in the early-morning hours, but Charlie was no Frank. Frank alone had the power to alter her soul if he cared enough to try. Lisa loved Frank, but he failed her. Frank lost his ambition, his drive. She had big plans before she met Frank. Plans before her heart nestled with his and on the eve of the big "4-0," she felt like her life was losing its hue. Frank had only managed to provide her with moments of greatness when she wanted a lifetime.

Those two words, "I do," changed everything. They changed Frank. Frank was a six-foot-four bronzed demigod. He was gorgeous, and for two decades, she'd been waiting for her husband to wow her, waiting for the all-consuming fire that she dreamed her marriage would be. Frank was the kind of man movies were made of, the kind that melted in your mouth. She just knew her life would be amazing, but that fire never really blazed. The memory was still fresh; still hurt. After only one week of marital bliss, Frank made a decision that changed their lives forever.

The Masons weren't ready to be parents, and since they had planned to honeymoon for a year via a private cruise around the world, they were obviously aware of this truth. Their parentage was a stipulation, a business move. It may have seemed cruel, heartless, but their lifestyle was one they individually and, in this case, collectively, went to great lengths to maintain. Frank proposed after a mere three months of dating, but Lisa didn't mind. She was relieved. Lisa Raine had plans for that 20 million; falling in love simply sweetened the deal. A chill tickled the skin, her black lace spaghetti strap, top left, exposed, causing the tiny hairs covering it to rise, but it wasn't the warm island wind that made her hold her arms for comfort. It was the thought of that day. Lisa would never forget it.

Mr. and Mrs. Mason went to meet with their attorney and friend, Jacob Wilson, expecting to sign a few papers to finalize the acquisition of Frank's inheritance. They *were anxious to begin their happily ever after when Wilson revealed an unexpected brick wall:*

The money would be released upon the birth of a child.

Lisa felt like she'd been blindsided by an armored truck. Had she not been sitting, she would have fainted with the news. Frank was stoic, however, like he'd known all along. The happy couple rode home in silence. *They had never discussed children—ever, but it wasn't the news of the child that now turned her stomach into knots. It was Frank's reaction. Frank didn't speak a word for nearly a week, not even hello or good-bye. Lisa still wasn't privy to the details, but one day, Frank came home with a new baby girl. In the blink of an eye, everything changed. Lisa grew to love Brianna, but women generally had nine months to prepare mentally, emotionally, and physically for motherhood.*

Frank gave her twenty-four hours.

He was cold, calculating. Too much for her comfort. The shimmer that she was accustomed to seeing was missing from his hazel eyes when he told her about the adoption. Every fiber of her being screamed out that something was amiss, but she made her peace with it and raised Brianna with all the love she could muster. There was no way she was walking away from her new life. She tried her best to give Brianna what she had not been afforded as a child. Though her many efforts to conceive with Frank had not been rewarded, she was proud of the intelligent young woman Brianna had become. Frank, however grand a father, had grown to be an absent husband over the years. He had slowly disappeared and withdrew from their marriage, a few broken promises at a time.

At the budding of the Mason family, the three would travel together. They shopped in Milan and vacationed in Paris. Brianna had been to Italy, Greece, and Egypt before she turned five years old. *They spent countless nights in exotic places. Once Brianna reached school age, they slowed down, traveled less, and eventually stopped altogether. Frank would go months without even touching Lisa, barely showing any interest. His every waking hour was consumed with Brianna. Although Lisa was not the jealous type, long stints of celibacy were cancerous to a marriage.*

On the contrary, she enjoyed the time they spent together as a family. Frank seemed to come back to life whenever Brianna was in the room. Lisa recalled a rare twinkle in his eye, and in those flashes, a hint of the man she married would push forth. It gave her hope that perhaps all wasn't lost, but those times were too infrequent for her tastes. There was only so much a woman could take before she drafted a new plan. For the next sixteen years, Lisa worked her plan: she'd give him what he needed and get what he wouldn't give her elsewhere . . . anywhere.

Lost in her thoughts, Lisa didn't hear Charlie come in and nearly leaped from the balcony at the feel of a gentle hand on the small of her back. Startled, she turned to meet Charlie's gaze and immediately felt naked underneath those doelike eyes. She quickly offered her lips to quiet her own questions. Charlie was not an imposing figure at five foot nine and a mere 130 pounds, but there was something that was always present in their time together that jarred Lisa. Charlie seemed to know things about Lisa that were only known to a select few. Charlie took her by the hand and led her to the bed—Lisa pushed the implications out of her mind. There was no way Charlie could know the truth.

Was there?

Chapter 2

"Armand, *get out!*"

"MK, I don't want to argue, OK? Just hear me out, please?" Armand pleaded.

Armand had never seen Michelle this upset and, frankly, it worried him. He slowly twisted the diamond-encrusted platinum band on his finger, ridding it of the sweat that coated his large hands. Nothing rattled Armand. Life had shaped his mind to anticipate, acclimate, and execute. Reality had caught him by surprise only once in his life, and the band was a constant reminder. It was the only symbol of a mother's love he owned, and the only piece of jewelry he wore; in this way, they traveled together. He carried that memory with him. His fiddling with it clearly showed that the situation with Michelle had really gotten to him.

There were things about Armand that Michelle Kaye had not been aware. Some of which, if divulged, would nullify this argument, but releasing that information could put Michelle at greater risk. His employers had a reputation that gave him access, and the freedom, to run in circles that could be dangerous for the average man. Lately, he had found it increasingly difficult to meet the requirements of the task he was hired to do. Though his employers had never threatened him, he did not think they would respond well to his failure. His moves were a calculated attempt to soften their expectation and buy him more time to sort it all out. Things had been going as expected. Armand had been very careful not to take things too far, but Sheila's antics rubbed Michelle the wrong way, and she was clearly on the verge of exploding. If he were a lesser man, he'd find that five-foot-six, fake-ass Taraji P. Henson and reshape her face. Not only did she fail to avoid Michelle as she left their condo—as instructed—but she ran into her, literally.

Michelle had pulled into the garage and parked in her usual spot. She gathered her things, safeguarded her Audi with the key fob, visually mapped out the quickest path through the maze of cars to the elevator, and started her trek. She began mentally preparing for the meeting scheduled with a potential client with mechanized precision, though it was still a few hours away, as she leisurely made her way to the elevator leading up to her condo. She weaved her way between the rows of cars, easily navigating the cold terrain of tires and plastic . . . when something grabbed her attention.

She paused to lay eyes on the owner of the shoulder-length blond, wavy weave whose whip action had interrupted her thoughts. Michelle felt an immediate familiarity that both intrigued and annoyed her. Even though several rows of cars separated them, Michelle was certain she knew her and could not help but stare as she sashayed through the parking lot. *Click, click, click . . .* The sound echoed off the walls marking each moment her heels connected with the cement floor. Michelle deviated from her route and opted for one that would allow her to walk by the woman, permitting her to get a closer look at her face. She was so focused on the girl that she failed to notice the car idling by with its reverse lights on. As

Michelle got close enough to get a decent look, the driver suddenly gunned the engine and quickly backed out of its parking spot. To avoid being hit, Michelle quickly scurried to the left, placing her directly in the woman's path. Ol' girl, unfortunately, was not paying attention, and the two collided.

Michelle fell to the ground and immediately started choking on the heavy fragrance that dwarfed her. Rather than assisting Michelle, the woman stood over her, brooding, showcasing her Manolo pumps that were visibly poised to strike. Michelle sprang to her feet, and the two engaged in an epic visual battle worthy of a heavyweight boxing ring. The hostility in the air was so thick that the large, three-tier parking garage felt like a broom closet. Ol' girl's purple contacts did little to dull the razor-sharp edge of the daggers she threw in Michelle's direction. Though she was taken aback by the animosity, Michelle stood her ground.

She had not lifted a finger to strike anyone in her life, but she was prepared to hit this chick, if necessary. The menacing glare painted on ol' girl's facial landscape hinted at the aggression waiting to be unleashed on Michelle, but surprisingly, *she* rolled her eyes, issued an awkward apology, and continued on her way. Michelle did not respond. She stood, transfixed, with a look of shock and confusion on her face. Why did this woman give her the evil eye? She took some deep breaths to regain her composure and inhaled another dose of the lingering fragrance the woman wore, which ignited a coughing fit all over again.

With slow, steady steps, Michelle made her way to the elevator leading up to her condo. Her breathing returned to its natural rhythm as she tried to make sense of the exchange. As she reached out to press the button to open the doors, the answer suspended her movement. She took a deep breath and inhaled the familiar scent. It was Armand's signature Polo Double Black cologne; ol' girl must have bathed in it. Images of ol' girl and Armand flashed through her mind, searing her memory. Michelle realized why she had looked so familiar: she had viewed her mug several times in the surveillance footage of her condo.

The realization hit her with the force of a sledgehammer. Michelle now understood why she had looked at her that way . . . She must have recognized Michelle from the various pictures hanging around the home. The same home that was leased to Michelle; the same home she shared with Armand. The same home she must have exited only moments before. The fine hairs on her arms stood in response to the swell of anger rising within her. She turned in a huff, nearly knocking to the ground a gentleman who had been patiently waiting behind her, sprinting back into the main area of the parking garage. She searched for the video vixen but could not find her. Livid, she took the stairs up to the condo and confronted Armand. Michelle's fury intensified as the scene replayed in her mental theater.

"This is *not* up for discussion," she seethed.

Armand found himself in an untenable situation. He did not want to lose Michelle, but he did not know how to repair the damage without blowing up the spot. Sheila was not supposed to confront or have any contact with Michelle. He had been explicitly clear on that point. All she had to do was arrive, be seen, and leave from the front door. Any qualms she had about that should have been addressed *before* she accepted his cash. He had gambled and lost. He was out of a thousand dollars, but more importantly, Michelle was up in the air. He never had a woman push his buttons like Michelle did; never had a woman that made him care. He didn't want to risk losing everything by telling her the truth too soon, deciding, instead, to let things play out and hope for the best.

"MK, I am trying here, but you knew my situation, and you said you could handle it."

Michelle collapsed into the plush, plum-colored chair and stared out the window into the street, refusing to meet his stare. She was amazed at the absurdity of the situation, ultimately resigning herself to the truth of it. She *did* know the kind of man he was, but she still expected some decorum. Michelle knew Armand would be trouble for her from the first moment she laid eyes on him coming out of Club Karma. Every step he made toward her spelled T-R-O-U-B-L-E in slow motion. Michelle was not the club type. She was pumping gas at the 7-Eleven across the street and found herself staring shamelessly at this man. Armand was a six-foot-two blend of French aristocracy and African rhythm. With his curly hair shaped by a fresh tapered fade, piercing light gray eyes, and a commercial-worthy smile, Michelle was helpless to defend herself. Though that night they only spoke long enough to exchange contact information, they had been inseparable ever since. That was two years ago.

Armand sat on the chaise directly across from Michelle, hoping to at least get her to reason with him. "I didn't know she would try to come at you."

"Is *that* supposed to make me feel better, Armand? I need you to leave."

"MK . . . Nothing happened. I need you to trust me."

"*Leave. Now.* This isn't working, Armand. It doesn't feel right, and I need some space." Michelle was done talking and wanted to be alone.

"MK, will you please look at me?"

Michelle rejected his appeal. His gaze was laced with kryptonite, and she did not want to grow weak beneath it as she had so many times before. Armand exposed a vulnerable layer in her that not even she was aware of, and she grappled with what it meant each time she felt its power. He opened her mind, journeyed the length of her person, and planted some part of himself deep within her soul. She enjoyed their closeness but despised it at the same time.

She continued staring out the window and into the street. The sidewalk was unusually crowded for this time of the evening, but the black sedan was eerily visible. She had seen the same sedan parked out there, in various places along her street, for the last several months, trailing her to the supermarket, the mall, and other random places. The sedan, which seemed to have no owner, no tickets, and ultimately, no history whatsoever. She wished she didn't have to do this with Armand right now. She could really use his help.

"Just go. Please leave. I need some space."

"MK, you know how much I care about you. Don't push me away."

Armand did care a great deal about Michelle. Her soft vanilla coating perfectly accentuated her five-foot-seven, slim frame. She had long black hair that came to rest just above her small, tight derrière. Michelle was a true beauty, but that's not what kept Armand around. She was the only woman that he could trust. He shared things with her that he had never said aloud to anyone. She was all the family he had. Armand simply couldn't give Michelle what she was asking for, at least, not yet.

Michelle rubbed her hands nervously along her pant leg, struggling, but eventually resolving to say what she felt. Feeling confident in her decision, she turned to face Armand and adamantly stated, "If you love me as you say you do . . . leave me alone until you are ready to *be* the man you *pretend* to be." With that, she stood and disappeared into the bedroom.

Armand strangled the urge to protest and thought that perhaps this time he could finally give her what she wanted. He loved her just enough to do it . . . even if it cost him his life.

Chapter 3

Michelle lay across her sleigh bed, lost in her feelings, wrapped in her lavender-colored feather comforter awaiting Armand's departure. She closed her eyes and gave way to the blackness resting just behind them, while the unconventional nature of their connection perforated her sensibilities and forced into question her judgment. This process, with more miles than she would like to admit, was not an unfamiliar one. The effort she exerted trying to make sense of it, their wayward love affair, left her with a kind of emptiness. A void that, she reasoned, would take much more than an ordinary viable explanation to even attempt to fill. It was not her beau's improbable infidelity that caused her emotions to swarm. The video footage from the security cameras substantiated his claims of innocence and had long thwarted any urge she had to end things prematurely. His bizarre desire to conduct himself as though he weren't innocent, however, that kept up the emotional upheaval within her.

Michelle considered herself to be a reasonably level-headed young woman but had somehow gotten finagled into being a willing participant in the insanity that characterized her love life. She could only imagine the number of Emmys she could have collected over the last year for her performances. Like the parade of women suggesting Armand's unfaithfulness, Michelle's hurt, the anger, and to some degree, even the distrust, was all for the stage lights. The fact that he needed this argument, this dysfunction, and this girl had infuriated Michelle.

Michelle had decided that ol' girl would be the first—and last—interaction she would have. Her demeanor had not exuded amity, and there was something in the way she tried to drill holes into Michelle's being that provided provocation for Michelle to attack the situation with an alacrity she lacked before. Moderation had been paramount in her ability to manage her reactions and affording her patience. Armand seemed to know intuitively where the boundary was and never crossed it, but this interaction was the tipping point.

The abhorrence colligating in the pit of her stomach confirmed her decision. It was time for her to focus on getting to the root of the issue and put an end to the charade. Armand was hiding something, and Michelle's investigative nature superseded her feminine instinct. She opted to play the part of the disheveled, unsuspecting girlfriend to find out what it was. Uncovering secrets was her business, her bread and butter, and there was no way she was going to let Armand keep his.

Armand was a *pretty boy* by most standards, and women fawned over him everywhere he went, whether it was the grocery store, gas station, or a trip to the Dumpster. Michelle was accustomed to getting the occasional hate, but the degree that these women took it to was ridiculous. She has had her car keyed, tailpipe stuffed, tires slashed, and had even been accosted in a bathroom at a restaurant. The craziness took some getting used to, but after a few self-defense classes, trips to the gun range, and some additional security features to her home, Michelle was fine. As much as it may have pained her to admit, she loved Armand LaCroix and was willing to deal with his psychotic groupies to be with him.

Pop. The main door slammed shut, confirming Armand's departure. Michelle emerged from the large bedroom and entered the room across the hall. She had converted the bedroom into a home office of sorts.

The expansive apartment had been her first grown woman move. She returned home after graduating from Rice University with a B.A. in journalism and spent months scouring the city for the perfect residence until she had finally settled on this one. She did not consider herself an interior designer by any stretch of the imagination, but she was pleasantly surprised at the amount of fun she had covering the walls of the three-bedroom townhome with art pieces capturing the Harlem Renaissance era. The likes of Jacob Lawrence and other notable artists of the time, such as Charles Alston and Henry Bannarn, adorned her walls.

Her father had referred to her as an "old soul," and she supposed that must be true. She had a quiet fascination with the past, especially the creative aspects of it. Artistic expression seemed completely unrestricted. There was an element of freedom present in the work of a creative mind that was not limited by moral constructs or capitalist motivations. Michelle sought to surround herself with their beauty. To taste, even in small doses, that liberty. She fancied herself akin to them and consciously tried to emulate their lives.

She wanted to mimic, not the manner in which they lived, but the essence of it, at least what they captured in their works: to live without inhibition. Her office housed her massive book collection, consisting of nearly 600 books amassed since childhood. She loved to read and research. The pages of a book kept her company during her adolescence and had been more faithful than any friend she could think of. Her profession, both as a journalist and an investigator, had been a natural path for her.

It was almost two o'clock in the afternoon now. She had a meeting in half an hour, and, as custom dictated, she reviewed her notes a bit more to be sure she was prepared. She was not very fond of surprises, especially in her line of work. She accepted that there would be some here and there, but she never entered into a situation without giving every conceivable angle the once-over.

Michelle might have been a successful freelance journalist if she focused and wrote consistently, but she simply could not. Her fascination with solving mysteries sparked her interest in journalism, but she found that her small private investigation business, in operation for only two months, had captivated her attention like nothing else had before. Being twenty-three years young and financially secure allowed her the freedom to fill her days with things that invigorated her. She had yet to dabble in anything comparable to the lure of unraveling a good mystery. To date, most of Michelle's cases were regarding adultery and nanny spying but never anything dangerous. She ran a simple ad on craigslist, which read: *I'll provide the truth in pictures. Send your requests to revealthetruth@gmail.com.*

Michelle got enough responses to keep her busy, and her rate varied according to the difficulty of the assignment. Recently, she received an e-mail from Brianna Mason, requesting her services regarding her boyfriend. She wanted to confirm whether he was seeing other women. Michelle had asked a few basic questions to get an idea of the type of person she would be working for. She had learned that Brianna, after interning throughout her college career, boldly started her own marketing company and had already landed her first high-dollar client. She was the only child of a rich, well-to-do family, and had been dating the guy in question for a few months. Michelle thought the request to be a little odd, considering they had only been together a short while, but Brianna had offered to pay three times Michelle's normal rate. Michelle was not walking away from that money.

The prominent lesson Michelle had learned since the launch of her business was that the client, more than the subject, was likely to confound her tasks. Her last client had gotten physical with her because she declined to comply with a request. The incident had forced Michelle to be even more selective. Michelle was a professional snoop, but even she had boundaries. Following a husband suspected of "freaking deacons" into a public restroom to snap pics was definitely beyond them. This particular assignment seemed simple enough, though. Brianna did not strike her like the violent type, but she still needed to get a feel for her before she would accept the job.

Michelle grabbed her purse, iPad Air, iPhone 5, and headed to Panera Bread. The restaurant where she would meet her new client was only twenty minutes from where she lived, and she wanted to arrive before her client did. The traffic was light, and she managed to make it with ten minutes to spare. As soon as she opened the door, her senses were overwhelmed with the tantalizing scent of freshly baked bread and sweet apple pie. She hadn't planned on ordering anything, but the slightly audible sounds of protest from her stomach changed her mind.

She stopped briefly at the counter, placed her order, and took her seat to wait for Brianna. She loved this quaint restaurant. It reminded her of her mother's Southern undertones. Despite its being a national chain, it still produced a level of intimacy and personality missing from most. Michelle was in the midst of enjoying a warm cup of skinny café mocha when Brianna arrived.

Suddenly, Michelle rubbed her eyes and shook her head frantically. She had to be seeing things. She looked away—and then looked back. Terror brought her heart to a standstill. Uncertainty shadowed every thought. Michelle was watching what felt like a mirror image of *herself* walking into the restaurant, but how was that possible? Was this real? Was she having an out-of-body experience? Her sudden befuddlement left her without words. She looked fretfully around the restaurant to see if anyone else saw what she saw. She pinched herself and winced slightly from the brief sting. No, she was not dreaming; this was definitely happening. She watched the woman as she walked cautiously toward her with a facial expression mirroring her own.

Brianna, usually a social butterfly, could not utter a word once she spotted the woman sitting at the third table from the back, per their arrangement, and took her seat in the booth opposite her. She wanted to say something—anything—but her communication prowess had abandoned her. Finally, Michelle broke the silence.

"Are you Brianna Mason?"

Brianna, eyes wide with disbelief, nodded her head slowly in confirmation.

Michelle's mind was all over the place as she searched for some explanation, inwardly rereading her notes and skimming their e-mail correspondence, but found nothing that would have prepared her for this. Brianna's e-mail wasn't out of the ordinary. There was nothing in it that suggested that after meeting *her,* that Michelle's world would be changed forever.

"You have my face," Michelle whispered. She was not directing it toward Brianna but rather stating it as a matter of fact. She verbalized what they had both been thinking. She had been an only child for twenty-three years. Who was this woman? Michelle felt like a little child. She didn't know what to do, say, or even how to feel. She placed her hands firmly under her buttocks. It was all she could do to keep them from stretching across the table to touch the unimaginable. This moment was the most tangible impossible had ever been.

Brianna was as bemused as Michelle. She hammered her fist on the table's surface. The hasty clamor jolted Michelle out of her trance. She reacted too quickly and wound up banging her knees underneath the table. A customer stumbled walking by, nearly falling to the ground with a tray of food, also startled by the abrupt noise. Michelle scrunched her nose as the stabbing pain spread from her patella, down her femur, coating her toes, and back. She gave Brianna an even more perplexed look.

"Sorry, I just . . . this is . . ." Brianna stuttered. She didn't know what to say. She was not even sure why she did that. Perhaps she thought the sound of the thud or sharpness of the pain would wake her up from whatever *this* was. Perhaps she was floating, and the bang would bring her down, but nothing changed. She was still staring at herself across the table. She didn't know if she wanted to hug her or hit her.

Michelle's smoked turkey sandwich arrived without incident, but her appetite had left her. She didn't even greet the mild-mannered server that carefully placed the plate in front of her. Sensing the tension at the table, the server hastily exited without bothering to offer Brianna anything.

The situation was surreal. It was like looking into a mirror; a walking, talking, breathing reflection of each other. They sat in silence in the booth for a while, unable to speak. Too many emotions were swirling. Too many questions.

For the two of them, life stopped as they both tried to make sense of the moment.

"I don't know what to say, Brianna. I never knew. I wasn't told . . ."

"Me, either. I had no clue."

"When's your birthday?"

"April second."

"Mine too. What time?" Michelle felt silly asking these questions. The answer seemed so obvious, but she still felt the urge to ask. It was almost like she needed to hear it out loud before she could accept it.

"I don't know. Around three o'clock. I think 3:04 a.m."

"I guess I'm the elder at 3:02 am." Michelle looked out the window and took a deep breath. She wanted to be happy, but she couldn't shake the ugliness of their union. Her parents had lied to her, and that fact was difficult to stomach. "Where do you live? I live near downtown, only a few minutes from here."

Brianna cleared her throat, but like the rest of her mouth, it was as dry as the Sahara, and the action offered her no relief. Her mental highway was a traffic jam, and she was not sure if anything could provide that relief. "I live out in Austin Ranch."

Darn it. Why was this happening? Brianna didn't want to answer any questions or talk at all. She wanted to run from the restaurant and put this entire ordeal behind her. The only problem was that her legs felt like cement blocks. She didn't have strength enough to move, no matter how much she wanted to. She was stuck.

"Have you always lived here?"

"Yes, aside from when I was away at college. You?"

This woman, whose personality and history were foreign to her, would not be disregarded. She could not ignore her. Brianna couldn't be rude to her without feeling like she was giving herself the shaft!

"Same. I cannot believe I have never seen you. I mean, I know this is a big city, but still . . ."

Michelle was filling the space between them with chatter, anything to avoid returning to that uncomfortable silence. Their obvious similarities made any questions futile. Brianna was inarguably her identical twin.

As their conversation grew, the typical movements in a restaurant became a distraction. They both needed quiet. Needed time to think and process everything. They ventured into the parking lot to continue their conversation.

"I'm looking at you, but it's still hard to digest." The energy between them was almost painful. Michelle's free spirit immediately embraced the peculiar closeness she felt to Brianna, who, despite their obvious kinship, was a complete stranger.

"I know. I cannot help but think . . . We might have never found each other if I hadn't e-mailed you." Brianna was dumbfounded, crippled by her inability to accept this new truth. She had come to get information on Javan, not her family, and certainly had not expected to discover she had a twin sister.

"I'm glad you did. I haven't even had my business that long. This was some cosmic coincidence."

"Well, someone actually referred me to your company, but the stars seemed to have aligned perfectly for this."

"Who referred you?"

Brianna's mind drifted off for a moment. She wondered if Uncle J knew about this. She hadn't thought much of his insistence on using this company before, but there was something there. He had been fairly adamant about it, and, although it didn't strike her as unusual at the time, in retrospect, his sudden passion and vigor were unwarranted for a little boyfriend inquiry. What if he had known all these years?

"My uncle J recommended you. He kind of insisted that I use you."

"Do you think he may know something?"

"I don't know, but I'm definitely going to ask."

Brianna and Michelle stood in the parking lot beside Michelle's 2013 black Audi, sharing their histories and discussing the future. They had the same almond-shaped brown eyes, same shoulder-length, jet-black hair, and the same honey-glazed covering. They searched for answers that inevitably led to more questions and eventually decided to call it a night. They exchanged phone numbers and went their separate ways but agreed to talk very soon.

Michelle drove home in shock. She could not believe she had a twin sister. She was not certain what that meant to her. Did that mean *she* was adopted? She decided to call her mother and try to get some answers.

"Mom?"

"Michelle, hey, *Number One!* How are you, love?"

"Fine, Mom." Michelle smiled faintly at the familiar sound of her mother's voice. Apprehension crept into her heart, and she momentarily lost her nerve and thought it better not to ask. Sophie was her rock, and if it turned out that she was not her mom, Michelle did not know what she would do. She could barely stand the thought.

"I'm not convinced of that. You need to come see me." Sophie's joy was evident in her tone. She always enjoyed hearing from Michelle.

"I'll be over there as soon as I can, Mom."

"Okay. It'll be good to lay my eyes on you."

"I love you too, Mom." Michelle let the line grow silent.

Sophie could tell something was bothering her daughter. The ridiculously chipper tone that she was so accustomed to hearing was missing from her voice. Whatever the issue was, she couldn't force it out. Michelle had always been stubborn, and Sophie had learned long ago to be patient with her, although she hated every minute of it.

"Michelle—"

"I have a quick question." Michelle teetered around her query, briefly considering whether this was something she wanted to discuss over the phone. It felt a little tacky, but she was desperate for an answer. "Mom, was I adopted?" Michelle blurted it out before she lost her nerve again.

"Adopted? What are you talking about, *Number One?*" Sophie understood the words, but she was confused by the question.

"Are you my mother?"

"Yes. Of course, I am. Why would you ever question that? Is this why you're upset?"

Michelle dillydallied a bit before she answered. She and Brianna had decided to keep their *discovery* to themselves.

"I just . . . I read an article recently, and it got me thinking, that's all."

"What could you have read that made you think you were adopted?" Sophie sounded calm, but inside she was screaming. Inside, her heart was beating so hard she thought it might break open her chest.

"It doesn't matter. It was simply a question, Mom. I just got home. I'm going to lose you in the garage."

"All right, Michelle, I love you, and we can talk later, okay?" Sophie sighed with relief. This was not the right time to have *that* conversation.

"Yes, ma'am. Love you too."

Michelle pulled into the garage, parked, and trudged upstairs to her condo. She dropped her tablet on the couch and wandered into her bedroom. She had never known her mother to lie to her. She didn't necessarily believe that she was, but she had to be. There was no other explanation. This woman was her twin sister, and she was raised to believe that she was an only child. She had no siblings. Michelle stripped down to her Vickie Secrets and crawled into bed. She was done thinking for the night. Perhaps a good night's rest would help her sort things out.

Chapter 4

Brianna woke up bright and early that Tuesday. She looked out her window and feasted on the beauty of the day. It looked like a normal day. Perhaps she had dreamed everything. She didn't *feel* like she had learned any life-altering news in the past several hours. Brianna shook her head and smiled, feeling slightly relieved at the notion of it being an awkward nightmare. But when she picked up her phone and saw she had a missed call from Michelle, she knew she had not been dreaming. Brianna had a twin sister.

Her family was not perfect, and she suspected her parents had kept things from her, but never in a million years would she have guessed that they would hide something like this. She had tried calling Uncle J last night, but she couldn't reach him. She hoped that he would call her back and shed some light on everything. Thinking about it made her anxious. She crawled out of her bed and went into the kitchen to fix breakfast. Brianna did not have an appetite, but cooking was therapeutic for her. Something about the methodology of it helped her to settle down.

After she ate and showered, she felt a bit better. She plopped down on her couch and prepared to give Michelle a call. She stared at her Android phone for several minutes and contemplated the implication of making the call. Absurd as it may have been, she felt that calling Michelle made things a little too real, and she simply was not sure if she was ready to do that.

She tossed the phone in anger, rejecting the idea that the family she had known all of her life had been a complete fabrication, watching the phone land at the end of the sofa. She was averse to believe her dad would lie to her about something so important. He would not do it; he loved her too much to lie to her. She picked up the remote and started flipping through channels. *Love Jones* was showing on TV One. Perfect. She always loved that movie, and she had turned to it in time to revisit her favorite line:

"When people who have been together a long time say that the romance is gone, what they're really saying is they've exhausted the possibility."

It never got old. Brianna stretched out and got comfortable. Two minutes passed, and she felt her foot vibrating. It was her cell phone. She let it go to voice mail, and five minutes later, it vibrated again.

"Ah!" Brianna was irritated and not in the mood to talk to anyone. She sat up and grabbed her phone. It was Michelle calling. Michelle may have been the last person Brianna wanted to speak with. While it was unfair to blame Michelle, she needed to hold someone responsible, and her newly found "sister" was an easy target. She held the phone in her hand until it stopped vibrating, but it wasn't long before Michelle called a third time. There would be no avoiding her.

"Hello?"

"Hi, I've been trying to call you." Michelle did not like stating the obvious, but Brianna made her feel weird or at least talking to her did.

"I saw I missed you. Did you need something?" Brianna was angry, and it was evident in her tone. She could hear her heart beating energetically in her ears. What was *wrong* with her? Michelle didn't do anything wrong. She had been blindsided too.

"I need the truth." Michelle had not slept all night. She tossed and turned. She couldn't settle her mind. Why had this happened? She needed to figure this out. As much as she may have been opposed to the idea, especially after hearing the poorly disguised vexation laced in Brianna's voice, she needed Brianna's help.

Brianna considered Michelle's words: *the truth.* Brianna wanted to pretend that she didn't care about the truth. Pretend that she could go on with her life as if none of this had happened, but she couldn't hide her head in the sand. She needed answers as badly as Michelle. "Do you want to come over and talk?"

Michelle was glad that Brianna wasn't fighting her. She was grateful the energy between them seemed to be changing. "Sure, can you text me your address?"

"I just sent it. I'll see you in thirty?"

"See you in thirty."

Brianna immediately e-mailed her assistant and advised that she would not be in for the remainder of the week. There would be no way she could put this out of her mind enough to focus at work and decided it was best that she just stay home. She tossed her phone on the sofa, fully intending to return to her movie, but she was no longer paying attention. Even sexy-ass Darius couldn't distract her from what she had just done. Brianna felt tears forming in the corner of her eyes as the realization sank deeper and deeper into her psyche, changing her identity in a traumatic fashion. The future was on its way to her house, a future that drew her parents' faces in pencil, making them accessible to change, and her twin's face in ink, the new permanent fixture. She was not sure if she wanted any of this, but it was happening, regardless of whether she liked it.

***

Brianna and Michelle were seated on the floor in front of the couch combing through their pasts. They had been at it for hours, looking at all the documents they could find, which weren't many, to try to put their broken history together. Neither of them had any real concrete answers, and they were beginning to feel the angst of frustration.

"Crap!" Michelle screamed. "This is so aggravating."

Brianna slapped her forehead and fell back on the couch. She was feeling pressed too. They had not been able to find anything tying them to each other. They compared their birth certificates, and, although the parental information varied, the hospital, date, and time were essentially the same. From that, they were able to confirm they were from Dallas. The "adoption" was obviously private because there was no traceable record of it. It was as though they were born into these families. Each document they came across suggested they were suffering from some form of dementia. Brianna would have sworn she dreamed it all if Michelle had not been beside her.

Brianna closed her eyes and took a deep breath. The whole thing was preposterous. Neither of them had any concrete answers, and she was running out of suggestions. "Maybe we should just confront them."

Michelle shook her head no. "I asked my mom last night, and she told me I was not adopted. They could have told us at any time, but they didn't. Somebody is lying."

"Obviously. The question is why. Why would someone intentionally do this?"

Michelle shrugged her shoulders. "I don't know, but I think we should keep them out of it until we find out more."

"We don't even know what we're looking for, Michelle."

"That may be true, but whatever it is . . . They are not telling us."

Brianna did not like the idea. Not one bit.

"I know, but they couldn't possibly lie in our faces," Brianna stated, swinging her finger from her face to Michelle's in a dramatic fashion. "I mean, come on, *really?*"

Brianna's point was valid, and it was not one that had escaped Michelle's construct. Michelle simply did not like confrontation. She, in fact, avoided it at every turn. She preferred a more subtle approach and wanted to get as many facts as she could before any accusations were thrown around.

"I think it would be better to wait until we have a little more information. It'll give them less wiggle room."

Brianna was not convinced that they needed anything more than their faces side by side, but she didn't mind trying it Michelle's way. This was her profession, after all.

"I asked my friend to keep an eye on them. Hopefully, he'll come up with something."

"Does he work for you often?"

"No, but I trust him, and I don't want to risk someone spotting me. It's better that he be the one snooping around this time." Michelle was not comfortable with spying on their parents, but she didn't see any other way to get some answers.

Either their parents knew and had intentionally hidden it, or they didn't know and would have the same questions they had. They needed to solve the puzzle without interference. Michelle had come up with the bright idea of getting a DNA test to see what kind of twins they were, fraternal versus identical. She saw Tia and Tamera do it on an episode of their reality show. Ironically, as much as she used to love their hit sitcom on the WB, *Sister Sister,* she hated that she was now living it.

Michelle was excited about finding out the results of the test, but Brianna remained indifferent. While Michelle had fully and completely embraced their sisterhood, Brianna was still resistant.

Brianna was trying not to stress out completely, but she was feeling overwhelmed by it all. Javan, *her splackavellie*, as she liked to call him, had been blowing up her phone and that did not help matters. She knew he was probably upset with her for ignoring his calls, but she didn't feel like talking to him. She needed some space, and he had been a little clingy lately. There was no way she was talking to him if he was upset; he would never let her off the phone. She and Michelle hung out for a few more hours, swapping stories and getting to know each other before she went home. Brianna was emotionally drained and passed out on the sofa shortly after. She didn't know what they would find, but she was certain she would not like it.

Chapter 5

Michelle sat down behind the large oak desk and opened her MacBook to check her e-mail. The wood floor creaked, offering its familiar grooves as her ergonomically designed chair rolled into place. It had been a few days since she visited with Brianna, and they had gotten a little closer. They were creating a new normal for themselves and getting more comfortable. She could tell that Brianna still had her guard up a little, but it didn't matter. They were both victims, and she honestly couldn't decipher what enabled her to adapt so quickly. She glanced over the usual suspects: responses to her PI ad, alerts from the video feed, and newsletters from various subscriptions, et cetera. Nothing special.

Ding dong. The doorbell sounded, interrupting her thoughts. Puzzled, she closed the computer and considered answering the door. Perhaps whoever it was would leave. She was not expecting company and was not in a hostess-type mood.

Ding dong. It rang again. Whoever it was wasn't going anywhere. Maybe Armand forgot his key. It was unlikely but not impossible.

Ding dong.

"I'm coming!"

She headed down the hall and around the corner to the front door. The back entrance, where she'd run into Armand's playmate earlier during the week, did not have that obnoxious doorbell. "Who is it?"

"I have a package for a Ms. Lewis," the stranger's voice announced. Michelle didn't remember ordering anything.

"Just a minute." She felt the back of her jeans for her iPhone and quickly signed into her security account. Sure enough, there was a delivery truck parked outside her stoop. No sedan in sight. Michelle turned the lock and opened the door.

"Sorry for the trouble, but this was my third and last attempt this week. There were express instructions for it to be delivered. Will you please sign here?"

"That's fine, Karl," Michelle said, straining to read his name tag in the evening light.

"Thank you."

"It's a little late for you to make deliveries, isn't it?"

"Like I said, ma'am, there were express instructions for it to be delivered."

Michelle took the envelope and closed the door behind her. She wandered over to the chaise and opened the package. She couldn't believe her eyes. She got the feeling that this may be something she needed to share with Brianna immediately, but she'd do a little legwork on it first. No need to get her hopes up if it's nothing, but if it's something . . . It could change everything.

Again.

Chapter 6

Frank did not understand what was happening. He felt his world closing in on him. Saturdays were supposed to be his time with Brianna, but now he would have this on his mind. Lisa had betrayed him. Next to his daughter, she was the best thing that had ever happened to him, and he did not want to believe she had done this. Frank realized he had fallen short of her expectations as her husband, but he loved her with everything he had. There were things he had done, a few, in particular, he had kept from his wife. But all that he had done was to prevent his family from crumbling in his hands. He had gone to great lengths to preserve it. Eventually, it would all come out, but Frank had tried to kill this one.

It had cost him millions of dollars, and this woman, whom he loved with all his heart, might have just undone everything he tried to do. He sat down on the leather couch in the white room of his Highland Hills home, meticulously looking through the paperwork he'd received by messenger. He was so caught off guard by the sight of his bank statements that he didn't even notice the photographs of his wife in various compromising situations. Being honest with himself, he didn't need to see any photographs to know that Lisa had not kept their vows. Frank was not a foolish man. He had been aware of her transgressions for a while, but this was worse.

Frank was on the verge of tears. He could feel his blood boiling, his body warming as his anger surged. His bank account was nearly empty. Millions were missing. He never checked the books himself. He trusted his wife to handle the finances. He only reviewed the bank statements, but nothing had ever seemed unusual; nothing that would have suggested *this*. He returned the documents to the manila envelope and placed them in his safe. It didn't make sense. Frank had recently reviewed the bank statements, and there was close to $10 million there. He walked into his office and sat down to look over the papers his wife had given him. He preferred his physical world to the virtual one, so he never bothered to sign in and check the online account that Lisa created, a fact he quickly started to regret. Sure enough, the statements read as he had remembered them, and as he would have expected.

He combed through them looking for any irregularities. He didn't stop with the most recent statements but continued to sift through each statement from the last several months, noticing huge, glaring errors. The errors were not exactly little things he would not have noticed if he had not been looking. Perusing through the statements with more vigor, he noted large monthly withdrawals for the same dollar amount, every single month. Frank was in shock. What was she doing with the money? She charged everything to her American Express Black Card; never used cash. Despite the large consistent withdrawals, the balance never teetered below the $10 million threshold. He was certain that was not by accident.

Confusion swept over him. He felt his body began to shake. He couldn't breathe and felt he might faint. He grabbed the corner of the desk to support his now heavy body weight. His vision blurred, and the room circled around him. He heaved and battled to give his lungs the air they so desperately needed. He tried to focus, but he only felt worse with each passing second. He couldn't believe he was leaving like this, with so many loose ends. He would die without his baby girl, Brianna, ever knowing the truth. This isn't the way it was supposed to be. Not what he had planned, but it didn't matter. It was too late. The room faded to black.

Chapter 7

Brianna tapped her fingers impatiently on the table. She had been waiting twenty minutes for the meeting to begin. She was extremely annoyed, and if the 508 Park Avenue Project wasn't so close to her heart, she would have walked out twenty minutes ago. She ran across an article about it, contacted the sweet souls spearheading it, The Stewpot/Community Ministries of the First Presbyterian Church of Dallas, and offered her marketing services. The piece reminded her of the 1986 film, *Crossroads*, which was inspired by the larger-than-life blues guitarist, Robert Johnson. Legend had it that Johnson sold his soul to the devil in exchange for his musical genius.

The 508 Park Avenue building's third floor held audience to numerous musicians in June of 1937, including the wicked stylings of Mr. Johnson. Brianna could hardly believe it. A remarkable piece of musical history right there in Dallas. According to the article, the plan was to renovate the building, and Brianna jumped at the opportunity to be a part of it. Javan Harris worked for Good, Fulton & Farrell, the architectural firm in charge of the renovations. The end game proposed that 508 Park Avenue would house a Museum of Street Culture, Open Art Program, and a Community Garden.

She was so excited about the project that she provided her marketing skills completely free of charge. She did everything on her own dime. These meetings were for the companies contributing to the renovations, unrelated to marketing, but Javan had insisted she be there. Normally, she didn't mind doing as Javan asked, but today, her patience was especially thin. Her mind was at her parents' house, hoping that package Michelle's friend had sent didn't arrive there without her. Brianna wasn't privy to its contents, but she didn't want her dad seeing it first. Brianna was ready to go. This was the worst possible way to spend her day off.

"Javan, I need to leave." Javan looked at her and shook his head.

"Brianna, I told you I need you to be here."

"Yes, but why? What does any of what you have to say have to do with marketing?"

"That will be covered once we begin."

Brianna's irritation mounted.

"We are already twenty minutes past the start of this *mandatory* meeting, Mr. Harris." The words failed to hide her frustration. Her tone was unprofessional, but she could not have cared less at the moment.

Javan looked around and noted the empty chairs. He walked to the end of the table and sat down beside Brianna.

"Bria, why are you being difficult, woman?"

Brianna grabbed Javan's hand underneath the table and squeezed it gently. It was their private conversation. Remembering the last time they found themselves alone in the boardroom, he felt his johnson thicken. He moved her hand up until it rested on his inflamed groin. He wanted her to touch him. He prepared to reenact the movie playing in his head and relished the feel of her thin fingers gently gripping the hardness barely covered by thin nylon polyester fabric of his dress pants. Brianna knew what he craved, and her eyes gave her away.

Javan felt he might burst as he watched her tongue trace the outline of her bottom lip. He felt his chest tighten as she bit down softly. Damn, she was too beautiful for words, and her every movement sent him closer to the edge. His body was on fire as the physical memory of their last time together overwhelmed his senses. He leaned in to kiss her, to taste the cotton candy-flavored lip gloss she often wore, but she resisted even this small measure of mercy. Left him in agony. Hungry. She had always been this way with him. Brianna was a tease in the worst way.

"Window-shop. You may not buy, Javan," Brianna prodded seductively.

Javan buried his face in the nape of her neck. "How about I lease with an option to buy?"

"Boy, you's a window-shopper . . . in the candy store lookin' at ish you can't buy . . ." Brianna teasingly rapped the lyrics to the rhythm of one of 50 Cent's biggest hits.

Javan let out a light chuckle. "Woman, you make me crazy. Why you got me like this in the office? Highly inappropriate."

"I did *not* do this." She slowly removed her hand from his body and placed it back in her lap.

Javan was the lead architect and thus, responsible for ensuring the renovations progressed on schedule. They met one day when Brianna stopped by the Stewpot to speak with Reverend Buchanan about the marketing direction as Javan concluded his meeting and was headed out. She thought she felt some static as they passed by each other in the hall. Her instincts proved true when she found him waiting for her in the parking garage an hour later. The two spent the next hour *working out* in Javan's Mercedes, and the rest is, as they say . . . history. Javan smiled knowingly and shifted in his seat, trying to suppress the urge to take her right there on the table.

"Bria, just a few more minutes, okay?" He cleared his throat hoping it would help him clear his mind that was suddenly full of her nakedness.

"Javan, where is everyone? This is infringing on *my* personal time."

Her facial expression masked the internal smile she wore at seeing his discomfort. His blanket need for her sweetness was so strong, she could see it visibly trapped inside of him, and it gave her a rush that could not be compared to anything else. It was exhilarating.

Javan would never admit it, but there was never a meeting on the schedule. He had only told her that so that he would have an excuse to see her. The weekends were usually *her time,* and in the four months they had been seeing each other, she had not recanted. Their allotted few days a month would sate him, but Brianna had been preoccupied even more than usual. While he had scarcely seen her over the last few weeks, he hadn't bothered asking her why. Brianna was the type of woman that shared the information she wanted to be known, and what she kept to herself *was for her.* He believed that woman could keep the Atlantic from touching the Pacific if she so desired. Javan couldn't handle the separation. She intoxicated him. He needed and accepted whatever agreement she offered, as long as it meant that he could have her.

"I'll give the others a few more minutes; then I'll call it."

This situation didn't sit well with Brianna. She didn't like that Javan had ignored her question, and it was beyond odd that no one had bothered to attend a mandatory staff meeting. Had it not been for his insistence, she would have skipped it herself. Something was off.

"Javan this is *my time.* I'm *not* getting paid for this."

"This was unexpected. What do you usually do on the weekends anyway? Why can't I see you?"

Javan regretted the question as soon as it left his lips and even more so when he saw the annoyed look on Brianna's face. He was not sure which question had upset her, but at this point, it didn't matter; the damage was done.

"Last I checked your little swimmers had nothing to do with my presence here. Therefore, my life is none of your business. If I wanted you to know, I would tell you."

She didn't answer the last question. Perhaps she hadn't heard it. He considered asking a second time but thought it would be best to leave it unanswered.

Brianna had remained single to avoid those questions. She did not appreciate Javan taking advantage of the situation. He was getting a little too comfortable with her. Maybe she needed to put some distance between them. She could tell that this was no longer a mere fling to him; he was serious. This was *exactly* why she was going to hire the PI. She needed to know if he was seeing anyone else and from the way he had been acting lately, it looked like she didn't need the PI after all. It was only a matter of time before he dropped the L Bomb.

She needed to cut him loose completely before that tragedy happened. Javan was a good guy . . . most of the time, but he wasn't consistent. He could be a real jerk sometimes. It was almost like he were two different people. Too messy. Too complicated. Overall, too much damn work. She had enough on her plate with the situation with Michelle.

After Javan called the meeting, Brianna made her exit. Saturday mornings were daddy/daughter time, and she cherished them. She was definitely a daddy's girl. He could do no wrong in her eyes. That was part of what made this predicament so painful. She couldn't fathom him lying to her, and the thought alone was too much to bear. As a child, he had made sure that Brianna never went without by giving her any and everything she desired. She adored him and would do anything to protect him. Her mom, on the other hand, was . . . *different.*

She did not trust her and would not have been a bit surprised if she had something to do with it. Brianna loved her mom, but there were times when she would feel like her mom was being less than genuine. She knew she was hiding something, and her behavior as of late had only increased her misgivings. It wasn't always this way. Before Brianna started school, back when the family would travel, things were better. They were happy. Typical. Ordinary. After that, things changed.

Over time, their family transitioned from the three musketeers to the dynamic duo. Her mom spent more time away from home and, on occasion, would disappear for weeks at a time. Out of the blue, she would just show up and go on like she hadn't been MIA for as long as she was. It never made sense to Brianna that her dad would simply let her return without any questions. His brave face failed to mask the pain Brianna sensed he felt. She initiated their Saturday morning routine so that he would know that at least one of the women he loved still loved him.

He always seemed to be in decent shape, but lately, his health seemed to be deteriorating, and Brianna was worried about him. He kept everything inside, and the weight of it all was surely killing him. Brianna thought for certain that her dad was dying from heartbreak. She wanted to evade *that* at all costs. It was plain luck that her avoidance would uncover a truth that irrevocably altered her life forever. If she had not been trying to spy on Javan, her life would be as she had always understood it. She was not sure what to think anymore.

Michelle's presence was bittersweet. Bria was over-joyed to have a sister but devastated by the possibility of her father's betrayal. She was not very receptive initially, but she began to warm up to Michelle. They were so much alike, it was uncanny. Over the past few days, the shock receded, and their bond forged immediately. On some level, it felt like they had never been apart. Neither of them could imagine their lives without the other. Besides her father, whose status in her life was questionable, at best, Brianna realized Michelle was the only other person she could trust.

Watching her father fall apart as a result of her mom's distorted expression of love left her on the defensive. If she had been willing to look past Javan's control issues, seeing that synchronized chaos between her parents was enough to discard the idea. Brianna finding Michelle had completely nullified any progress he made. Bria had no use for him. She sympathized with him, but it stopped there, and she had plenty to distract her. Presently, her mind was on that package at her parents' house. She was extremely worried about its contents.

Michelle took complete control of the situation, spear-heading the search for their birth parents. Since Michelle lived off of a monetary gift she received from her mom after graduating from college, she could afford to take time off and concentrate her energies. Michelle's friend had come across something useful about her parents, and so Michelle had suggested that he send it directly to Brianna. The staff meeting had forced Brianna to cancel the exchange, and the friend overnighted it, insisting that she had to have it this morning. She hoped it wasn't too bad. She considered the possibility that her dad could be involved in something shady, but it seemed more befitting of Lisa. She hoped it was not anything criminal.

Chapter 8

"Frank? Franklin, are you home?" Although Lisa enjoyed Saint Maarten, it did feel good to be home. After a long week with Charlie, she was looking forward to some alone time with her husband. The house felt unusually cold, though. Her body was still warm from the Saint Maarten's rays. She walked into the bedroom and dropped her bags down on the floor. Frank was probably in his office. To be unemployed, Frank spent a ridiculous amount of time in there. She was anxious to see him, but, always the lady, decided to bring Frank to her. Her *welcome home* was one of the few things Lisa looked forward to enjoying.

She powered on the media system and listened to the soft tunes travel through the speaker system and pour into all five bedrooms of their home. Their bedroom was her favorite spot in the house. She savored the feel of the velvet carpet on the soles of her feet when she walked. It would be at least another hour or so before Frank joined her, and since Maxwell wasn't the only one with a "Bad Habit," Lisa used that time to cleanse herself of hers. Frank always appeared less than enthusiastic when it came to satisfying Lisa, but after a long separation, he managed to drum up some energy for her.

Lisa showered and dressed, but Frank still had not come to see her. She was peeved. Maybe he wasn't home, but where would he be? The hour had lapsed twice. She left the bedroom and went looking for him. This was typical of Frank to disappoint her, but something felt wrong. It was *too* quiet. No television chatter, phone conversation, no sign of Frank. The kitchen was empty except for what looked to be the beginnings of a sandwich on the island. The living area and den were vacant. Lisa yelled out for him. "Franklin! Franklin, where are you?" She quickened her pace and searched her memory. She thought back to the small table in the foyer, where they left notes regarding their whereabouts, but there was nothing there.

Lisa was growing increasingly impatient as she headed from the white room down the long hallway toward Frank's office. Her mood was completely blown. No nookie for Franklin.

"Franklin! Fran—" Fright gripped her heart as she neared the open door. This couldn't be . . . She had to be mistaken. "Oh my God, Frank!" Lisa could see Frank's body stretched across the wood floor behind his desk. She ran to his side and fell to her knees. Shaking him and crying uncontrollably she continued screaming his name. "Frank, wake up, Frank! Please." The room swirled around her. Panic-stricken, Lisa grabbed the office phone and dialed 911. "Help me, please, my husband . . . He's not moving! Oh my God . . . I don't know if he's breathing. He's so cold . . . please . . ."

Lisa was hysterical. Heartbroken. Confused. She dropped the phone and cradled Frank's face in her lap, sobbing aloud. She was not thinking. She was feeling. Feeling guilty about lying to her husband, stealing from him. She did not hear the ambulance pull up. Did not hear the EMTs enter the home, nor register that they had entered the room to assist.

"I feel a faint pulse," one of them said, but Lisa did not hear him.

Her mind flashed back to metal poles and stage lights. Just sixteen years old, naked, alone, and afraid. The air stank of lust and liquor. Hands all over her body, on her breasts, her thighs, between her legs. Her eyes burned from the smoke in the air. Inside, she was screaming, terrified, but her body rebelled against her trepidation. Survival outweighed her instinct to run. She was dancing. Trying not to die. Trying to live. One second from locating the nerve to find the Reaper and offer her soul. Death presented itself as a favorable alternative, by far, and it was at that precise moment Lewis drifted into her biography. The specific day was lost to her, but the tactile sentiment dredged within her person the instant his Kodak smile seemed to reach into the abyss and pull her out and into him; it was something she would never forget.

Vividly, she recalled how rapidly her heart beat within her chest the first time he entered her, the first time he made love to her. Lewis had filled her womb so completely; their bodies fit together so perfectly, she was convinced they were designed for each other. She felt their souls connect, and she dreamed of forever. For months, Lisa lived under the haze of love, completely immersed in the little world she and Lewis fashioned.

Inside the chaos that fueled their lifestyle filled with broken dreams, empty bottles, and fast cash, she found a small but immensely viable measure of peace with him. Lewis had her heart, and she would have done anything for him . . . until she realized that she was only one ride in his amusement park—a hard brush with a reality that permanently snatched the stars out of her eyes. From that point on, she looked out for herself. Lisa wanted out, and Frank had been her hero draped in dollar signs. Her door marked "exit." Her way out of the amusement park. He had saved her, and she loved him for it.

"Ma'am . . . ma'am . . . We need to get him to the hospital now. Are you coming?"

The EMT interrupted her thoughts. Brought her back
to the present. Back to Frank. She nodded, got up to
follow them, and hoped with all her heart that she hadn't
lost Frank forever.

Chapter 9

Lewis pulled into the hospital parking structure and picked a spot as isolated as possible. He wanted privacy. He sent a text to let her know he had made it and reclined the seat in his E-Class to relax and wait. Things had been rocky between them lately, but it didn't bother him much. He simply wanted his money every month. The garage was dimly lit and devoid of people. He cracked the driver-side window and decided to light one. The sweet scent of his Black & Mild filled the car. He closed his eyes and let his mind wander. Pretty soon, he heard a light knock on the passenger-side window. He looked over to find Lisa motioning for him to unlock the door. He hit the switch and sat up to speak with her.

Lisa slid uneasily into the passenger seat. The Mercedes was her choice, her flavor, and everything in it from the custom seats with *LL* stitched into the leather, the sunroof, limo-tinted windows, and the state-of-the-art BOSE stereo system was her design. The memory brought a faint smile to her face, relishing how inseparable they were back then. Time had certainly changed things.

"Lewis."

"Lisa."

"Still a beautiful car." Lisa looked intently in Lewis's direction as she spoke but allowed her gaze to rest on the column outside the driver's-side window behind him.

Lewis was surprised to find that her beauty still captivated him. He wanted to keep it business, but his eyes betrayed him. His gaze was heavy with the lust of his loins. He could tell her he loved her, but he'd be lying. The truth was, he loved what she could do for him. He looked at her with a challenge in his eyes. Could she resist him? Lisa returned his stare and answered his challenge; she certainly could. Time froze as they ran into their past. Desire rapidly replaced the dissipating smoke, leaving the air wet with moisture from the heat emitting from their bodies. The carnality of their relationship was rearing its impious head.

Lisa felt her heartbeat steadily increasing, and her breaths grew shallow. Lewis took his finger and traced the outline of her arm. She shuddered as her body responded to the feel of his finger against her skin. Even that small contact was nearly too much. She felt herself falling under his spell, and her body grew ripe with want. She missed his touch. Lewis, trying to seize the moment, leaned in for a kiss, but the movement snapped Lisa out of her trance. She pushed him back into his seat, pulling them back into the present.

Lewis was disappointed but not surprised. Their studio sessions came to a grinding halt at her insistence. That was her idea, not his. He complied after she insinuated that, at the time, her fiancé was growing suspicious and felt it might jeopardize their money. As far as he was concerned, however, Lisa would always belong to him.

"Reminds me of you." Lewis recently parted company with a woman and wasn't pressed for the goods, but if Lisa was willing, he would rise to the occasion.

"Frank is upstairs, lying in a hospital bed."

She didn't want to hear it. Things were different now, and there was no sense in going down memory lane. She still loved him, but she was in a different space. Her husband was upstairs fighting for his life, and she didn't have time for this. Lewis was no longer of any use to her; he was a nuisance.

"Sleek. Sophisticated. Black and gorgeous."

Lisa rolled her eyes. "I really should get back to him."

"We were good together."

Lisa didn't know what had him feeling so sentimental all of a sudden. He had not spoken to her like this in years. Attraction was never the issue.

"It was business. The minute I tried to cut it off, you flipped."

Lewis scoffed. "Tried to cut what off? My money? Damn right."

Lisa cut her eyes at him. "Why did you call me down here?"

"Payday."

Lisa should have known it was about money. It was *always* about the money. She wondered if he cared about anything else.

"I still have two weeks."

"Not anymore."

Lisa groaned in frustration. She needed more time to figure things out. "Well, I don't have it now."

"You got jokes?"

"No, I'm serious. I don't have it."

Lewis sighed. Lisa was tripping. He didn't like her fucking with his mind—or his paper.

"That's not cool."

"I don't know what else to tell you."

"Tell me you'll have my money." Lewis was losing patience. He knew she had the money. Lisa would not do that to herself. She *always* had a backup in place.

"I just don't have it. I'm tapped out. I'm not working. What did you think would happen? All this money going out and nothing coming in?"

"Fuckin lyin'. Cut the bullshit. I know you, or did you forget?"

Lisa sucked her teeth. She had a stash, true enough, but she had no intentions of sharing that with him.

"Lewis, I need more time. Either you give it to me, or your ass's out."

Without flinching, Lewis reached across the seat and grabbed Lisa around her neck. He squeezed until her deep honey-colored skin changed to a blistering red.

"Don't fuck with me, Lisa. I want my money. *Now*." He squeezed harder. "I don't want to have to do this."

Lisa scratched at his hands trying to loosen his grip, but he wouldn't budge.

"Just stop. There's no use, baby."

Lisa stopped clawing and stared at him with fire in her eyes. She was petrified but refused to let him see it. She didn't want to give him the satisfaction of seeing her cower.

Lewis smiled at her fight. He loved that about her. "That's better." He released his grip and spoke to her calmly. "I don't want to hurt you, but I will. Get me my money. I don't care what you do, but get it. One week."

Lewis's tone was tender, light. If it wasn't for the sinister intent, his words could have been mistaken for sweet nothings. Goose bumps traveled the length of her body. She didn't know if it was the threat or the slight hint of pain she heard in his voice that made her nervous as she grew increasingly uncomfortable.

"You'd *kill* me?" Her voice was calm, but she feared the answer.

"What do you think?" His cryptic answer did nothing to soothe her apprehension.

She knew the answer. Money was a nonnegotiable with him. She had not known him to kill anyone, but she didn't think it was that he wasn't capable. He had simply never been put in a position to do so. Lisa rubbed her neck and settled her pulse, slowed her breathing and looked back at Lewis. She wanted to scratch his eyes out. She couldn't believe he put his hands on her. He had done that to other women before but never to her. She grabbed the door handle and pulled it to open the door, but Lewis stopped her. She refused to look at him and kept her back to him. Whatever he needed to say he could say it to the back of her head. She was done with him.

"The love was real."

"I don't even know who you are anymore." Lisa was serious, and her words were heartfelt. She was on the verge of tears, pissed that she had ever loved him. "Those days are long behind us."

"They don't have to be. We can go somewhere and start over."

Lewis was wrong. Lisa would never feel safe with him again. Her scars were fresh. Lewis had crossed the line, and as far as she was concerned, they were over for good.

"And your wife, Lewis? Are you now willing to leave her?"

"She'll be fine. She never needed me. You did. Besides, you know I was only there for my daughter, Lisa. There was no way I could let her grow up without her dad."

"Staying for the kid said every man who has ever cheated anywhere." She turned to look back at him. "You left your daughter a long time ago. The only person you have ever truly been loyal to is yourself."

"Lisa . . . Don't talk about my daughter, and you know how I feel about you, wife or not."

Lisa shook her head. "Lewis, I may have needed you before, but I don't need you anymore."

Those words cut him. He hated that. He was married, but he felt that he and Lisa had a connection. He understood her. They were from the same world, and his bond with her had been different from what he had with any other woman. Though he would never admit it, he resented her for leaving him and playing house with that lame ass, Frank. Her relationship with Frank was supposed to be business, but she made it personal. He couldn't compare to Lewis, and she knew it. She was too much like him . . . Money over everything.

"Fine. Get the fuck out. One week."

Lisa opened the door and closed it behind her. Lewis nearly hit her as he powered the car, revved the engine, and sped out of the parking structure.

Lewis had been driving around since his visit with Lisa trying to calm down. He didn't want to take his anger and disappointment into his home with Sophie. She would ask questions, and he did not feel like talking. He had been attempting to reach Charlie for the last few hours and had come up empty. He did not like being ignored. Charlie's absence was a huge snag, especially since Lisa said she didn't have any money. That was information Charlie should have provided to him. He had better hear something soon. Otherwise, things would not bode well for her.

"Started from the bottom, now we're here . . . started from the bottom . . . now my whole team fucking here."

Lewis pressed the button on his steering wheel to answer his phone.

A soft, sultry voice echoed through the car speakers. "Lewis, I got your messages. I was—"

"Where are you?" he questioned. He was not in a talking mood.

"Omni Hotel. Room 1520." Lewis considered going home where his wife, Sophie, was probably waiting and decided to make her wait longer.

"I'm on my way."

He disconnected the call. He'd deal with that when he got there. The forty-minute ride from the Agg town to the Omni would give him time to order his thoughts. He felt mildly remorseful about making Sophie wait. Mildly. He loved Sophie, mainly because she gave him Michelle. Michelle was his baby girl. Everything he did was to protect her, even if she couldn't understand him enough to appreciate it. It is true that he had been away from his family more often than he liked, but he was trying to provide the life they deserved. The financial liberties they enjoyed came with a price, and he didn't mind if they hated him for it.

Lewis was a hustler. He sold anything and everything profitable, from clothes to DVDs, tickets to games, concerts, whatever he could flip. Over the last several years, he refrained from the small-time money and focused his energy on one score. It was the biggest of his life, and it had served him well. Lisa had been his greatest investment to date. He was not a stranger to the local hot spots around town, but Onyx was his spot. He had his pick of the women wherever he went. People often mistook him for Morris Chestnut. Lewis gladly bedded the women but scoffed at the comparison. He had at least four inches and roughly 100 pounds on "Ricky," from the movie *Boyz in the Hood*, and if asked, way more heart.

It was never a question of whether he could have Lisa, but what he would do with her once he had her. She never offered resistance, although her reluctance was evident. Lewis chuckled, thinking about how frigid she was their first night together. Granted, there wasn't much space in the back of his Rover, but he put in some of his best work that night. After a few shopping sprees and a few *studio sessions,* Lewis had his way with her. She needed him, and he knew it. Lisa looked young, but he never inquired about her age. He put her up in a loft downtown and paid for all her weekly pampering. He watched her slowly shed her naiveté and embrace her femininity, her power.

Lisa was stunning, and Lewis wanted her to understand and accept that truth. He had learned from his time at Onyx that fantasy paid. The bigger the fantasy, the higher the profit. He had watched men shell out thousands of dollars for a mere hour of a woman's time. It wasn't long before he learned how to capitalize on the give-and-take. He schooled Lisa on the finer points of providing the fantasy: tease, seduce by suggestion. He drilled her the same as he had done with other women before her, but Lisa's mental capacity separated her from the rest. The arrangement was simple: Lisa would give him a percentage of whatever she earned dancing, *or otherwise,* in exchange for his protection. Lewis was driven. He loved anything that made him money, and Lisa kept him laced. She brought in $2,000 on a slow week.

For months, things rolled smoothly between them. It was a beautiful situation for him. As with all things, though, the good times didn't last forever. As time went on, Lisa became more and more vocal about her desire to quit. Lewis wasn't having it. There was no way he was going to let her disposition stop his cash flow, but he didn't want her unhappy, either. He wasn't overly concerned with her feelings, but a happy woman was a more productive woman. Period.

There had been whispers about a young guy trolling the bars, throwing his paper around, and he needed to get Lisa in on the inside track to who this dude was. He sent out feelers to get more information so he could plan out his next hustle.

It didn't take him long to learn the young man's name: Frank Mason. According to his sources, Frank was in the area finalizing plans to claim the remainder of his inheritance, reportedly some $20 million. Part of that plan required a paramour, as it were, to close the deal. Lewis was not one to pass on money, and regardless of the other gold diggers plotting to secure the ultimate payday, he had the perfect woman for Frank. Lisa wanted out of the stripper life, and Frank could give her a new one, so Lewis simply needed to convince Lisa that Frank was her ticket out. If he could pull this off, the Lisa/Frank combo was going to make him millions.

Surprisingly, all Lewis needed to say was yes.

One night, after a late night *studio session,* as they lay entwined across Lisa's sleigh bed, breathless and wet with love, it was Lisa who made her move, and with a plan of her own. She began by letting him know that she would no longer dance, *privately* or otherwise. Before Lewis could respond, he felt her tongue lightly graze the tip of his manhood. His objection wedged in his throat; he was no longer possessing the ability to think or speak. With the skill that came with being an impromptu "working girl," she worked her way down his hardness until his ten inches were no longer visible. His body tensed. Lisa had never behaved this way before, and she wouldn't stop, despite his pleas. Lisa's head game was masterful. She learned the dance all too well. Lewis was outmatched. For what seemed like an eternity, she licked, sucked, and swallowed every part of him, leaving him twisting, turning, and throbbing with need. He needed to release, but she wouldn't allow it, taking him to the edge of bliss before yanking him back without mercy.

With each trip, she laid out the details of her plan: she would marry a man named Frank Mason, a young guy with old money. Lewis couldn't discern or remember in great detail exactly how she planned to do it, but if it was comparable to what she was doing to him, he believed it would certainly work. Lewis was in a whirlwind. He couldn't breathe. He shook and fought the urge to grab a fistful of her long, black hair. He tried to contain himself, but resistance was futile. She showed him firsthand how she would convince Frank Mason that she was *his* woman. Lewis didn't know how she knew of Frank, but he could not have cared less at that moment.

She told Lewis that once she was with Frank, her payments would change from weekly to monthly. Large enough to make it worth his while but small enough as to not be missed by Frank. Considering the amount Frank spent every weekend, she offered to give Lewis ten thousand a month for the first few months. Lewis did not protest; he could *not* protest. Lewis was in agony, longing for the curves of her face, the softness of her lips. He could scarcely think of anything else.

He loved her and hated her, unsure of which emotion ruled him more. When she was done laying out her plan, she asked if the terms and conditions were agreeable to him. She sucked, looking for his reaction before asking. Sucked. Asked.

He shouted, "Yes, whatever you want!"

He would have given her his firstborn if it meant she would free him. Now Lisa decided to relinquish control. She relented, leaving him in the calm of his release. He couldn't believe what just happened, but he was low-key about his excitement regarding it. Lisa making the proposal was completely unexpected, and he realized for the first time that he had completely underestimated her. The way he saw it, she had anticipated resistance from him and concocted this scheme when she was sure he would be most susceptible to her advances. *I'll be damned; she set me up,* he thought to himself, grinning at the execution. From that moment on, he viewed Lisa in a completely new light.

She had managed to do something no other woman could: earn his respect. For the first few months, Lisa paid the agreed-upon amount, increasing it to twenty thousand each month thereafter. Things were going well . . . until Lisa decided that stealing from her husband was morally deplorable. Nearly six years into their agreement, she tried to buy Lewis out with a $4 million lump-sum payment. She hoped the buyout payment would be enough to satisfy him, but she didn't take into account his insatiable greed. Lewis figured if she could afford the buyout, she could give more. Mrs. Mason might have been feeling remorseful, but not guilty enough to confess the whole truth. Lewis took advantage of the newfound leverage he had over Lisa, *offering* to relieve her burden by sharing their secret with her husband. Lisa was horrified by the blackmail attempt, but her reluctance to resolve the situation herself forced her hand. In order to keep Lewis from crashing the world she'd meticulously built, she increased his payout per month, nearly doubling the payment. With thirty-five thousand being funneled into his accounts, she was sure that there would not be any problems. For a time, there had not been any glitches . . . until *now*, that was.

Lisa's availability had waned in recent months, but since she was still paying on time, he was not concerned. He did not like surprises, however, and set up his own version of an insurance plan: Charlie Gray. Charlie was desperate and would do almost anything for a leg up. Lisa's questionable behavior had provided the perfect opportunity for Charlie to prove herself, and she jumped at the chance. Charlie had been on assignment for three weeks and hadn't reported anything of any value to Lewis. He began to think that Charlie didn't take him or his money seriously, convinced that Charlie had lost focus. He wasn't sure if she rolled that way or not, but he also wasn't sure that she wasn't distracted by Lisa's curves and feminine wiles. Lewis could understand if this was true, but he would not accept it, even if she was attracted to her. He did not mind spending money to make money, but he never threw a dime away.

I-35 North was clear, and his Mercedes E-Class always made for a smooth ride. He parked and headed to room 1520. Charlie had some serious explaining to do. Lewis was ready to cut his ties and move on. He didn't believe in paying someone to do a job that they were ill-equipped to do. He thought that maybe Charlie was not the woman for the job. Besides, there were plenty more where she came from. Lewis called Charlie from his cell, but she did not answer. He disconnected the call, taking a moment to collect himself. He felt his rage rising. His time was precious, and Charlie knew he was en route. He called again.

"Hello?" Charlie quivered.

"Open the door; I'm outside."

"I'm not in my room . . . I, uh, had to make a run."

"Open this damn door! I don't have time for this."

A member of the janitorial staff dropped his things as he passed by, obviously startled by Lewis's outburst. Lewis cursed under his breath, realizing he was drawing unwanted attention.

"I'm sorry, but something came up, and I couldn't wait."

"You couldn't call and let me know before I wasted my time driving out here? Huh?"

"I was going to call you but . . . It was simply last minute."

Lewis stood outside the door, leaning in to place his ear against the wood to listen for movement inside. He felt disrespected and considered the consequences for kicking the door in, deciding against it. He had spent enough time with "Dallas's Finest."

"Charlie, I am giving you today, are we clear? Do not try to leave town. I *will* find you, understood? *No one* disappears with anything that belongs to *me*." He hung up the phone before she responded. He would deal with her later. What in the hell was going on—first Lisa, now Charlie? Shit, he hoped that Sophie would not try him. He was ready to pop.

Chapter 10

Michelle sat in silence, trying to make sense of what she heard. What was her father doing here? What had just happened? How did Charlie know her father? So many questions swirled through her mind. The package she received came with a note that suggested she reach out to a Charlie who was staying at the Omni Hotel. Charlie apparently had been spending a generous amount of time with Lisa and might be able to shed some light on her history. She had a few questions regarding the old photographs she received and hoped Charlie could help her put some of these puzzle pieces in her head together. She found the hotel where Charlie was staying and came by on a hunch that she might be there. She had expected to get a few answers but not this. Michelle pondered what angle she should approach Charlie with. She did not want to reveal who *she* was, but she wanted to know the relationship between Charlie and her father.

"Is everything okay?"

"Yes, it's cool." Charlie held her stomach unconsciously, worried about what Lewis might do to her. She said the wrong thing before, and he nearly killed her.

"Are you sure? Whoever that was sounded pretty upset."

Charlie considered confessing her horror. Telling this complete stranger how she had misrepresented herself, scheming and plotting and now was in so deep she couldn't tell which way was up anymore. "What can I do for you? Earlier, you said you had questions about Lisa."

Charlie wasn't forthcoming, and Michelle couldn't press harder without arousing suspicion.

"I came across some old photographs, and I was hoping you could help me identify some of the people in them. I think that Lisa may be in a few."

Charlie glanced at the photographs spread across the bed.

"Where did you get these?"

"Is that important?"

"Not really, I guess. Just curious."

"Someone sent them to me with a note directing me to you."

Charlie tried to mask the urgency in her voice. She lied about the origin of the pictures being important. It was very important. Someone figured out who she was and where to find her. The thought made her even more nauseated. She did not know a lot of people in the area, especially anyone who would have access to these pictures. They were old photographs, sending Charlie down memory lane. She could not recall most of the people in them, but one did catch her eye. She picked it and passed it to Michelle.

"How did you find me?"

"The pictures came with a note." Michelle passed the note to Charlie. "Here it is."

Charlie examined the handwriting. She recognized it but couldn't remember who it belonged to. She could only think of a handful of people that knew where she lived, but they wouldn't have these pictures, and even fewer knew about her and Lisa.

"That is a picture of Lisa from high school."

Michelle's eyes widened in surprise. Her note had given her the impression that Lisa and Charlie had only recently begun spending time together.

"Exactly how long have you known Lisa?"

"Oh, we grew up together, more or less. I lived down the street from her. We were neighbors, not friends. That particular picture was at a house party. She didn't even know who I was, but I knew her. She never missed a party."

"She was a party girl?"

"I thought so at first, but after that night . . ." Charlie's voice trailed off.

Michelle glanced up from the picture and peered at Charlie; the question manifested itself in her eyes.

Charlie hesitated to answer, but the look in Michelle's eyes made it difficult to ignore her. "Lisa had gotten unusually wasted. A few of her friends took her home around one that morning."

Uncertain of her words, Charlie sheepishly shrugged her shoulders. She busied her fingers with the buttons on her chiffon blouse, trying, unsuccessfully, to draw strength from their firmness. She wanted nothing more than to allow their solidarity to inhabit her entire being. To feel confident and secure in all that she had to say.

"I can only speculate on the time, but her screams woke me up around three. I could see into her bedroom window from my house across the street."

Michelle took note of the subtle but swift change in her demeanor. The lavish modern art decor of the room exchanged its exquisite caravan of Sunkist oranges, fire-engine reds, and cherry browns for a mild, less intrusive gray scale as the temper within grew heavy with Charlie's malaise.

Charlie paused, fought back the tears, and wondered if she wanted to share this story with a stranger. Michelle moved to the bed and placed a comforting hand over Charlie's, offering it as a palliative, encouraging her to continue, prodding her to go back.

"I couldn't make out what was happening at first. I only saw a lot of movement. Everything was blurry. I'm visually handicapped without my glasses, especially from that distance, but it was dark in my house, and I couldn't find them right away. I didn't want anyone to see me, so I left the light off. It took me a second, but I found them and . . . part of me wished I hadn't found them. I can never un-see that."

Charlie started openly weeping, unable to hold back the tears any longer. "The bastard was raping her!"

This was the first time she had ever shared the horrific scene from that night with anyone, her emotions letting loose from carrying that guilt around with her all these years. Michelle did not respond. Besides, she didn't know what to say. She held her questions and gave Charlie the floor.

Charlie's cries subsided, and she spoke again. "I was scared for her. Hurting for her. I should have yelled for help or something, and I was going to, but then I saw *her*. She just stood there. Watching."

Charlie's body shook as she spoke. Disgust was etched across her face. Nausea threatened to visit her. Michelle grabbed a cold towel from the bathroom and handed it to her. The cool, damp towel returned some of Charlie's face back to its natural color. Her eyes were swollen, and her face was red from crying. "I was in shock, I guess. I couldn't move. Watching her standing there . . . I kept waiting for her to intervene, to save her daughter, but she never did. She stood there, watching her ratchet husband rape their only daughter."

Michelle was stunned. No, mortified was the more appropriate reaction that she could describe. This was horrible. She immediately thought of Brianna. How could she tell her? She changed her mind, realizing that it was not her story to tell. If Lisa wanted Brianna to know,

Michelle decided that Lisa would need to be the one to do it. Charlie lay across the bed, emotionally drained, visibly exhausted. Michelle thought of what this could mean. This was not going at all as anticipated.

"Charlie, why did you tell me this?"

Charlie massaged her temples with the tips of her small fingers, warning the impending migraine to stay at bay. It was a vain attempt to buy time for her mind to assemble some plausible explanation, something to justify her sudden candor. Maybe it was Michelle's convivial demeanor that permitted her to speak, or maybe the weight of it all had simply become too much to bear.

"I'm tired of living a lie. I feel like I've lost myself."

Michelle nodded. She understood what Charlie meant. Life was like a delicate fabric, and it doesn't take much to alter it. Charlie had cut so much that she no longer recognized the material; she lost *Charlie*. Michelle recognized her dismay because she too had fallen victim to the same thing.

"I was in love with Lisa . . . I am in love with Lisa. She disappeared that night, and I blamed myself. I thought maybe if she knew she had someone in her corner, she could have stayed, maybe even get some help. I heard awful things. I worried, but I was too young to do anything. I never forgot about her. I had been looking for her off and on. I travel a lot, and in every city I stayed, I looked for her. After I got to Dallas, I got into a little *legal* trouble. I knew this lawyer, Jacob, from around the way, and I stopped by his office for a consult. To my surprise, I saw a picture of her. Well, it was a picture of her, this guy, whom I later found out was her husband, and their baby."

Michelle perked up. That baby must have been Brianna. This provided a window to get more of a definite timeline for their separation. Depending on how old Brianna was in the picture, they must have been separated fairly soon after they were born.

"She looked happy. It did not take much prodding to get Jacob to talk about the lovely family. Once I had her name, Lisa Mason, I looked her up. I didn't think I'd have any chance of getting close but after a few months of uh . . . monitoring, I saw a crack in the door."

Michelle was not surprised that Charlie *monitored* Lisa. She couldn't label the energy, but something was certainly not kosher. She continued to listen to Charlie as she divulged more details of her stalker-type behavior. "I noticed that she would meet with this guy every month at a certain club. I figured that would be my best shot. I didn't know what they had going on, but he had 'ladies' man' written all over him. It wasn't that hard to get his attention. We only messed around a few times, but I tried to stay close, you know, like, make myself available. Dude was real disrespectful, and it was difficult for me to be around him. When I was at the point to where I was about to give up, he propositioned me. He was *loaded!* When he came at me with dead presidents, I knew he could make it worth my time."

"Wait, wait; hold on a minute." Michelle was not sure if she wanted to hear more. She had already learned more than she ever thought she would. Frankly, she wasn't sure she could take any more, especially if this dude was who she thought he was. She had to find out more information for her own version of "connect the dots."

"So you're telling me that your catching up with Lisa, here in Dallas, was completely coincidental?"

"Well, yes, umm . . . Well, I had been looking for her, but it's not like I had any idea where she was. I was only hoping to run into her one day, like in the movies. I had imagined the whole thing for so long. A magical reunion."

Charlie chortled and shook her head, amused with the absurdity of her imaginings. That would have never been possible. Lisa didn't even know her.

"So the guy . . ." Charlie met Michelle's stare. "He paid you to get close to Lisa?"

Michelle offered her last thoughts as more of a factual statement than a question. Charlie nodded, confirming her thoughts. "He pays for everything. Every trip I take her on, every dinner, every gift that I give to her, he took care of all of it. Dream come true, right?"

Michelle sensed Charlie's angst and understood her sarcasm. The way she saw it, Charlie had gotten herself into an impossible situation. While her love for Lisa was genuine and ever-present, the entirety of their affair was predicated on a lie, not to mention the fact that Lisa was married.

"Right, dream come true." Michelle couldn't fret over Charlie's issues. She had enough of her own. She stood to leave. "Thank you for speaking with me. I appreciate it."

Charlie grasped the full severity of her disclosure and sprang to her feet. If Lewis ever found out that he had been a pawn in her chess game, or that she played him to get close to Lisa and took his money in the process, he would not take it well. The scar-drawn necklace he left around her neck from her last admission served as a constant reminder of what he was capable of. She glared at Michelle, her nostrils flaring as her hands flexed into fists. "If any of this ever gets out, I'll know who's to blame."

Michelle shrugged, ignoring the threat, slightly confused by her abrupt change in attitude. She smiled halfheartedly before she closed the door behind her. "The dude that hired you to get close to Lisa, that's the guy that was here earlier, right?"

"Yes, that's him," Charlie answered. "He can never know what I've told you."

Michelle was grateful that Charlie could not see her face, where her bewilderment was so poorly masked. What did all of this mean? What was her father into? She never saw him much growing up, but he had seemed to be a decent man, and he always provided for her and her mother. Now she wasn't sure what to think or how to feel about him. This situation was evolving at an uncomfortable rate. She didn't know if the new information had anything to do with her or Brianna. She still had a lot of digging to do, and something told her she was not going to like what she unearthed.

Chapter 11

Lisa grabbed a towel and dried her face. She hardly recognized the woman staring back at her. Her eyes were puffy, hair disheveled, and she desperately needed a bath. She had been by Frank's side for the past two days. He had suffered a severe anxiety attack, and the doctors said that he would be fine, but the whole ordeal had taken a lot out of her. Since Lisa was unable to confirm how long he had been unconscious, they admitted Frank for observation to determine what, if any, long-term damage he might have incurred as a result. Lisa was relieved but still shaken. As quietly as possible, she eased the door of the tiny sterile bathroom closed and tiptoed to the sofa bed to lie down.

It was pretty late at night, and Frank had been sleeping for most of the day. He hadn't spoken at all except for a few inaudible ramblings. Seeing him so vulnerable forced Lisa to think over the choices she made, both during their brief courtship and their marriage. She had gotten with Frank to better her own life. It wasn't about love and commitment to her but survival. In many ways, he rescued her. She trusted no one but Frank. He had provided for her and allowed her the space she needed to feel comfortable in their relationship. She had not been faithful to him, but she did not want to be without him. Despite her indiscretions, she didn't think she could handle that. Who else could love and accept her as Frank had?

Buzz . . . buzz . . . Her phone vibrated. Lisa rolled her eyes in annoyance. It was Lewis again. He had called at least ten times in the last few hours. She wasn't in the mood to talk to him. She was still reeling from his last visit and, frankly, she did not see cause to speak with him. She had no idea how she was going to come up with the money, and she was fairly certain Lewis knew something. He had an uncanny knack for being able to tell when she was holding out. He always seemed to be a few steps ahead of her. Lisa was still salty about him refusing to let her out of their agreement after she gave him the four million. She couldn't talk to him without having a plan in place and certainly didn't want anything to happen that could worsen Frank's condition. Her past needed to stay where it was. She had done all she could to give herself a new life, and she wasn't going back.

Buzz . . . buzz . . . Her phone rang again. This time Lisa answered.

"Momma!"

Brianna's voice came screeching through the phone. Lisa kept a low even tone when responding. Brianna had a tendency to be a bit dramatic, and Lisa didn't want the conversation to get out of hand.

"Sweetheart, your daddy's okay. Take a deep breath. He's going to be fine. Are you okay?"

Lisa could hear Brianna trying to regain her composure, faintly talking aloud to herself.

"I'm fine." Brianna lamented, but Lisa was not sure how true that was.

"I've been trying to reach you. I was getting worried."

"I've been busy. My schedule has been pretty full lately with the 508 Park Avenue Project and everything."

"Oh, okay, I figured it was something along those lines." Lisa assumed Brianna had simply been avoiding her, as usual. She was skeptical about why her daughter was telling the truth . . . or not, but the thought that she was busy gave Lisa some comfort, if only for a moment.

"What happened to Daddy?"

"Well, he had an anxiety attack and was unconscious for a little bit. They are holding him for observation, but his vitals are good."

"Anxiety attack? Over what?"

"I wasn't home, but whatever it was must have had something to do with money."

"Why would you say something like that?"

Lisa heard the venom in her question. The attitude Brianna never could hide from her, and, if she was honest with herself, maybe her daughter never tried to hide it. No one could say anything wrong about her daddy. Lisa envied their relationship and wished that Brianna could come to *her* defense just once. To have someone that would love her blindly and without condition was something that Lisa coveted more than anything. Unfortunately, no one ever had, not even her own daughter. Her response was tepid. "It's one of the two things he loves most in the world. The other is you."

"Well, I'm coming up there. Are you at Baylor?"

"There is no need for you to come up here now. We'll probably be headed home soon."

"Are you sure?"

"He's fine. We'll see you soon."

"All right."

"Oh, Bria, can you go by the house and make sure everything's okay? I left hastily, and I can't remember if I secured the house."

"I'm here already."

"Oh, you're there now?"

"I have been here since Saturday."

"Ah, yes, well, OK, great. We'll see you when we get home. Love you."

"Love you too. Kiss Dad for me."

Lisa gripped the thin mattress of the sofa tightly, entering into her own interrogation room. Her mind raced, contemplating what information had caused Frank to respond in such a way. Different scenarios coated her memory, coaxing her deepest fear to the surface.

"Where is all our money, Lisa?"

Frank's voice cut through the air like a knife pressed against her throat. Lisa's heart sank. She gasped and turned to Frank. She searched his face, prepared to grovel but found him sound asleep. Frank was still heavily medicated. She expelled the air that had gotten trapped in her throat with his question. She took a deep breath and tried to relax. When she settled down, she remembered that while he had moments of lucidity, they never lasted long. The medication he was on made him extremely drowsy. Still, this last question shook her to the core, but she couldn't figure out why the question rang like a church bell in her ears. Had she summoned the question with her own fear? How could Frank know that their millions were gone? She hoped she was only dreaming, but something told her otherwise.

Chapter 12

Brianna sat in her dad's office chair, looking over the papers he had left strewn about. She realized that he signed for the package, but she couldn't find it anywhere. She had spent the past couple of days looking for it. Whatever was in it must have upset her father enough to trigger an anxiety attack. Now she wanted to find it more than ever. She was glad it was not a heart attack as she had suspected. She had several missed calls from her mom, and when she finally got around to checking her messages, she was too upset to call her back. She decided that, whatever it was, her mother was probably to blame. She couldn't figure out how to address her mom without tipping her off that she knew something was going on. She searched everywhere she knew her dad might have kept important packages, but she hadn't come across any information that seemed particularly startling.

"*Next to Me . . . ooh hooo . . . Next to Me . . .*"

Brianna picked up her phone and read the display. "Hey, Michelle."

"Bria, I just got your message about your dad. Everything okay?"

"Yes, he's OK. I haven't seen him, but Lisa has been at the hospital with him."

"Well, what happened, Bria? Don't keep me in the dark."

"He had an anxiety attack. I think he saw whatever *your friend* sent me. I've been looking all over the house for it, but I cannot find it. I know he has a secret spot, but I have never been able to locate it."

"Guess that's kind of the point," Michelle giggled over the phone.

"Soooooo, not helping." Brianna relaxed and fell back into the chair laughing.

"Give me the address, and I'll come help you look. I miss you anyway."

Brianna didn't expect her parents for at least another day or so, and she could use a fresh pair of eyes. Michelle had an unnatural knack for finding things.

"Sounds good. I'll text you the address. See you in a bit." She disconnected the call, relieved that Michelle was on her way.

Chapter 13

Lewis was greeted by the unsavory scent of Pine-Sol and bleach when he gingerly pulled open the back door of his home to enter into his expansive kitchen. It was hard to determine if it was the fragrance or what the scent implied that beckoned Lewis back to the car. The house was Gotham, he was Batman, and that smell was his signal to leave. Sophie was upset about something, and he did not feel like dealing with whatever it was. Lewis did, however, want something to eat, and he didn't need to turn the light on to see that his wife had not cooked dinner. He was going to blow a gasket. The women in his life seemed to be losing their minds. Lisa was ignoring him, he still had not spoken with Charlie, and now, Sophie? Enough was enough. "Sophie! Sophie! Where are you?"

Lewis yelled out for his wife, walking through the house in a desperate search, peeking into each of their six bedrooms before finding her in the den, barely visible, in the dark.

"Sophie, why haven't you cooked dinner? I'm starving."

Sophie did not respond, and Lewis felt rejected. He felt the distance between them. Something was wrong; he could sense her sadness. It was heavy and blanketed the air. Lewis felt weak. The floor offered itself as a soft place to land, and he momentarily regretted insisting on the hardwood floors over Sophie's desired carpeted ones. He remembered the time when Michelle had been hospitalized during a bout with pneumonia. She was only a toddler at the time, and they nearly lost her. That was the last time he had seen his wife this way, and he dreaded what she may say.

"Sophie, what is it? Did something happen to Michelle? Oh, God . . . Is she OK?"

Lewis found his wife in the darkness. Even on his knees he still towered above her. He felt the tears on her face, and while releasing his own, he tried to pull her close to him. She resisted his touch, gasping at the feel of his calloused hands against her soft, ivory skin.

Confused, Lewis fell back on his haunches, trying to read her face in the moonlight. That's when he saw them: the photographs she held in her hands. He snatched them away from her and looked through them, frantic to know the contents of the evidence that caused her pain. Lewis was in every frame. The last three months of his life all caught in the flash of someone's camera. Faceless women and how he *loved* them. He felt his world crashing around him. He furiously tore what pictures he had into pieces, frustrated at the irony. Those very same pictures that now lay in pieces had ripped and left Sophie's heart in the same condition. He looked at his wife and wished her heart didn't tear so easily.

"Sophie, I never meant to hurt you," he whispered. "I love you."

He continued, but Sophie did not have anything to say. There were no words that could accurately describe her angst. The absence of light allowed his chocolate frame to disappear into the darkness. Only his pearly whites were visible, and she was tempted to snatch all thirty-two of them out one at a time. Sophie was dangling off the edge of nowhere, and Lewis's Hallmark utterings only served to pry her fingers loose. Her heart physically ached with each breath as she felt a thousand needles invading her chest.

She received a package earlier that day and had been awaiting Lewis's arrival. Perhaps they could have discussed what she had seen had he come at the expected hour, but Lewis was more than two hours late, and the wound was no longer fresh, or raw, or susceptible to the touch. It no longer needed treatment or attention. The injury started to mend itself. She reached the point to where she no longer required an explanation. She wished with all her heart that she had left when the opportunity presented itself. Perhaps more than ever before, she wished she had taken that money, and Michelle, and run far from Lewis.

She hated him, and probably more so, she hated herself for loving him, for choosing him. She had long since stopped asking herself the obvious question: why. Each time, a little of her power dissipated as she bothered to dredge up an answer. Regardless of whatever fancy verbiage she dressed it in, the bottom line was obvious: She had made a mistake. Lewis presented himself as the man of her dreams. He was her every fantasy in real time and had given her everything . . . except himself. A beautiful, two-story brick home. A beautiful daughter. Financial security. But the one thing that she desired most—his heart—was never even on the table. She thought her pregnancy would open the door to his heart, that conceiving a child would allow for a deeper connection, but nothing changed. Had it not been for the love she felt for her daughter, she may have had no feeling at all.

They had been together for the better part of a year when they learned of the new addition. Her family forced her to choose: either abort the child or leave. She remembered the events like they happened last week.

Richard dismissed the help to their quarters in the west wing of the house after Sophie gave him and his wife Katherine the news. It had been too much for

Katherine to process, deciding to go to bed early. He thought it was best anyway. She did not need to be present for the conversation he planned to have with Sophie. He closed the large oak door to his office and now stood in front of his desk, trying to rope in his emotions before speaking.

"Damn you. Did you learn nothing from your sister, Sophie? I will not allow you to smear our family name! I won't have it!"

He spewed his words with such venom it made Sophie's ears bleed. She blinked back the tears that began to well up behind her eyes, trying to pretend that she didn't see the shame squared into his jawline or notice the malice in his heart.

"Why are you saying these things? Angela and I are not the same, Dad. I have done everything you have asked of me. Everything. This was not my fault. You told me to date him!"

Sophie had been careful not to cause the same kind of crisis as her older sister. She followed instructions with military-like precision, including her relationship with Lewis. Her every move had been drawn out for her. She didn't deserve his punitive disregard.

"No one told you to sleep with him! Can you imagine? My daughter behaving like some dirty little thug's whore? And you want to have the bastard's baby? You are going to see Naomi at Planned Parenthood—and that's final!"

Richard looked incredulously at his daughter. He thought she could handle this. It was feasible to infer that he acted prematurely. Sophie was not yet a woman, although he treated her as such. To his credit, this was no different than what he had asked of her before. What made this boy special? Why now? The two, she and the boy, were only meant to be seen together to bolster his popularity among black voters in Dallas, but this was not part of the plan. He was in the midst of his mayoral run and would not risk losing his most generous campaign backers because Sophie failed to keep her legs closed. The Freemont family had sacrificed too much for him to allow his naïve daughter's indiscretions to undo everything.

"Dad, I didn't intend to get pregnant, but I'm keeping my baby."

Richard grabbed his putter and swung in no particular direction. Sophie fell out of her chair and toppled to the floor. She balled herself up into a knot, afraid to move. Richard stood a good three feet from her, but his shadow loomed over her, covering her completely.

"Not in this house, you won't. I will not allow you to ruin this for us. That child will never be welcomed here!" With each word, his putter tore through the air. Sophie scrambled to the door, jerked it opened, and scurried to her room. Fearful of his wrath if she found herself in his line of sight, she remained there the rest of the night. Lewis came for her early the next morning.

Everything she was permitted to take fit nicely into her Louis Vuitton carry-on. Her parents refused to bid her good-bye. Their front porch was empty except for Nanette, the maid, who braved the tide to offer one last plea. To Nanette, Sophie was her daughter. Though she had none of her own, she practically raised her. Watching her depart that way was nothing short of devastating.

"Don't do this, Luce. They'll come around, chile."

The lie started her stomach churning something awful and left a bitter taste in her mouth. She had seen the underbelly of the Freemont clan. She knew where all the skeletons were buried. Image was everything to Richard as the patriarch of the family, and he would likely never change his mind, but at seventy years old, Nanette simply did not care what he wanted. She had taught him to cherish his family above all else, but that wretched Freemont blood had taken his mind and poisoned his heart. Lucille needed to stay home where Nanette could guide her until she was ready for the world. She had already lost Angela, and she did not want to lose Sophie too.

"Nan, I'm going to miss you most."

Her parents were dead to her. Richard and Katherine had relinquished their titles. No one ever discussed her sister, not even Nanette. Sophie was not going to hang around and allow the same thing to happen to her.

"This just don't feel right at all. You're just a baby. Not nearly a woman. Ain't the proper way to do thangs."

Nanette wanted to drag her back into the house and lock her upstairs in her bedroom. Had she been a few years younger, she would have done exactly that. "I was the one that named ya. Sophie Lucille Freemont. I raised ya like you was my own. I know what's best. I would never tell ya what to do. It's your life, but maybe you could stay until he's settled some. That boy got a lot of livin' left in him. I can see it in his eyes. Now, I'm tellin' ya what I know, chile."

Nanette's frail body shook as she spoke. Tears were streaming down her face. But she tried to smile for Lucille, to give her some joy to take with her.

"I love you, Nan, and I'll keep in touch. Promise."

"Just as stubborn as your papa. Be careful, ya hear? Be careful. If you need anything, call. Write. Something. Don't disappear on me. My heart can't take that."

"I won't, Nan. I won't."

"I love you, Luce."

"I love you too, Nan."

Sophie gave Nanette a reassuring hug and joined Lewis in the car.

That was the last time she had any contact with any member of the Freemont family. She left with Lewis, believing that he would take care of her. Instead, she spent most of her pregnancy feeling abandoned and emotionally starved. It wasn't long before she realized Nanette had been right: Lewis was not ready for a family . . . not even close. Many times she attempted to leave but did not have the finances to do so. Her pregnancy forced her to accept a very difficult truth: her financial security rested solely with Lewis. She was completely dependent upon him. She could not go home and had no technical skills and no formal education to strike out on her own. Sophie was broken spiritually and dying slowly.

She needed a way out. The life forming within her womb kept her alive. She never missed a prenatal appointment. She ate healthy, balanced meals and always took her vitamins. Sophie was perhaps the healthiest, physically, that she had ever been in her life. She had significant weight gain, in her opinion, but the doctor assured her that it was completely normal. Lewis never inquired about how things were with her. His affairs were always more important and took precedence over all else.

Lewis was noticeably absent when Sophie went into labor. He was home when she showed the early signs of labor but dismissed her request for a ride to the hospital, saying he had *business* to tend to. That was the last straw. Sophie's screams and cries of desperation did nothing to warm his cold disposition. He left her holding her full belly, round with his only daughter, in the worst pain she'd ever experienced. Sophie waited for over an hour for Lewis to return, wishing he would have a change of heart. Instead, she ended up taking an ambulance to the hospital. Imagine her surprise and shock when the doctors informed her after she had given birth to Michelle that another child was on its way out.

Sophie couldn't believe it. She had been pregnant with twins! She didn't understand how that was possible. The doctors tried explaining to her that sometimes the second child was not visible because it was hidden behind the first. Sophie nearly went into shock, crying uncontrollably. She was not prepared two raise two children all alone. She was only seventeen! How would she ever break the news to Lewis? She still had not been able to reach him and was sluggish to accept the reality of her situation. It seemed that the universe somehow answered her prayer, however. Something aligned exactly right and sent a man into her room with an offer she could not refuse.

She didn't even know his name or why he had come into her room, but his words were cemented into her memory. He told her that he and his wife needed and wanted a child, her child. Faced with no other alternative, Sophie did the unspeakable. The stranger swore that her daughter would grow up in a good, loving home, that she would have nothing but the best. Sophie thought this proposal was her way out, though she couldn't have foreseen the irreparable damage her emotional decision would do to her psyche.

She didn't realize that when she took the $5 million from the pleasant man and gave him her baby girl that she would lose a part of herself. To this day, she still does not know where he came from or how he knew she had twins. She never said a word to Lewis about it. She had been at home, alone in their dingy, one-bedroom apartment with Michelle for over a week before she saw him again. The power of her own transgression kept her from asking where he had been, why he hadn't bothered to at least return her phone calls. Her pain brought her silence.

She thought she could take the money and move away with Michelle, but once Lewis saw her . . . She realized she could not take her away from him. He was *different* with her. It was obvious how much he loved his daughter. She would not dare tell him that she sold one of their children to a complete stranger. She hoped every day that she might see her somewhere, but she did not. She guessed they must not live in Dallas. Her daughter was gone forever, and she had only herself to blame. The guilt fed an awful postpartum period which she barely came out of. She did not keep any of the money for herself, instead, giving it to Michelle as a gift after she graduated from college.

Sophie had kept her dreadful secret and lived with the repugnance no amount of Suave or Dove could remove. She had played the part of the good and faithful wife and doting mother. She accepted Lewis's disrespectful behavior; the weight of her truth anchored her. Now, after seeing with her own eyes her husband's truth, being forced to face his philandering ways firsthand after all that had happened, Sophie was finally ready to go.

Lewis was still on the floor, begging for her to acknowledge him. "Sophie, talk to me."

He was fuming inside, but he would not direct his anger at Sophie. This was not her fault. He would save it for whoever *was* responsible.

He did his best to repeat his question without arousing her anger. "Sophie, where did you get these?"

She turned to face him. Even in the dark, he could feel her eyes boring into him.

He was undeterred. "It's a logical question. Someone is trying to destroy our happy home. Don't let them do this. I know you're disappointed, but haven't I taken care of you? Have you ever wanted for anything?"

Sophie rolled her eyes at him, irritated at his arrogance. "Unbelievable." Sarcasm was evident in each syllable. "Seriously, what is *wrong* with you? Do you know what I gave up to be with you? My parents. My family. They disowned me, Lewis! I walked away from my life to build one with you. I was only seventeen. A child. This house is the very *least* you could do!"

Sophie turned on the light and walked around the den, pacing, trying to calm down. It was no use. "All the crap you promised me! I loved you, and you do me like this? How could you?"

"Sophie, I know that, all right? I know you gave them up for me, and I busted my ass to give you the life you had! But it's never enough . . . I could never be enough for you."

Sophie laughed. "You bastard. Of course, make this about you. You are *not* the victim here. Don't you dare try to blame me because someone got the *ladies' man* on film."

Lewis was speechless. How did this happen? How did the situation spiral so far out of his control? It was true that Sophie's family, with its strong, old-money, Anglo-Saxon heritage, had rejected his rich African ancestry and exiled his wife. He did everything he could to make it up to her by being certain that she wanted for nothing. He would not apologize for his decisions. He did everything he was supposed to do as her husband. In his mind, the liberties he took were his right as a man.

He walked to the minibar in the far corner of the room and poured himself a glass of Louis XIII. He drank it quickly and poured himself another. Sophie was irate and was not the soft-spoken, docile women he married. She had been angry before but not like this. Regardless of whether he felt she deserved to feel how she felt—he could not handle her being disrespectful. Not without a little help from his "friend," that is. He looked at Sophie motioning toward his drink. She waved him off and left the room, clearly frustrated.

Chapter 14

Sophie hurried to the kitchen cursing Lewis as she stomped down the hall. "*Son of a bitch*. I could have gone on to college, married, and lived happily! But, no . . . I got knocked up and fell for his crap. I don't need this. I don't need *any* of this!"

Her eyes bounced along the stucco wall darting in between various family pictures that hung on each side. She came upon a photograph they had taken during one of their prebaby trips, her round belly on full display. She gingerly removed it from the wall, reminiscing for a moment about a happier time. They were on day three of their four-day getaway at Silver Leaf Resort and someone, smitten by their obvious adoration for each other, insisted on capturing the moment. Lewis stood behind Sophie, his long arms cradling their bundle of joy. They had forever ahead of them.

Craaaaack! Sophie smashed the frame against the wall, sending big chunks of glass flying everywhere. *He's such a liar!* She let the frame fall to the floor and with her hands, frenetically tore the picture into tiny pieces. She held the shreds in her hand, closed her eyes, and like a flower girl in a wedding, resumed her walk, dropping the pieces along the way.

She switched on the fluorescent light, illuminating the kitchen as soon as her feet hit the black-and-white tiles. The floor's shine temporarily impaired her vision, but she kept moving like it did not affect her at all.

Some people went to church, to confession, engaged in meditation to calm their nerves. Sophie went to the kitchen, her sanctuary. Lewis was a piece of work, and she needed to invite the calm before things got any worse. With the door of the fridge slightly open, she grabbed a pitcher of fresh lemon water from the morning and placed it on the marble countertop. Then Lewis sauntered into the kitchen. Sophie watched him in the reflection on the stainless steel face of the dishwasher as he dragged his large frame to the island in the center of the room. He plopped down on a stool, wasting the small amount of liquor remaining in his glass.

"Tell me the truth, damn it!"

Sophie opened the fridge to return the pitcher to its place after pouring herself a glass of water. Her eyes never left Lewis. A fresh cauldron of bile started swirling around in the base of the small fleshy pouch that replaced her taut tummy when her body had extended itself into motherhood. Lewis should not be this intoxicated so quickly. He was sauced and could barely keep his seat on the round bar stool. But this emotive aggravating her senses stretched beyond inebriation and into something larger, more profound. She denied her legs' request to run and her arms' request to find some cookware that would suffice as weaponry. There was no need for either of those things. Lewis was drunk and being an ass as usual, but nothing more.

"Lewis, I have told you everything."

"Liar! Dirty liar!"

Sophie smacked her head against the door of the fridge in frustration. "Lewis, please, drop this."

Lewis continued slurring his words and speaking incoherently. "Why you be stupid, Sophie? Don't be stuuuupiiid."

Sophie was on edge. Lewis had successfully stolen her peace. It jetted out of the room the moment his foot entered. She didn't want to talk about any of this and decided to go to bed. "I'm not stupid."

"Whatcha say?"

"I am not stupid, Lewis."

Lewis stared at Sophie through his bloodshot eyes. The room was spinning a bit, but he felt in control. Sophie was going to tell him what he needed to know.

"Who are you protecting? Huh? Whoo aree yyoouuu pro . . . tect . . . ting?"

He got up and wobbled around the island until he was close to Sophie, leaning against the edge for support. His consumption of hard liquor was evident in his breath and nearly made Sophie lose her lunch. The stench consumed the air between them, making it unbearable. Suffocating seemed better than to allow that putrid gas into her lungs.

"Tell me where you got the damn pictures, Soph."

He poked her shoulder with each word. She moved slightly to her left, toward the door, to avoid his touch.

"I told you the truth."

"Liar!" he spat in her ear.

She screamed as a bomb exploded in her head. The tension erupted into the largest fireworks display Sophie had ever witnessed. Variant hues of the color spectrum danced before her eyes as a migraine attacked her with the force of a tsunami wave. She staggered, weakened by the pain shooting through her head as she covered her ears and turned to leave. Lewis grabbed her arm and pulled her back across his body. The counter kept her from hitting the ground, and she paid for its service. *Craaaaack* . . . Pain ripped her insides as her rib connected with the counter.

"*Ahh!* Lewis, what are you doing?"

Lewis snatched her off the counter by her hair and tossed her to the ground.

"Lewis, stop!"

"Tell me!"

He stood over her, straddling her body, as she tried to scoot away. He grabbed another fistful of hair and lifted her to her feet. "Give me his name!"

"I don't know!" Her cries bellowed against the walls of the spacious area.

His hot breath warmed the tears flowing from her eyes. Taking advantage of her position, she rammed her knee into his family jewels and tried to make a run for it. But the liquor turned his gems to steel, and he felt nothing. Lewis remained on his feet and sidelined her before she could flee the tight space between the island and the counter. Her head took the brunt of the impact as her body collided with the ground again. Lewis pestered her for more information, asking questions she did not have any answers to.

"Why did they send these? Huh? Who was it, Sophie?"

Bam! She felt his foot find a soft spot in between her bruised ribs.

"Please stop, Lewis. Please."

She wormed her body away from him, disregarding the avalanche of hurt consuming her and rose to her feet. Courageously forcing her legs to hold her upright, she faced her husband, the man she had shared the majority of her years with, and for the first time, she feared for her life. She saw Lewis as she had not ever seen him before . . . as the raging monster he was. She quickly scanned the room for something to defend herself but found nothing. She cursed her OCD. The kitchen was spotless.

Smack! Lewis slapped her with such power that the force immediately caused her nose to bleed and her lips and eye to swell. She stumbled backward, nearly falling, but managed to stay on her feet. Blood covered her hands, and there was not one part of her body that didn't ache.

"Sophie, just tell me." The clarity in his voice alerted her to a scary conclusion: her husband was sobering up.

He was no longer slurring his words. With each blow, the effects of the alcohol left him, and Sophie could plainly see this. It was perhaps what frightened her most. Though he was no longer under the influence of his adult beverage, the look in his eyes was still that of a possessed man. Lewis was drunk with power.

Her lips were so swollen she could not answer. Not that she had anything new to say. Her jaw hurt too much to move, and it wasn't even worth the effort. Lewis started closing the space between them, and her mind shifted to Michelle. She had loved Michelle with all of her heart, and she was proud of the young woman she had become. Michelle would be fine. Sophie felt a peace pass over her with the thought. Lewis put his hands around her throat, but Sophie didn't make a sound. If he was going to kill her, she was ready. She only hoped he would make it quick. She had nothing left to say.

Chapter 15

"Hey, love . . ."

"Armand, before you start, this is *not* a social call."

Armand had been hoping that Michelle would come around. She usually did, and although he suspected this time would be different, it had been a little over a week since she asked for space.

"That's unfortunate. Forgive me, already. You know I only have eyes for you."

Michelle had to stifle her laugh. This whole thing was utterly ridiculous, and as far as she could tell, unnecessary, but if he wanted to play, who was she to stop the game?

"All right, Armand. I love you too. Can we move on now? That package you sent to my client, what was in it? The package was intercepted, and some unauthorized parties may have viewed its contents."

Now it was Armand's turn to laugh. "What, are you auditioning to be the next Bond girl or something? Okay . . . uh, that's terrible, Agent Lewis."

"Hush and answer the question. Someone else got what you sent and hid it. Now, what was in it, Agent LaCroix?" Michelle could joke too, but she needed to know what she was dealing with before she got to Brianna's.

Armand cringed. He was afraid that would happen. He didn't know that family, but he knew that what he had found had the potential to rip it apart. Michelle had asked him to handle this for her, and it seemed simple enough. However, once he started doing surveillance, he found some disturbing things, and, frankly, he didn't even want to share what he'd seen with Michelle.

"That's not good," he stated.

"What did you find out?" Michelle didn't know what to expect given all that she had learned from her conversation with Charlie.

"Let's say I've seen people get iced over less. This would not have happened if you let me meet with her."

"Fortunately for you, she canceled that morning."

"Look, I know what your instructions were, but it all seemed ridiculous to me, and that stuff was important."

"I understand, but my request for you to remain anonymous was important too, Armand. She saved your butt. I'm still a little angry that you were going to meet with her after I gave you express instructions not to do it."

"I don't know how lucky it was, seeing as though she didn't get it."

Armand was right. Maybe she should have let him meet with Brianna. She wasn't sure if she was ready to tell Armand about her, and it's not like she could keep a secret after they met. A twin was not something you could lie about. "What else can you tell me about what was in there?"

"Nothing. Talk to your client. It is not my place to issue the information."

"Oh, *now* you want to follow my directions? Typical."

"Yep. Agent Lewis knows best."

Armand was not going to be the bearer of bad news. Michelle had never forbidden him meeting clients before, so he knew this one was special. He would keep his distance until she told him why. Besides, he had enough on his plate.

Armand didn't want to tell her. Thankfully, she did not press for details at the moment. She already had plenty to ponder.

"Okay. Hopefully, we'll find it. Listen, I didn't tell you because I didn't want to alarm you, but I think some guys have been watching my place."

Armand panicked. "What? Watching your place? Have they tried to do anything? What makes you think that?"

"Well, I noticed them awhile back, but then they left for a while, but now they're back. Black sedan, license plate 75Y6TH. Could you look into that for me?" Michelle asked.

Armand agreed to look into it for her, but he didn't need to. He knew who it was and was trying to take care of it. He had already made his first move by sending the pictures he'd collected to the home of Leonard Lewis. He was hoping that doing so would be a show of good faith to those watching. His meeting Michelle may have begun as a job, but his feelings for her were genuine.

The people that hired him had suspected as much and had *him* under surveillance. He thought they would stop watching her place once he was no longer there. The brothers were dangerous, and he feared for her safety. The women he brought into their home were meant to serve as a distraction to them. Armand simply did as instructed and tried not to ask them too many questions. He didn't want them to question his loyalties, and either the ruse didn't work, or they weren't watching him.

They were watching her.

"Michelle, please be careful. I love you."

"I am. I love you too."

Chapter 16

Brianna could hear Michelle's car pull up in the driveway. More importantly, she could see her through the peephole, where she had spent the last few minutes anticipating her arrival. She opened the door just as Michelle rang the doorbell.

"Michelle, I'm so glad you're here," Brianna said with a smile on her face.

"Hey, doll, I am too," Michelle replied, giving Brianna a big hug.

"So, let's get started, shall we?"

Brianna grabbed Michelle by the hand and led her to the white room.

"My dad has two favorite places in this house: his office and this room," Brianna stated as she took off her shoes and entered the room.

Michelle slipped off her shoes and entered behind her, her eyes quickly surveying the room, searching for anything that looked out of place. White was definitely an appropriate adjective. The carpet, couch, table, walls, and fireplace were all white. Nearly everything in the room was white except for one painting that hung above the fireplace. Michelle decided to start there. Brianna took a seat on the couch to watch her work. She loved watching Michelle's brain sort through things. It was a real treat for her. Michelle pulled the painting from the wall far enough to peer behind it . . . and found exactly what she was looking for.

"What are you thinking?" Brianna asked.

"This is the only thing that doesn't seem like it belongs here. If your father has a hiding place, it would be somewhere near here."

"Oh, okay."

"I also thought this painting is really awful," Michelle joked. "Come help me move this. There's a safe underneath it."

Brianna got up and helped Michelle remove the painting, placing it alongside the wall. Then Brianna turned her attention to the safe and began trying different numerical sequences hoping to unlock it. After several unsuccessful tries, at Michelle's suggestion, she unlocked it using their birthday. Not the most imaginative idea but Michelle figured that Frank was not versed in criminology enough to know *not* to use a numerical sequence so easily attained. Michelle peered into the safe and studied its contents.

There were a few rolls of cash, birth certificates, a diary, and few other nonessentials.

"I think this is it," Michelle stated as she pulled out a manila envelope similar to the one she received. "My friend told me that there's some unfavorable information in here. Are you sure you're ready for this?"

Brianna had already considered the ramifications of her probing and decided that truth was better than the comfort of whatever lies she may be currently living in. "Michelle, we found out a week ago that our parents have been lying to us our entire lives. I doubt there is anything in there that could be worse than that."

Michelle shook her head, still not wanting to believe that, but accepting its truth at the same time. "True enough." She opened the envelope and spread its contents on the floor around where she and Brianna were sitting. In it were bank statements, photographs, and what looked to be a lockbox key. Michelle grabbed the photographs, recognizing some of them from the package she received earlier. The others she couldn't bring herself to even speak about.

"Brianna, looks like you were right."

Brianna tried to swallow the air that materialized in her throat. She only suspected that her mother had been unfaithful, but to *see* her infidelity, in print, was a different beast altogether. Brianna felt like she held her father's broken heart. She wiped the tears forming in the corners of her eyes with the back of her hand.

"These must have been what my father saw. It was too much for him." It was a simple statement, but her tone posed an important question.

Brianna needed confirmation that Michelle understood and agreed with her reasoning. She needed her sister to remind her that she was not crazy for having her mother followed like some common criminal. That it was not merely right but the only feasible course of action. However, Michelle was distracted by *her* own thoughts. For the moment, the only father she could be concerned with was her own. Leonard Lewis, whose features were prevalent in too many frames for Michelle's comfort. Her shock was obvious as she studied his silhouette as it draped with Lisa's, drawn in a lovers' embrace, trying to come up with a palpable reason for his presence . . . and finding none.

She was even more confused now. First, a connection to Charlie she could not explain, and now this? If he had already been intimate with Lisa, why did he hire Charlie to get close to her? Although she could barely stomach the knowledge of his betrayal, a more ominous question remained unanswered: How could he do this to her mother? She was glad that her mother would never have to learn of this. Her body shuddered as the truth rose into her consciousness and embedded itself in her bones. She had no idea who her father was. Michelle shook her head to reclaim her mind and return to her *here and now*.

"Bria, I know who some of these people are."

Brianna looked at Michelle with curiosity rooting itself in her deep brown eyes. Michelle picked up a photo of Charlie and Lisa venturing through the North Park Mall. "This woman is Charlie, an exotic dancer."

"Lisa's a stripper?" Brianna closed her eyes and fell backward onto the floor. Her temple throbbed incessantly as the depravity of Lisa's betrayal waged war on her sensibilities. Hot tears streamed down her face as her pain and anger mingled. Brianna truly had no clue who Lisa was. Michelle continued.

"I spoke with Charlie today before I came over. She's known Lisa since grade school. From what she told me, they recently began *hanging out*."

Brianna was hurting, and Michelle could see it.

"Lisa is sleeping with a woman too? I don't understand. I know it's 2014 and all, but *really?* She and my father have been married for twenty years!" Brianna exclaimed. "This is not happening, Michelle; it can't be. My mother's gay?" Brianna was not looking for an answer. She wanted to understand, but more than that, she wanted it all to be a fictional tale.

"Bria, I know this is hard to hear, but we'll get through this together. You are not alone in this."

Michelle grabbed another picture and held it near Bria's face. She braced herself for the words that would come out of her mouth. "That man is my father."

Brianna sat up so fast, she almost knocked Michelle down in the process. "What!"

"My father and Lisa know each other somehow, though I'm not yet sure about the nature of their relationship." Brianna was dumbfounded. Michelle wasn't completely

honest. Intuitively, she felt that Lisa and her father had
a sexual history, but she couldn't bring herself to say it
aloud, much less share that information with Brianna.

"Michelle . . . I . . . I . . ." Brianna stammered, trying to
process this information. The possible affair was a hard
enough pill to swallow, but that wasn't what had her
speechless. Michelle's eyes confirmed that they had seats
on the same train of thought. If their parents had known
each other, how was it that neither had ever come to
realize that their children were identical?

"Bria, this is crazy. This entire situation is crazy! I don't
know what to think, literally. I keep calling this man
my father, but I don't know he is." Michelle shook her
head. "We don't know who our parents are, biological or
adopted. These people that have loved and raised us are
not who we thought they were."

Brianna shook her head in disbelief. She did not know
what to make of things either, but she knew that no matter what *the truth* was—Frank was her father. "Regardless
of whoever our biological parents are . . . these people . . .
They are still our parents. They paid for our college edu-
cations, taught us everything we know. We need to try
to hold on to that." Michelle allowed Brianna's words to
imbue her judgment, fostering a temporary base, a solid
place from which she began again. "I was starting to feel
like I lost something, but now that I think about it, I have
only gained."

Timidity left her words as she spoke, finding clarity
in the spaces. "This has always been our reality. The
difference is that now we're aware of it. Now that we are,
we have the power to change it."

Brianna listened intently while Michelle spoke, but
questions continued to inundate her thoughts. "I guess
I'm just freaking out a little. What if Lisa and Lewis are
our parents? What if this was some whole diluted scheme,
and they all conspired to keep us apart?"

"Sure, Michelle, and why would they do that?"

"I don't know. Hell, it all seems a little ironic, don't you think? They are having a secret affair and each of them . . . has one of us?"

"I cannot think about that. This is already heavy enough. Let's not add stuff without any proof."

"What else are you thinking about? What's bigger than this? Why are we here?"

"How about my dad lying up in the hospital with a lesbian wife at his side? How about *that?*"

Michelle needed to calm down. She did not want to argue with Brianna. This was a lot for them both. Frustration was taking over.

"Bria, I . . . I feel like I don't know who I am. I don't know what to believe. Nothing is off-limits. All I have is speculation. I'll use that to find the truth. You have to draw a path to walk one; otherwise, you could end up anywhere."

Brianna looked at the picture of Lisa, her mother, with Lewis, and the other picture with Charlie, still reeling from the hard evidence. Secretly, she hoped this venture to be a frivolous one. She wanted to be wrong. She could tell Michelle was fighting to hold on to her sanity. Her eyes left her exposed and gave Brianna access to her private musings.

"Brianna, I mean, you don't find it odd at all?"

"Of course, I do, but what does that mean? What does it matter if I do?"

"The odds were against us ever finding each other. How random was it that you chose my ad on craigslist?"

Brianna stopped breathing. Small bumps the size of iodized salt crystals climbed her arms as her body chilled from the inside out. How could she have missed it? She had completely forgotten about him in the midst of everything else that had been going on. "Not random at all, actually. Uncle Jacob—"

Michelle grabbed Brianna's arm and finished her sentence. "I know a Jacob!"

Brianna stared at Michelle excitedly, energized by Michelle's sudden burst of glee. "Jacob Wilson. He's a lawyer, right?"

"Yes!"

The hype resided, and Brianna's wheels of thought began to turn. "He recommended your company. I never thought anything of it until now."

Michelle could not believe it. The odds were too great that he would send Brianna to her and Charlie to Lisa without knowing anything. He had to know something. "Wait, how do you know him?"

"Charlie knows a man named Jacob."

Michelle paused briefly to be certain that Brianna was following her.

Brianna nodded her head, signaling that she understood.

"If he is the same person, which I presume is the case, he also told Charlie how to find Lisa."

Brianna saw where Michelle was going. "He must know something. This is entirely too coincidental. He's been a friend of my father's for years. I used to have play dates with his daughter all the time. He's been like an uncle to me."

Brianna rehashed every conversation she could remember, looking for clues, things she might have missed that could help them now. She would not call him again. He had twenty-two years to tell her . . . She paused in the midst of her thoughts . . . Something told her that this was his way of telling her. He led her directly to Michelle in his own way, without confessing a single word.

"If I ever get the chance to meet him, I think I'll hug him and thank him," Michelle spoke from her heart. She meant every word. She loved Brianna.

"I am grateful for that, but if he sent Charlie to Lisa, then he's complicit in her affair as far as I'm concerned. I don't know how I feel about him right now."

Michelle didn't even want to broach the subject given the probable romance between Lisa and her father. She thought it best to move on and quickly. "Let's take a look at some of these papers."

Michelle picked up the bank statements. "Umm . . . Bria . . . I think these are your parents' bank statements."

Michelle handed the papers to Brianna. After perusing the paperwork, Brianna's jaw dropped. It *was* her parents' bank statements, but the dollar amount could not be right. There was less than $50,000 in there. "Michelle, if this is correct, my parents are damn near broke. My dad never gave any hint that he had anything less than a few million dollars. What is going on? Millions are missing!"

Brianna was floored. Her parents were, in large part, responsible for the lifestyle she enjoyed. Her company was only a few years old. If their money was gone, things would certainly change for her too. She racked her brain trying to postulate some solution. She snapped her fingers as the answer dawned on her. "My mom has a secret account. Uncle Jacob told me, inadvertently, awhile ago that 'a smart woman always keeps an umbrella because the rain will always come; every drought has an end.' I think he was telling me that my mom has another account. One my father does not know about. We need to find that account number."

"What is your plan? Why do you want to find it?"

Brianna grinned mischievously. "Perhaps we can use it to get some answers."

"Blackmail?"

"Whatever it takes."

Michelle did not contest the suggestion. Their parents had forced them to live in an alternate reality, to exist in a negative space with no intention of ever removing them from the black room. But as more of the picture developed and the images came into focus, one thing was very clear: the deception ran deep, and their quest for the truth was not only rewriting their notion of their family but altering them as individuals as well. They simply needed to find out how much of their truth was fabricated.

Chapter 17

Frank was relieved to still have his life. For a moment, he was convinced he was losing it. When his world went black, and he found his breath leaving him, his last thoughts were of Brianna. He would move heaven and earth for her. He looked to his left and saw his wife, Lisa, asleep on the sofa bed. If he could speak, he would have hurled every curse word imaginable at her. He had accepted a great deal from Lisa. He thought he had been a good husband, especially since he had overlooked her various affairs, but the thought of her stealing from him was unforgivable.

Why would she need to do that? She had full access to whatever her heart desired. He had made sure that she had the best of everything. His money was always *theirs*. There must have been a reason, but he could not think of one. Maybe it was Karma for the shameful thing he'd done so many years ago. The lives that were forever changed. If that was the case, Frank would accept his punishment. His beautiful daughter was a constant reminder of how desperate and callous he had behaved in the pursuit of the millions that were now missing. Each time he looked at her face, a part of him died. The guilt tore him up inside. As if the deed itself was not enough, he had to pay a lot of people to cover his tracks.

Thinking of it all reopened wounds that never healed properly. He used to attribute it to destiny. Finding Brianna's mom that day and convincing her that Brianna should be his was both the best and most awful thing he'd ever done in his life. Money had never been an issue for him; Frank was accustomed to paying for what he wanted. Out of all the things he'd purchased in his life, his college degree, his wife, homes, cars, etc., Brianna had been his greatest purchase to date. Frank couldn't regret the manner in which he came to father Brianna since he had never loved anyone as much as he loved her. Besides, he had kept his promise; his little girl received the best of everything.

He paid to have a false birth certificate created, to have the legal documents granting the adoption drafted, and even paid Jacob to keep his trap shut about the whole thing since he was the facilitator. Brianna being ignorant of the fact that she had a twin sister out there, as beautiful and probably as sweet as she, was the only part of this that left a bitter taste in Frank's mouth. He could no longer stomach his hypocrisy. He possessed the information about the whereabouts of her sister; he'd had it since they brought her home from the hospital. He had gone out of his way to make sure that their paths never crossed, and it wasn't a cheap secret to keep.

Frank had been paying the "Marx Brothers" a hefty amount of money to keep tabs on Brianna's twin's family, specifically her sister. He had been able to ensure that Brianna never happened to run into her by knowing her twin sister's exact location at all times. Now, with his money gone, he had no way to keep this in place. Even if he did want to keep this from Brianna, he did not know how he would be able to do so. He could only hope that the Marx Brothers would accept that their arrangement had run its course. Frank may not only lose his daughter but his life as well.

Chapter 18

It had been a few days since Michelle had last seen Brianna, and her mind was still perplexed with the onslaught of information. Not only had they discovered a possible affair between Lisa and her father, Lewis, but Brianna's parents were broke in comparison to their usual standards. Millions of dollars were missing from their account. The two sisters had found another set of bank statements in Frank's office that said something completely different. Something was definitely not right. One set had been altered and did not reflect the true account balance. Michelle could only surmise that it was Lisa's doing. What if Lisa had a private account *for her eyes only?* It would make sense if she did.

She did not know what the misrepresentation of facts had to do with Lisa's past as a dancer, but she would soon find out. Charlie had not mentioned anything about Lisa stripping, only that she had seen the dude, or Lewis, as Michelle confirmed, and Lisa meeting at the club several times. Michelle could not think of any reason they would choose to go there unless they both had some connection to it. She needed to check it out; maybe it would lead to the man behind the curtain. Someone or a group of persons got all of this started, and Michelle intended to find out who. There was way too much dirt for no green to exchange hands. Locating "Oz" would be the true test, and it was imperative that she passed. Her gut was telling her that "Oz" would know exactly who their parents were.

Between the pictures she received and those Armand sent to Brianna, she was convinced that someone had to know something. Armand had recent pictures, but those she received were dated from high school. Who would even know to send those to her and with a note telling her who to talk to? The one woman she had not spoken with was her mother, Sophie. Sophie had always been able to read Michelle like a book. They were so much alike, and Michelle knew that her mom would pick up on any slight change in her voice. She needed to regroup before going to her house.

It had been over a week since they last spoke, and if she waited too much longer, she knew her mom would get upset and start bombarding her with phone calls. Given everything she had learned about her dad, she did not want to cause her mom any grief. Michelle looked out her bedroom window to find the black sedan back in its usual place. Armand still had not contacted her with any information about it, and although they had not tried anything, their presence made her uncomfortable. She called the police and had them send a cruiser by. That usually got them to leave. She did not want them following her to her parents' house. Michelle showered and got dressed, preparing to head home, wondering how far down the rabbit hole she'd have to go.

Chapter 19

A few days passed, and Sophie had calmed down considerably. Lewis had never put his hands on his wife before the other night. He surprised himself by doing so. He had not intended to hurt Sophie and didn't feel responsible for what happened. If Sophie had given him the information he wanted, it never would have happened. All she had to do was let him know where she got the photographs, but she stuck with her anonymous messenger story all night, and Lewis could not accept that lie. She was going to give him the name, even if he had to beat it out of her. Turned out, that was exactly what he did. He beat her like she was a man . . . like he would a stranger, but he still didn't get an answer.

His friend Louis XIII had rid him of any inhibitions he may have had. The sight of his wife's black eyes, her swollen, bloodied face, colored with variations of blue and purple, paralyzed him for a second. Lewis actually had to admire the beauty of the palette. Sophie fought back at first and showed some real courage, a little grit, but near the end . . . Even her tears had deserted her. Pathetic. Not only had she failed him, but she had failed herself.

He pitied her, and it disgusted him. He wondered how he ever married such a weak woman. Eventually, he simply gave up and left her to lick her wounds. Sophie had been avoiding him and had not said much of anything since the incident. He heard her asking Michelle not to come by earlier that morning. He wanted to see his daughter, but it was probably for the best that she did not see her mom in that condition. He could swing by her place later. Lewis still had a real issue: he did not know how Sophie got those pictures, and he was not comfortable with the notion of someone watching his every move. That warranted his prompt attention.

Sophie slept in one of the spare bedrooms, obviously not wanting to be in the same room with him, much less sleep with him. He was still angry and didn't want to be bothered with her anyway; he needed space to think. Lewis was aware that he had made enemies over the years. People didn't like to see you getting money unless you're willing to share it, but this was personal. He couldn't think of how the destruction of his marriage would be beneficial to anyone. He reached out to a few friends, but no one heard anything.

Knock ... knock ... knock ...

"Come in," Lewis told her.

Sophie walked slowly into the room, still in pain from their altercation a few days earlier.

"Lewis, I know that you're still mad, and I wish I knew who sent the pictures, but I don't. I'm sorry that I disappointed you." Sophie's demeanor was understated, her face downcast. "I want you to know that I still love you, and I know that you didn't intend to hurt me. You never have before."

Lewis was pleased. He *had* been good to her, and he was glad that she realized that she had brought what happened upon herself. Perhaps she was telling the truth and really got the pictures by an unknown messenger.

"You don't know where the pictures came from?" he asked one last time. Sophie shook her head. "Okay, I believe you, sweetheart." He motioned for her to come to his side. "I'm sorry this happened. I love you, and as long as you're honest with me, it won't happen again."

Lewis pulled Sophie's face to his and kissed her softly. Staring into her beautiful blue eyes, he was reminded of how deeply he loved her. He pulled her into the bed with him. He was gentle as he loved her. Trying to be considerate of her tender body, he took his time and ravaged her slowly. Kissing her neck, circling the outline of her breasts, and planting soft kisses across her flat stomach. Sophie moaned with pleasure, returning his love with as much fervor as her body would allow. She cried out softly at the feel of his tongue on her aching breasts. It had been such a long time. With his hand, he explored the depth of her wetness, probing her first with one, then two, and finally, three fingers.

Sophie relaxed and gave in to the moment, pushing away her angst, swallowing her disgust, and freed her body to enjoy her husband's touch. She felt his hardness pulsing between her legs. She took her hands and dug her nails into his back. Tasting the salt layer covering his hard chest, neck, sucking his fingers, whatever her lips could find, until the salt turned to sugar. Sophie gasped when Lewis entered her. His strokes were slow and deliberate, their lovemaking passionate and extensive.

Her breath heavy in his ear, her legs up over his shoulders, Lewis pushed into her womanness until he was saturated with her natural juices. He felt her contracting around his member, and despite his efforts to delay his climax, he would not last too much longer. Their bodies emanated so much heat, their bedroom was now a steamy sauna. The aroma of sex and deception fragranced the air. Lewis's strokes grew more intense, rapid, defining, and more purposeful. His body screamed as his heartbeat quickened. He felt a warm sensation spreading throughout his body, euphoria beckoning to both of them. After they had climaxed, they lay breathless, blanketed in silence, each lost in their thoughts.

Sophie wanted to cry, to grieve for the years she lost when *this man* had chosen *not* to be present, to not be a part of her. Things could have been different if *this man* had shown up more often.

"Lewis, would you like breakfast, babe?"

Lewis kissed her. It was music to his ears. He heard his stomach growling in anticipation. This was the Sophie he married. "Of course, I would."

"I can bring it to you if you'd like."

"That would be great, honey."

Sophie grabbed her robe and left to get his breakfast. She was still sore, and it hurt very much to move, but this breakfast was important to her. She needed to show Lewis that she was capable of serving him in the way that he deserved. She had gotten up early that morning and cooked quietly in order not to disturb him. After warming his food in the microwave, she placed his scrambled eggs, bacon, grits, and two slices of lightly buttered toast on one plate, his short stack of pancakes on another. She wavered for only a moment before placing those plates with one glass of orange juice and one of water, all on a tray, and prepared to take it into the bedroom to Lewis.

She took a deep breath and concentrated on not dropping the tray. She did not want to upset him again. It took several minutes, but she made it without mishap and placed the tray in front of him. He eyed the food, licking his lips as he anticipated sating his hunger pangs. He seemed genuinely grateful for it. Sophie almost remembered how good it felt to be appreciated by him.

Almost.

"I hope it's to your liking," she said.

Lewis was too busy eating to notice that Sophie grabbed a chair and now sat beside the bed, facing him.

She attempted small talk as he nearly inhaled his meal. "I had to get up early because I wanted it to be perfect for you. It's taking me a little while to move around here lately."

Lewis heard her, but he wasn't listening.

Undaunted by his ravenous appetite, she continued to engage in the one-sided conversation. "Michelle called this morning upset about something, but I assured her she'd figure it out. You know Michelle . . . always digging into things."

Lewis was a bit surprised by his appetite. The events over the last week must have taken more out of him than he realized. He couldn't get enough. "Sophie, this is really good, girl. It's been awhile since you've cooked like this. All my favorites too."

Sophie smiled. "Thank you. I wanted you to enjoy it."

Lewis picked up the glass of water and drank it. Something about the food had left him thirsty. He immediately regretted his decision. Lewis started coughing, gasping for air but failed to fill his newly punctured lungs with the oxygen he needed. He was suffocating, looking at his wife for help.

"Everyone deserves a good last meal—even a jackass like you. Putting your hands on me was a mistake. I have taken a lot from you. I put up with your infidelity, your absence. I raised your daughter alone, and perhaps I would have gone on and continued to do so, but you got greedy. Thought that you could beat me and still live? I don't think so."

Lewis was in shock. What was happening? He wanted to speak, but he couldn't. Sweat dripped from his brow, burning his eyes, but he stubbornly kept them open, staring intensely at Sophie, searching her eyes for an answer, but he found none. He didn't see any life at all.

"Don't be afraid, love; it will be over soon. You really shouldn't be so predictable, Lewis. Why would I apologize for you beating me? I cannot believe you fell for that.

I guess I should thank you for the . . . *studio session* this morning. That's what you refer to it as, isn't it? I hadn't planned on it; then I thought, why not? It was one of the few things you always did well."

Sophie shook her head and laughed loudly. Lewis understood he was going to die. He abandoned his toil and looked at the woman he married. No one deserved this, he thought, not even him. The end was near and watching Sophie's eyes as they showed him the way seemed cruel. She enjoyed his suffering.

"You made this too easy. I almost hate to tell you that Michelle is not an only child. It's so anticlimactic."

Lewis tried to sit up, but he could not. His body was still weak from their lovemaking, and his health deteriorated at a rapid rate. While he heard the words Sophie spoke, he did not understand. What did she mean by Michelle not being an only child? Of course, she was. Sophie could see the confusion in his eyes. She decided to twist the knife and began to stab into his heart. "That night, when you didn't bother coming to the hospital? I gave birth to twins."

Lewis began to cry. He had another daughter? He could not believe he had been so blind. This woman was pure evil.

"Don't cry, Lewis. I was promised that she would be taken care of, and I'd like to believe she has. Of course, you'll never truly know, will you? Shame. Things could have been different. Oh well . . ."

By now, his breaths were shallow, empty. His life flashed before his eyes. His mother and daughter . . . Lisa and the women he bedded . . . the day he proposed to Sophie. He lived a fast life and enjoyed every moment of it. He did not have one single regret. Maybe it was fitting that he left this way. He only wished he had a chance to say good-bye to Michelle and see his other daughter. He was sure she was as beautiful as her sister.

To Sophie, he only had one last thing to say—if only he could have had the ability to speak for one final moment. In his mind, he cursed her before attempting to take his last breath. *I'll see you in hell, bitch.*

Chapter 20

Michelle felt uneasy, convinced something was wrong with her mom, but she didn't want her coming over. She could only hope it wasn't too bad. She needed to relax. Michelle hadn't heard from Armand for a few days, either. It wasn't like Armand not to call to at least say hello. She had spoken with Charlie a few times despite her warning at the close of their last meeting, though she had not gotten a whole lot of new information. She was only able to confirm that her dad had a sexual history with Lisa, Charlie, and several other current or ex-strippers.

According to the information, he would put them up in a hotel suite and cover their expenses. She did not know where he got the money to do all of this because she knew he didn't have a conventional 9-to-5 career, but it didn't matter much in the grand scheme of things. Michelle was appalled by his behavior. Besides, the bruise around Charlie's neck was hard to miss. Lewis was a monster, and she was ashamed to be his daughter. For the first time since fate brought her and Brianna together, she was happy with her probable adoption.

"Is it bad that I never made love . . . I never did . . . but I sure know how to . . ."

"Hey, Bria, I was just thinking about you. So glad you called."

Brianna explained that she wanted to go out of town. This situation was stressing her out, and her dad had not been released from the hospital yet. Apparently, he had contracted some sort of infection, and they were keeping him longer. Michelle, realizing that she was wound up a bit too tightly herself, thought perhaps a vacation would be exactly what the doctor prescribed.

"Sure, love, we can go for the weekend. I could use a break too."

Michelle hung up the phone and called her mom. The phone rang for a little while, but eventually, she answered.

"Mom, are you sure you're okay . . . Well, I'm going out of town for the weekend. I'll have my cell on me if you need anything. By the way, have you spoken with Lew—I mean Dad lately? Oh, you have? Is he there with you? No . . . oh, okay . . . Well, I'm going to get ready to head out. I love you."

Michelle looked out her window. The black sedan was there, as usual. She decided to call Armand. "Armand, can you come over, please? Thanks." She needed to clear the air before she left. It was time to get to the bottom of whatever was going on with him. She couldn't play this game anymore.

It took Armand a little under thirty minutes to get to the apartment. They sat across from each other in the living room, staring each other down, wondering who would speak first. Michelle decided to take the initiative. "What is going on with you, Armand? Why are you faking infidelity?"

Armand was caught off guard but not completely surprised. He looked at her with raised eyebrows, fell back into the couch, and threw his hands up in surrender with a big grin on his face. "You're right; I would never betray you that way. I love you."

Michelle smiled. "I know that . . . plus, I had security cameras installed, in case the sedan ever tries anything."

Armand did not know that. He laughed at the thought. She had known this entire time but had argued with him like she hadn't.

"I knew you were lying, but I thought if I went along with you, I could figure out why on my own."

Armand took a deep breath. "Of course, you did. I only did it to protect you. The people I work for . . . They aren't good people."

Michelle looked toward the window. "You work for the black sedan?"

"Somewhat, yes. Unfortunately, I don't have a great deal of information to share with you. I . . . I . . . ." Armand was afraid to confess the whole truth. He did not want to tarnish what he and Michelle had, but he didn't have a choice at this point. "Our meeting was not by accident. I was hired to get close to you."

Michelle felt like the wind had been knocked out of her. Their entire relationship had been a lie? She could not accept that. "No, Armand. No, that cannot be true." Tears fell like hot wax from a candle, creating intimate pockets around her collarbone. "We have been together *two years,* Armand! All this time you were only pretending? I can't . . . "

Armand got up to take a seat beside her. "Michelle, it may have started out that way, but my loving you is real. Don't you see? I was not supposed to fall for you, but I did. Now, I'm afraid for you."

Michelle tried to focus her thoughts. She felt faint. Did she know anyone anymore? Everyone and their damn secrets!

He continued. "It was about your dad. They wanted to get to him."

Of course, it was about him. Everything seemed to involve him lately.

"Look, the Marx Brothers are not to be played with. I brought the girls here because I was trying to throw them off."

Michelle shook her head. This mess was too deep. "What do they want with my father? Why didn't you tell me instead of lying all this time?"

"What was I supposed to say, MK? 'By the way, babe, two years ago I was hired to keep tabs on you'?"

"Yes! That's *exactly* what you should have said! These people may be dangerous. I could have been killed! You don't even know what they want, Armand!"

"I think, if that was the case, they would have done it by now."

"What type of backward-ass logic is that? They haven't killed me because they haven't killed me? Do you even *hear* yourself?"

"I don't know what they want, and I'm sorry I didn't tell you, but after a while . . . I simply didn't know how. I never thought it would get this deep between us. Thought I could get out of it, give them something so they would go away."

"Oh yeah, Armand? How is *that* working out for you?" Michelle was furious. Armand had known all this time who these people were and had not said a thing to her about it. "I'm calling the police."

"Wait, what? No, you cannot call the police."

"Why not, Armand?"

"I think getting the DPD involved would make things worse for us."

Michelle didn't want to admit it, but he was right. She watched her mom deal with the police over her father more often than she liked through the years, and it was never pretty. It took them forever to do anything, but she still would have felt better being able to turn it over to them. "All right, fine, so what should we do now? Do you know why they chose you?"

Armand shrugged his shoulders. "I honestly don't know. They approached me with a picture of you. Told me they'd pay me to kick it with you. I would have done it for free, but I took the money. At the time, I didn't see the harm, but after a while, it changed. It was a strange request, but I really needed the money at the time. I was desperate."

Michelle looked out the window. The black sedan was no longer parked there. "Well, they are not here now."

"Michelle, I know how all of this must sound to you, but it's the truth. I love you."

"Not at all. I think I need a drink."

Michelle's last statement made her start laughing. She had never had a drink in her life. Armand thought maybe she had lost it, but he caught the bug himself and got lost in a good laugh.

Michelle's joyful tears turned into painful ones in an instant. Armand held her tightly and let her cry softly. She needed to release the tension in her body. He needed to hold her. For a moment, for Michelle, everything was as it should be. Armand was her safe place. Although their beginning had been orchestrated, she refused to let that destroy everything they had built together. The love between them was strong enough to survive a less-than-perfect start.

"Armand, so much has changed. I'm overwhelmed by it all."

"What's going on?" He braced himself for what she had to say.

"Ha! Where do I start?"

"The beginning." Hearing that made Michelle chuckle again, but Armand was serious.

"I'll give you the condensed version. I have a twin sister, and we recently learned that our parents have been sleeping together or slept together at some point. Lisa is Brianna's mom."

"Twin sister?"

"Yep."

"What do you mean your parents have been sleeping together? Like a big orgy or something?"

"No, nothing like that, not from what we can tell." Michelle wasn't sure, but she could not rule out that possibility, though.

"My father and her mother have been . . . involved."

"What does that mean, then? Is this Lisa your real mom?"

Michelle shrugged. "I thought I was biracial until I met Brianna. My mother is white! Lisa is black. I honestly don't know what to think."

"Wow. I know this is a lot, but I'm confident that you'll be fine. We'll figure this out together."

Michelle was grateful to be able to discuss things with Armand. Keeping it from him had been extremely difficult. "So, the Lisa Mason you had me follow . . . that's the same . . ."

"One and the same."

"Then Lisa may be in trouble."

"She *is* trouble."

"No, seriously. The woman she's been hanging out with is bad news."

"I met with her."

"What?"

"I got a package with a note telling me to look for her."

"So you do random shit by yourself now? What the fuck, Michelle?"

"I didn't know she was dangerous."

To be as intelligent as she was, Michelle was capable of doing some really stupid shit. Armand wanted to know every detail. "Did you notice anyone following you?"

"Not that I remember. Why?" Michelle continued to let the wheels in her head spin as she watched him pace back and forth.

Armand continued his pacing, wondering why the Marx Brothers had not tried to contact him lately. He thought something was wrong. Now he was certain.

Michelle could sense his nervous energy. "What is it, Armand?"

"I think you need to leave town for a while."

"I'm already headed out of town for the weekend."

"Good, but that may not be long enough. Are you going alone? Where are you headed?"

"To Cancun with Brianna, but why do I need to leave?" Alarm bells started ringing in her ears all over again. "What aren't you telling me, Armand?"

"I don't know how everything is connected yet, but I get the feeling that I am no longer of use to them. If that is the case . . . I know too much. They are not going to let me walk away. I need to know you're safe until I can figure this out."

Michelle was worried and felt her heart rate increasing. "Armand, do you think someone might try to kill me?"

"Michelle, just breathe. I won't let anything happen to you. Go with your sister, try to relax. You should be safe there. I want you away from all of this."

"Armand, how am I supposed to relax if some Marx Brothers people are trying to kill me?"

"You will be safe as long as no one knows where you are, all right? Just trust me on this. Don't tell your mom. Tell Brianna not to tell anyone. Just go."

Michelle looked around, succumbing to the thunderous wave of panic begging her to sleep.

"Michelle . . . Michelle! Don't check out on me." Armand grabbed her shoulders, trying to pierce through the glaze in her eyes. "MK. MK! Can you hear me?"

"I hear you. I hear you. I need a minute to process this." She sat back, resting her head on the couch for a few minutes. Then she picked up her cell phone and hit a button on speed dial.

Armand raised an eyebrow. "Michelle . . . Who are you calling?"

Michelle brought a finger to her lips to silence him. "Brianna . . . What time is our flight? Six o'clock this evening? All right . . . Don't tell anyone we're leaving, okay? I'll explain when we land. Love you too."

"Michelle, listen, I don't—"

"We're going to Mexico. We'll be there for at least the weekend."

"Michelle—"

"If I can convince her to stay longer, we will, but for now . . . It's the weekend."

Armand conceded, realizing that he could not win. He couldn't worry about that now; his mind was already thinking ahead, plotting his next move. He could not let anything happen to Michelle. He would protect her at all costs. He needed to speak with Lewis. He may have started out being an indirect target, but now he would become his ally.

Chapter 21

It was nearly time to take Frank home. The small infection cleared, and he was ready to be released from the hospital. He was awake and alert but still had not spoken to Lisa. She was not sure how to interpret that but thought perhaps it was best that he not say anything, especially if what he had to say had anything to do with their financial situation. What would she tell him? *"Sorry, love, but I've been robbing you blind to pay my ex-lover to keep quiet about my stripper past?"* Right. She could not see a scenario in which that would go over well.

Lisa really wanted to see Charlie. She always managed to help her relax. She wanted to cut her off, but she couldn't. Charlie was an addiction; she knew exactly how to touch her. Everything she liked and hated. Sometimes, it felt like Charlie could see into her soul. She also had not heard from Lewis. It was not like him to go without calling her, but she could not say she wasn't enjoying it, though she wasn't sure if his absence was a good thing or a bad one yet. Time would tell. Lisa was stressed.

"Lisa." Frank's voice pierced through her thoughts, startling her.

Lisa quickly grabbed her chest. She had hoped to at least make it home. The silence was preferred over the uncomfortable conversation she assumed they were about to have. She could not even face her husband, afraid of what he had to say.

"Lisa, look at me."

"Franklin—"

"Don't do that . . . Don't do that. Turn around."

Lisa turned to meet her husband's stare, his hazel eyes filled with tears. "Frank, what's wrong?"

"Don't do that. You know *exactly* what's wrong. I asked you what happened to all our money, and I have been waiting for an answer. For over a week, I have waited. I am *still* waiting."

Had Frank been awake? Had he really asked? Lisa was shaking. How could he possibly know? Her lips quivered.

"Franklin . . . sweetheart—"

"Stop calling me that! Only my *wife* calls me, that and you are *not* her! I don't know who in the hell you are, but you are *not* the woman I married and loved for twenty-something years." Tears streamed down his face.

"Okay, okay, Frank, you need to calm down. You're still in your hospital gown, for Christ's sake."

"What did I do to you, Lisa? What did I do that would cause you to steal from me? I gave you everything!"

"Frank, look, we can discuss whatever it is you're upset about when we get home, okay?"

Lisa began getting his things together, getting her things together, preparing for the ride home, when she heard something that nearly cut her to her core.

"You are not welcome in my house."

Lisa stopped, turning toward Frank. Surely she had heard him incorrectly. "What did you say?"

"What are you confused about? I don't want your lying ass in my house."

Lisa closed her eyes. Her fists clenched involuntarily, and her thin lips trembled. Her face was flushed and red with fury. She had been afraid of this conversation, but now that it's happening . . . screw it. She was not going to cower and run from it. Everything that meant something to her was dangling in front of her.

"Are you sure you want to do this here?"

"I asked, didn't I?"

A nurse walked in, saw the situation, and sharply turned around, closing the door behind her.

"Franklin, let me be clear." The fright gripping her insides was hidden well behind her cold stare. Lisa faced her husband. Though she was well aware she lied, she would *not* allow him to disrespect her. Right or wrong, when she spoke to him, she did so in her full authority—as his wife. Regardless of whether he liked it, they were equals. "When we married, you did not love me. You hardly even knew me. So, you are right, I am *not* the woman you married, as if you had a clue about who she was! I was not even old enough to buy a fucking drink, but I *was* old enough to be a wife. I knew I was just one of the many purchases you'd make, and I didn't mind. I needed a change and didn't care how it came. So don't act like it was all love, because we both know that isn't true."

Frank was livid, but he could not refute her words. He had not loved her in the beginning, and he had gotten her like he did everything else in his life, with his money. That still didn't stop him from unleashing the anger in his heart. "Woman, I trusted you with my family's money, and you blew it! Where is it, Lisa? *Where is it?*"

"Is that all you care about? After all these years, Frank? Still? I cannot believe this."

"Lisa . . . You don't realize what you've done. You just don't—"

"I'm not finished. I knew you were only with me for that money, but I wanted the money too. Don't look so surprised. Get over it. At least have the courage to say it. I married you for your money, but I did love you. I grew to love you. I was in a bad situation coming into the marriage, and if you had taken the time to get to know me before you wedded me, maybe you would have known it too. You were so busy throwing your money around; you never bothered to ask *me* anything."

Frank was at a complete loss for words. He had no idea that Lisa had known all these years. Perhaps he really did not know her after all.

It was Lisa's turn to unleash the malice and contempt that resided in her heart. "And Brianna . . . That adoption should be in the *Guinness Book of World Records* because it was the quickest one I have ever heard of. One week's time, Frank? Where did you *buy* her? That *is* what you did, isn't it?"

Stunned, Frank got up from the bed and rushed at Lisa. Lisa's instincts took over as she lifted her leg and kicked him as hard as she could in his groin.

"Franklin, don't ever try to come at me—ever!"

Frank was lying on the floor in pain. His whole body hurt. It felt like the entire lower half of his body was on fire, and it spread throughout his limbs. He'd snap Lisa in half if he could only move. "Shiiiiiit! You dumb bitch!"

"Fuck you, Franklin. You deserved it. Don't ever come at me. Do you know who I was before I became Lisa Mason? Lisa Raine Wilson."

Frank stopped moving for a moment. He sat up as the pain subsided, trying to determine if he had heard her right. "Wilson? What are you talking about?"

"That's right . . . Lisa Wilson."

It was a coincidence. It had to be. Jacob had been *his* friend.

Lisa watched with satisfaction over her deceit as the horror crept into his face as the speculations swarmed through his mind. "Jacob is my foster brother, but we don't talk much. He kept whatever little secret he's sharing with you. It's funny and kind of ironic too. That day in the office, he didn't even recognize me, but I recognized him . . . immediately."

Frank wanted to speak, but it was obvious that Lisa no longer wanted to talk. Her demeanor changed. The temper previously displayed was replaced with an eerie calm. She purged her soul and was in the process of freeing herself. Her spirit felt lighter with every word. "As if I could ever forget him. I ran from one rapist, only to land in a foster home with another one. I didn't trust anyone when I first got there, but after a while . . . I trusted *him*. He was always nice to me. He stuck up for me with our parents and kept me from running. They weren't always nice to me. Jacob was older, and I felt safe for the first time. No one had ever done that before.

"Then, one night, with one thrust, he undid all the progress I had made. He ripped my innocence to shreds all over again. For years when I slept, I used to see him, long after he could no longer touch me. I was miles away from him, and he *still* had power over me."

Frank thought he would be sick. He could not believe what he was hearing. Jacob had been his close friend for years. It was hard to believe that he would be capable of doing something so cruel. This news repulsed him. He got up from the floor, reaching out to Lisa, unsure of how she would respond, or if it was even the proper thing to do.

"Lisa, come here, baby. Come here." He took her into his arms. "I am so sorry, Lisa. I had no idea. I really didn't."

"Frank, I need some space. I'm going to stay with a friend for a few days. Can you get home? I cannot do this right now."

"Listen, we can talk about the money later. All right? I'll handle it. I just . . . Let me be here for you now. Let me be here."

Frank still needed to know where the money went. He had not forgotten, but they could discuss that later. Lisa clearly needed him, and for probably for the first time in their marriage, he was able to see exactly how much.

"Frank . . . I need to get out of here."

"I'll give you some space, but I will come to get you. I love you." Frank was serious. He was not letting her go.

Lisa left the hospital room and called Charlie to pick her up. She needed her now more than ever. Jacob was the closest thing to family Frank had, and Lisa had never wanted to take that away from him. Even if she could not forgive Jacob for what he did to her, he did seem to be a different person, or maybe she just wanted him to be. In either case, the truth was out now, and Lisa felt better. She didn't need to be the victim anymore. She was reborn. The new Lisa wanted to see the woman that loved her, that seemed to know her. The last thing she wanted was a man.

Frank sat on the couch in his hospital room feeling woozy from the emotional roller coaster Lisa had taken him on. He went from hating her, to loving her, to wanting to protect her. He could not believe he had lived with this woman for over two decades and had been so ignorant of her life. He thought he loved her . . . that he had been a good husband, but he was no longer certain of that. His family had always handled things financially. It was simply what he had learned to do. Money made the world go 'round.

It was clear he had missed something. His wife had needed something that he had failed to give her: intimacy and understanding. He had been her business partner and not her friend. He did not know if he could be something he had never seen. He still was not even sure if it was his marriage or his ego he wanted to salvage, but one thing he did know: he needed to see

Jacob. Frank experienced an urge to seek something he never had before: retribution.

Frank knew where Jacob would be. He left the hospital and went directly to him. He made the forty-five-minute drive in twenty minutes. Things had not been the same between them for years. The tension had been building since Jacob suggested that Frank tell Brianna the truth. Frank politely reminded him that it was none of his business and if he should ever forget, perhaps the board would like to know of Jacob's side dealings, reminding him of how interested they might be in hearing about all the backdoor deals Jacob used to fund his lavish lifestyle.

That was about five years ago. Jacob had attempted to orchestrate a meeting between Brianna and her sister here and there; Frank shut it down every time.

After Jacob got Brianna's voice mail, he expected him to show up at some point. Since Jacob had caused Brianna's reunion with her sister, Michelle, he expected Frank to come and see him. He expected a civilized conversation, a meeting of the minds, but Frank was not in a talking mood. He, in fact, did not say a word. Jacob sat behind his desk at the back of the room in his office. Frank barreled through the halls of the one-story building with the force of a tsunami wave.

Jacob heard Frank before he saw him, the raised voices of a few young men, legal aides, vainly attempting to stop him . . . his assistant's screams as Frank tore past her, bursting through the large oak door into Jacob's office. Jacob stood at the sight of Frank's six-foot-four frame filling the doorway. Jacob subdued the urge to react defensively. Frank was visibly angry, and he did not want to make the situation worse, but Jacob had grossly underestimated the depth of Frank's rage.

When he opened his mouth to speak . . . *Bam!* Frank covered the six feet of distance between him and Jacob in seconds. Jacob's open mouth caught the full weight of Frank's 230 pounds carried in a nasty left hook. Before Jacob could respond, Frank leaped over Jacob's desk and connected with a right hook, breaking Jacob's jaw and sending him crashing to the ground. The sound of Jacob's jaw breaking echoed off the walls of the carpetless office.

Shock rendered Jacob immobile as Frank rained down blow after blow. Frank saw crimson as Jacob's blood soon covered his hands, face, and his clothes. Had he been in his rational mind, the blood would have caused him to stop, but it did not stop him or even slow him down. He imagined the red sticky substance on his face were *her* tears, serving to intensify his fury. Some of the associates had called the authorities, and the sirens sounded loudly outside as they breached the building. Frank did not hear the sirens; he only heard Lisa's screams muffled by Jacob's burly hands. The sound of her clothes as they ripped; her sense of security and self-worth shattering like glass cutting the sheets of the bed as Jacob violated her. He saw a young girl crumbling under the weight of a grown man. He wanted to stop Jacob, to prevent any pain from coming to her, but he could not. No matter how many times he hit Jacob, he could not save Lisa. He could not end her heartache.

After being shot with a drive stun gun twice and being Tasered, four officers were eventually able to restrain him. Jacob's face was hardly recognizable, and he was barely breathing. By the time the paramedics were able to get to him, the assessment of his injuries was astonishing. He suffered three broken ribs, a broken nose, a fractured jaw, his eyes were swollen shut, and his lips were busted. Frank sat emotionless, handcuffed in the back of the police car. He could only see Lisa's face. He remembered the numerous times he made love to her. How tender and soft her body had been. The way she felt, how she smelled of lavender and honey. It enraged him to think of Jacob being with her—his wife. Jacob had known all these years and never said a word to him. The mere thought that he had ever been friends with Jacob disgusted him. He worried about Brianna now and what he would say to her. He thought of Lisa and where she had gone. Frank was not sorry for what he did. He was certain that, had it not been stopped, he would have killed him.

Chapter 22

Cancun was exactly what Brianna needed. Javan had been blowing her phone up for three days straight and had shown up unexpectedly at her place the night before her flight left. She had hoped to avoid having the conversation with him altogether, but he clearly had different plans. With everything going on, she simply did not have time for him. She honestly did not want to hurt him, and as much as it pained her, she had to let him know that their relationship had run its course. He did not take it well, and she nearly called security to have him removed, but Michelle's call seemed to calm him down. With her attention diverted elsewhere, it gave him time to compose himself.

Some part of Brianna cared about Javan, but that thing she wanted at the moment was not a relationship. She didn't want to have someone else she had to fret about. Her parents' situation was reason enough for her to stay single for the rest of her life.

"Bria, come in here."

Michelle called Brianna in from the patio, back into the room where she was sitting at the table with her MacBook.

"What is it? I was trying to relax. It would behoove you to do the same. After all, we are in Cancun."

Michelle could not relax. She was still antsy about the Marx Brothers and hadn't figured out how to tell Brianna yet.

"I can't. I need to figure some of this out."

"Well, what did you find, Carmen?"

"Carmen?"

"Yea . . . you know . . . Where in the world is Carmen San Diego?" Brianna sang.

Michelle could not help but laugh at that. "Cole, you stupid. Anyways with an *s* . . . I called you in here to let you know that your dad was arrested yesterday."

"What? He was in the hospital!"

"Well, not anymore. Now, he's in Lew Sterrett."

"Let me see." Brianna pushed Michelle to the side and plopped down in front of her computer. "What does it say?"

"I don't know; you took the computer." Michelle pulled the MacBook closer to her. Brianna picked up her phone and called her dad. "His phone is going to voice mail."

"It says he's being charged with assault of a local attorney . . . *Jacob Wilson!*" Michelle was beyond shocked. "What in the world?"

"He must have found out that he told us somehow, right? What else could it be?"

"Are you serious, Bria? It could be *anything* else. I seriously doubt he knows anything about this," Michelle stated, motioning toward the two of them.

"I'm calling my mom. I cannot believe she didn't call me and let me know."

"Don't tell her where you are."

Brianna waved a dismissive hand in Michelle's direction. "I remember. She's not answering anyway. She must have had something to do with this."

"She might, but you need to be reasonable. It's not like she can force your dad into doing something he doesn't want to do."

Brianna rolled her eyes. "Whatever, *MA*chelle. I need to go see my dad."

"We just got here yesterday." Michelle did not know what else to say, but even she knew that lame excuse would not sway Brianna.

"And? I need to go and see about him. He was just released from the hospital."

"According to this article . . . He is not the one in need of care. Jacob is in the ICU."

"Oh my goodness . . ." Jacob's condition had not even registered with Brianna. "He fought Uncle Jacob? I don't understand this. I feel like I'm in a twilight zone or something." Brianna was perplexed. Even if her father somehow found out about her and Michelle, would it warrant a beat-down like that? She didn't think so. Her dad rarely ever raised his voice. It had to be something really big to provoke that type of violent reaction. Michelle thought that Brianna was making her mom a scapegoat for everything, and maybe she was, but she had been right to do so thus far, and she was convinced that this situation had something to do with her. Brianna went to her bag, grabbed the envelope Michelle's *friend* had sent her, and rejoined Michelle on the couch.

"I think there may be something in here we're missing."

"Well, you may as well add these into the mix." Michelle took the pictures she had received out of her computer bag and handed them to Brianna.

They both began sifting through pictures before Brianna saw something that caught her attention. "Michelle, I think this is Uncle Jacob. He's much younger, but I'm pretty sure that's him."

Michelle took the picture and looked it over. She thought it could be him, but the angle was not right, so it was difficult for her to tell. If she squinted a little and looked at it from an acute angle, it kind of looked like him. "It could be him, but the only picture I have for reference is this leaked hospital photo. So, what if it is?"

"Well, this picture is from the group that you were sent. Someone knew Uncle Jacob and Lisa when they were younger."

Michelle started to understand what Brianna was hinting at. "It could even be the person that sent the pictures in the first place."

"I think it is, but who could that be?"

"It's the wizard." Michelle was slightly annoyed. They were making connections but still finding more questions than answers.

Brianna needed a breather. The trip to Cancun was supposed to be an escape, but now she felt even more stressed. "I'm going for a walk."

"Where are you going? I'll finish this up and catch up with you."

"I'm headed toward the beach. I'll walk slowly."

"Cool. I shouldn't be long."

Brianna did not know exactly where she was going, but she knew she couldn't stay in the room any longer. She took the elevator down to the first floor of the hotel. She did not notice the two men trailing her as she made her way through the busy lobby and into one of the many on-site stores. Brianna wanted to grab a pair of shades and some more sunscreen. She had already started to burn a little bit from her time on the patio earlier. She made her purchases, and then made her way to the beach just out behind the hotel, hoping that a little stroll would help her to relax. The two men were not far behind her.

Michelle was glad Brianna went for a walk. It provided the perfect opportunity for her to call Armand. It was getting late, and the sun was setting. The scene from their patio was really beautiful. The sky was filled with gorgeous shades of lavender, pumpkin orange, light pinks, and deep crimson. Michelle wished she wasn't so preoccupied so that she could really enjoy it. This was her first trip away in years.

"Armand, what's going on? Have you made any progress?"

"Yes and no. The Marx Brothers have been calling me, but I've been avoiding them until I figure out some of this stuff. I'm trying to stay low and out of sight for now. I've been looking for your dad, but there's been no sign of him. It's almost like he disappeared. He hasn't been at any of his usual spots."

"Well, I talked to my mom before we left, and she said he wasn't home. I can try to see if she's heard from him."

"That's not necessary." Armand considered whether to let Michelle know where he currently was at that moment. "I've been sitting outside your house for a little while now, and there's no sign of your dad here."

"I'm not overly comfortable with you watching my mother like that, but at least she's safe. I find some measure of comfort in that."

"Of course. What's going on with you guys there? Everything all right?"

"It was . . . until we found out that Brianna's dad is in jail."

"In jail? What's his name?"

"Frank Mason. Have you heard anything? I only know what the news printed."

"Nothing I'm sure you don't already know. Where is your sister?"

"She went for a walk."

"You let her go alone, Michelle? What are you thinking?"

"You said we should be safe out here. I told her I'd catch up."

"You still need to take precautions. Does she know the danger you're in?"

"Did it follow us here?"

"That's not the point."

"Then make it plain, Armand. If you lied—"

"Did you tell her anything?"

"I didn't tell her . . . I—"

"Michelle . . ." Armand sighed in frustration. "Hold on."

Michelle could hear Armand pressing buttons.

"Why would you keep this from her?"

"I couldn't figure out how, and besides, she's already worried enough. Who were you texting just now?"

"No one. MK, this is too important. Go find her and tell her what's going on. This is *not* a good time for all these damn secrets. Why are you acting like a child?"

"*Excuse me?* I am just . . . This is a lot. I don't know what to do."

"You need to snap out of it. I'm not trying to be harsh, but we don't have time for you to clam up. Pull yourself together. Go find your sister. I'll see what I can find out about Frank, and I'll call you later."

Michelle felt awful. Armand was right; she did need to pull it together. She was not behaving like herself. She checked the time. Bria had been gone about twenty minutes. She quickly splashed some cold water on her face and took off to find her. She didn't want to tell her the danger they were really in, unsure of whether Brianna could handle more bad news, but she didn't have a choice. She needed to know.

Chapter 23

Lisa was relaxing in the hot tub at the Hilton Anatole. She had been with Charlie since she came to pick her up after her fight with Frank. She turned off her phone and decided to take some much-needed time away from the men in her life. Charlie hadn't asked too many questions, and Lisa was grateful for that, not wanting to discuss the situation. She needed to keep things as light as possible. She had been on edge since she found Frank lying on the floor in his office that day. Charlie kept things simple for her, and she needed simple.

In moments of severe stress or confusion, she craved Charlie, the peace and calm she felt in her presence. However, none of these things were enough for her to enter into a relationship with her. Lisa was not certain if she wanted a relationship with anyone. She had loved Frank, but she had not been happy with him for a considerable amount of time. This argument may have given her enough fuel to leave him for good. She had a sizable stash hidden. Money only she had access to; it was her emergency reserve. She was never going back to her old life, and she put cash aside as insurance.

Lisa's skin began to wrinkle. She grabbed her robe, slid her feet into her sandals, and started the trip back to Charlie's room. She used her key to open the door and found Charlie pacing the floor. Lisa wished there was some way to avoid inquiring about the reason for her obvious panic without seeming rude. She could not think of one single thing she could do.

"What's wrong, Charlie?"

"Jacob is in the hospital," Charlie spoke without thinking. She looked at Lisa and saw it was too late to take it back.

"Jacob?" Lisa searched Charlie's face for an explanation. She could tell by the uneasiness in Charlie's eyes that they were talking about the same Jacob. "Exactly how do you know Jacob?"

"Lisa, I think you need to sit down."

"I think I'll stand." Lisa felt the hairs on her arms react to the drop in room temperature. What was Charlie about to tell her?

"Lisa, I am not who you think I am . . . not completely."

"What are you talking about? What do you mean?"

"I have known you for a long time. I knew you before we met at the club that night."

Lisa closed her eyes and shook her head in protest. "No, I am good with faces. I would have remembered you. We never spoke before that night."

Charlie took a deep breath and sat down. She only uttered one word. "Indiana."

Lisa fell back into the door, banging her head against the wood. A loud ringing noise filled her ears, and all she could see were pieces of light. She could feel Charlie gently turning her around on the floor, with her small arms wrapped around her chest, pulling her toward the bed. Lisa did not want Charlie to touch her, but she was too dizzy to protest. Charlie stretched Lisa across the bed and propped a pillow beneath her feet for elevation, grabbing a cool, wet towel to cover her forehead. Lisa was conscious but not completely coherent. Disoriented and faint, it took everything she had to keep her eyes open.

Now Charlie was on the phone with someone. Lisa could scarcely make out the conversation. She could only hear bits and pieces, but Charlie was scared. She could hear it in her voice.

"What . . . He's dead? Are you . . . sure? . . . For how long? Murdered?"

Lisa could only hear every couple of words or so, and it was hard to concentrate. She gave up and succumbed to her thoughts. *Indiana.* That was the last word she heard Charlie say clearly. The only way Charlie could have known anything about Indiana was if she had been there, but what were the odds that they both would end up in Dallas? Texas was a big state. Lisa had to consider it, though. The odds were the same with Jacob, but they were both here. She tried to think back to her days in Indiana.

Many faces passed through her mind, but she could not place Charlie there. Not that Lisa could recall too much of anything from that time with any decent amount of clarity. It all seemed to be one long, alcohol-infused block of time. Too much pain awaited her there. The night she found the courage to run, she vowed that she would not look back, and she kept her promise. She foolishly attempted to remain in contact with her mom for the first few months but to no avail.

Lisa suffered through many phone calls, listening to her mother complain and blame her for leaving her alone with her husband, Lisa's father, who now lavishly adorned her with the same emotional and physical scars previously reserved for his daughter. Sometimes, she even begged and pleaded with Lisa to come back. Even though her mom had failed to protect her, Lisa still loved her and felt responsible for her misery. Lisa's father was a sadist, and her mother was easily manipulated. If Lisa had not left, her father would have surely killed her, and her mother would not have lifted her voice in protest. One day, Lisa called and her father answered the phone. She never called again; she knew that her mother was dead.

Lisa did not want to be her mother and made some questionable decisions in an effort to avoid it. It did not matter to her. She could not be completely at the mercy of another person—ever. She would always have an exit clause in every social contract.

Lisa was groggy and succumbing to the lull of sleep. "I need to get my money from . . ." She drifted off to sleep again.

Charlie was no longer on the phone and sat in a chair, watching Lisa rest. Things went from bad to worse. Jacob was in the hospital, and Lewis was dead. Charlie was not Lewis's biggest fan, but she needed him, especially now. She did not have a backup plan, and Lewis was her sole source of income. His demise did not help her situation, even if it did free her from his toxic hold. She would soon have to move again, and she only recently took up residence at the Hilton from the Omni.

Lisa rambled something about money in her sleep. Charlie thought maybe she could convince Lisa to help her out. Charlie figured it was more likely that Lisa would run as soon as she realized the truth. She didn't think Lisa ever truly considered her an option anyway. They never discussed Lisa leaving her husband, and Charlie never asked or inquired about him at all. She hoped that Lisa would decide on her own that Charlie made her happier than anyone ever did. No one ever chose Charlie. Her lifestyle had left her alone and isolated from her family. She had not let anyone touch her in the way that Lisa had.

Desperation lent itself to bring her the deepest connection she had ever had with another person and simultaneously caused her to sever that very same tie. She wasn't certain if she could stomach Lisa's outright rejection. Time revealed all truths, and it was beckoning this one to the surface. Charlie had no choice but to sit and wait.

Chapter 24

Brianna was enjoying the salt air and the cool breeze along the beach's edge. She carried her pink flip-flops, one each in hand, and savored the feel of the gritty white sand beneath her feet. Things had gotten complicated, and it was refreshing to return to something so basic: a beautiful sunset and the sound of an ocean wave. She had been walking for some time and thought herself to be alone on the shoreline. She did not notice the men that had trailed her from afar were slowly, but surely, closing the distance between them.

She thought about her dad sitting in jail and could not understand why Michelle was so adamant about their staying in Cancun. Brianna could not shake the urge to go to him, but there wasn't anything she could do for her dad anyway. If their staying a few extra days would help Michelle to relax a bit more, she didn't mind staying. It wasn't like she had much to go back to, anyway. She was losing her walking path to a forested area and her light to the starlit night sky.

She paused briefly to take in the scene. The moon's light seemed to dance across the water's surface. As she turned to make her trek back to the resort, she bumped into a man. She jumped backward, startled by his sudden presence.

"I'm sorry, I didn't see you standing there. Excuse me."

She attempted to walk around him, but he quickly wrapped his arms around her, pinning her arms at her sides. Her legs sliced through the air as the adrenaline pushed its way through her veins, forcing her to fight. Instinctively, she began to scream, but her voice could not travel the mile or so down the beach to the nearest ear. The second man immediately gagged and taped her mouth. Terrified and disoriented, Brianna twisted and squirmed violently, trying to break free. She managed to wiggle an arm loose enough to grab a fistful of short black hair which she pulled as hard as she could.

The bigger of the two men screamed, grabbed her hands, and threw her to the ground. Brianna landed on her back, sharp pains surging through her body from the impact.

"John! Why did you do that? We agreed not to hurt her."

"That shit hurt, Mike."

"I don't care what she did, stick to the plan. Period."

"Fuck you."

"You need to cut that anyway."

Brianna was forced to listen to the senseless babble, to endure their lighthearted chatter, as they bound her hands and tied her legs together, forever changing her life as she knew it. They had destroyed, in only a few minutes' time, her sense of security, rewriting her reality. She lay there, helpless and afraid. Tears began to stream down her face before she heard her name. It was faint, at first, but it kept getting louder.

It was Michelle! Michelle was coming! "Brianna! Brianna! Someone, help!"

Michelle's cries slashed through the air like lightning, igniting Brianna's fight, giving her a little bit of hope. Maybe she could get out of this and away from these men.

"Brianna! Brianna! No! Stop! Let her go! Bria!"

John turned toward the voice and could make out someone sprinting toward them. "I thought she was alone, Mike."

"She was. I only saw her."

"So, who in the hell is Flo-Jo?"

"I don't know, but we need to get out of here."

"Aren't you glad we moved the car to this end? I'm too pretty to run."

"Why would we run? Scared of a woman, man?"

"No, but I don't feel like dealing with her. Do you?"

"Nah . . . Let's move."

"Come on."

The men picked Brianna up from the ground and began to carry her to the car that was just over the hill waiting.

Brianna started struggling again, her will revived by her sister's voice. She did not know that it would help or anything, but she had to try. She wiggled and threw her body to the left and the right, to no avail. She could still hear Michelle screaming for her as they closed the door to the car. She closed her eyes and cried in silence. What would happen to her now?

Chapter 25

Michelle ran until she could no longer see the car. Then she fell to her knees and screamed in agony. Brianna was gone, and she had no clue how to get her back. Breathless and overwhelmed, she collapsed into a heaving mass of tears. She reached for her phone and remembered it had fallen along the beach somewhere while she ran. This was her fault. She should have told Brianna, and perhaps she would not have wandered so far from the resort. Michelle lay on the beach weeping until she passed out.

The sun greeted her. She sat up and looked around the beach. Not a soul in sight. She looked around for Brianna, hoping for a moment that maybe she dreamed the ordeal. That maybe her sister was waiting for her over the hill. She realized she wasn't being rational, but she couldn't help herself; she was heartbroken. She got up and walked up the hill, looking at the parking lot where the car had been waiting that drove her sister away. From where she stood, she could see a small puddle of oil; it must have been leaking while it sat. She turned away, downtrodden, and headed back down the beach to find her phone.

She found her cell buried in the sand about a third of the walk back. She only had a little battery left. She called the only person she could think of . . . Armand.

"Michelle? I thought I told you . . . I would call you. It's not . . . safe . . . Michelle? Babe, what's wrong? Are you crying? What happened?"

Michelle was overcome with her tears again as she fought to tell Armand. "Brianna . . . They took her. They took Bria." She cried harder.

Armand took a deep breath and tried to stay composed. He was not in a place where he could speak freely. He had to be careful not to escalate the situation. Michelle was hysterical, and he needed her to focus because he had more bad news. "Michelle, sweetheart, this is not your fault. I need you to take a breath."

"I should have told her and maybe—"

"They did it. It was the Marx Brothers, and they alone are responsible. We will get Brianna back, but I need you to calm down, okay?"

"I just got her, Armand! I just got her."

"I know, just . . . I'm so sorry this has happened." Armand couldn't have explained to Michelle that there was nothing she could have done. He felt bad about Brianna, but he was relieved that it wasn't Michelle. "I know this isn't easy to hear, but the reality is that they would have taken you both had you been with her."

Michelle understood what he was saying, but it didn't help. The truth did not ease her pain or settle her mind. Brianna's absence hurt, and each step she took toward the resort felt like a step farther away from Bria. "I know, but I'm just so scared for her, Armand."

"We'll get her back. Trust me." Armand meant every word.

"I trust you."

"Good, because I need you to come back, but I need you to do as I say."

"Come back? They could have Bria here somewhere, Armand! You need to come here!"

"They are not there. I'm almost positive they probably left last night soon after the grab."

"Soon after the grab? Armand, that's my *sister!* Don't talk about her like that. I don't even know who *you* are."

Michelle never pegged Armand to be knowledgeable about this type of thing, but he seemed to have all the answers. How could he be so calm at a time like this? It was one thing to suggest they hide. That made sense to Michelle, but this was different. Brianna had been kidnapped. This was some next level ish. What did Armand know about that?

Armand bit his tongue. Michelle was really in her feelings, but he understood. This was a huge ordeal for her; it would be big for anybody. Regardless of whether he liked it, her words were true; there was a lot Michelle did not know about him, and it was for her own protection; he needed her to focus.

"I'm sorry, love. I didn't mean to sound insensitive. I love you. We will get your sister back. I will. You didn't lose faith in me that fast, did you?"

"Of course not. I just wish this wasn't happening. I miss her so much, and I have no idea if she's okay. She was fighting, but I couldn't get there in time. I tried . . ."

"Stop beating yourself up. Refocus your energy. Our best shot at saving her is for you to keep it together. You need to survive this."

"I am trying, Armand. I'm trying. I'll come home."

"Chances are they think they have grabbed you, and so you can't go back to your apartment right now."

Michelle was listening, but her thoughts were scattered. She kept thinking about Brianna. "I don't know if I can do this. She must be so scared. Oh my goodness, I just—"

"Michelle . . . Michelle."

"Where am I supposed to go, Armand? What am I supposed to do?"

"Listen to me. Take the next flight out and take a taxi to the Hilton Anatole downtown. I'm going to reserve a room for you there. It'll be under Marie LaCroix. Don't call anyone."

Armand wanted the information about her dad to come from him. He couldn't chance her calling her mom and getting the news. He wanted to be the one to tell her. She was already in a fragile state, and he did not know how she would take it.

"How will I let you know that I made it back?"

"I'll know."

Michelle's phone was about to die. The beeps were getting closer together.

"Be careful, Michelle. I love you."

"I love . . . you too—" Michelle's phone died before she could finish the sentence. She hoped it would not be the last time she spoke with him. She went back to her room and booked the next flight out. At least it wasn't the Omni. No chance of her running into Charlie. Michelle did not know what to expect, but she hoped Armand could work a miracle . . . She had a feeling that it would take one to get Brianna.

Chapter 26

Lisa sat up and gingerly swung her feet off the bed, trying not to exacerbate the nausea threatening to overwhelm her. Her head was pounding a bit, but she could manage. She looked around the room; there was no sign of Charlie. She walked to the bathroom and splashed some cold water on her face. It did not help. She laughed, thinking that only worked in the movies. Charlie apparently had more movie magic than Lisa. She had vanished, along with all of her things. There was barely any evidence that she had ever been there.

Lisa did not fully understand what was going on. She stumbled through the ferocious baseline wreaking havoc on her mind to recall the things she heard before her head collided with the door. She remembered it had something to do with Charlie, Jacob, and Indiana. Indiana . . . That was what shocked her and knocked her off her feet. What did Charlie know about her life in Indiana? After her mother passed, she tried to erase that horrid time from her memory altogether. Something was not right about the entire situation. Too many questions, and now, Charlie had disappeared with the answers.

Things must have been pretty bad to send Charlie into hiding like this. Lisa needed to know where she had gone, and she needed to know now. She looked around the room for some clue about where Charlie might have gone. Luckily for her, she did not have to look long. Charlie left a note on the table where Lisa remembered seeing her last. Lisa picked up the note and sat down to read.

Lisa,
I know you are probably confused. I wish I could have stayed and explained it all to you, but I'm just not as strong as you, I guess. I cannot answer all of your questions, but I will speak on the more important ones. Those that will bother you most. I knew you before Dallas . . . way before.

You may not remember me, but I have searched for you since you left Indiana. My real name is Charlene Grae, and I lived in the house across from you.

That night . . . The night you left, I saw what happened. I saw him, Lisa. I tried to get to you, but when I saw your mom . . . I couldn't. I'm so sorry. I felt like I owed you, and I've been looking ever since. So, this is my penance . . . my confession. I owe you the truth, so, here it goes: Jacob is an old friend of mine from the old block. I found out where you were from a picture in his office. He's hurt really bad; currently in the hospital, but I don't know what happened yet, honest.

I'm hoping it had nothing to do with Lewis. Before you ask . . . I met Lewis at the club. He wanted someone to keep tabs on you, and I offered myself. I wanted a chance to be with you. Don't hate me, please. I did it to protect you, Lisa. He's not who you think he is. He's a monster. I don't know what the arrangement is between you, but whatever it is . . . get out. Get away from him. Please, leave him alone. I heard that he might be dead or something, but I don't know if it's true.

Lastly, I love you. Everything between us was real, genuine. I had to leave. I couldn't handle your rejection. My heart can't take it, and there is so much going on.

The doctor said the stress isn't good for me. I'm going away for a while. I know you deserve more than this letter, and you'll get it, but not today. Be safe.

Love always,
Charlie

No, this was *not* cool. Lisa's emotions were swirling. She had never felt so betrayed. It was a good thing that Charlie, or *Charlene,* had taken off; Lisa felt like she could strangle her. No wonder Lewis seemed always to be two or three steps ahead of her; Charlie had been spying the entire time! She didn't need Charlie to warn her about Lewis. She wanted nothing more than to get away from him, and if Lewis was dead, then it would be her lucky break.

But Jacob being in the hospital? None of this made any sense. She jumped at the sound of her phone vibrating. She picked it up and saw she had sixteen new voice mails. Most were from associates from the strip club, trying to confirm whether Lewis was dead, but the two from Brianna rocked her to the core. Frank was in jail with an aggravated assault charge. Suddenly, the queasiness she had tried to avoid sent her running to the bathroom.

She prayed to the porcelain deity as the realization hit her. Over and over again, she vomited until there was nothing left in her stomach. She held herself and cried aloud. Frank must have gone to Jacob after she left the hospital. How could this have happened? Frank rarely raised his voice. He was simply not a violent man; in fact, he was the complete opposite. He was so docile and easygoing that Lisa often questioned his emotional connectivity and wondered if he actually cared.

This should not have happened, and Lisa had no one but herself to blame. Jacob was in the hospital, and

Frank was in jail. The weight of it all was nearly too much. Poor Brianna. She must be worried. Lisa attempted to call her, but like Charlie's phone, it went straight to voice mail. Lisa sat on the tiled floor of the bathroom with her head propped against the tub. Her thoughts were all over the place, and she was uncertain of her next move. This was not how she wanted things to go.

It was not Jacob's apparent health concerns that bothered her; Frank's incarceration was not a part of her plan. She had no choice but to adjust to the new situation. Lisa felt remorseful, but there was an emotion stronger than that coursing through her, something deeper and more profound than guilt. She felt relieved. Perhaps this was the break she needed to start over. If Lewis was gone, with Frank out of the picture, Lisa could leave unhinged. She did not want to leave Frank, initially, but given everything that had transpired over the last few days, the idea did not seem to be a bad one.

She recounted her last words to Frank. She had not intended to lie to him, but it happened all the same. Nothing had ever happened between her and Jacob; the story was false. The details were true: she had been violated in the worse way by someone that should have protected her. An incident that sent her on an unfathomable road of self-destruction, but it was not Jacob's face that colored her nightmares . . . It was that of Ronald James, her father. She could not share that with Frank. It was too close, painful, and embarrassing.

Jacob's name had slipped out unexpectedly. Out of all the names available, even she was surprised that it was Jacob's that the universe offered her. She briefly considered confessing the error, but that meant admitting she lied. How would she explain that type of mistake to Frank without destroying her credibility? Besides, Frank had taken the bait, and once she had him where she wanted him, she could not relinquish her position. Jacob seemed to be a safe substitute, and as she spoke, the words came easily. It felt natural. Frank and Jacob hadn't been close in years. Frank was angry, and she needed to neutralize him, to turn the tide and evoke some sympathy; soften his heart. She never, in a million years, expected this.

Frank had given her more attention that day in the hospital than he had in the last several years. In truth, she relished it, even though the exchange was unpleasant. She had never intended to disclose that part of her past to anyone, but, at that moment, she was desperate. She expected Frank to be angry about the money, but not to *that* degree. Hearing him telling her to move out struck a nerve. She simply could not allow that to stand. Sure, she made mistakes, but he was not without his imperfections. She kept her head down about them during their marriage, unwilling to do anything to jeopardize her good thing; her version of the American dream. But he backed her into a corner, and she came out swinging.

She had planned to confront him when it seemed most advantageous. The situation would have been entirely under her control. She could not make her move unless she was confident that she could sever her ties to Lewis. Once that was in place, Frank would have had two options: he could either move with her for a fresh start in a new place, or she would leave without him, but Frank had forced the issue. On some level, she wished he would choose to accompany her, but she had enough stashed away that it would not have bothered her, financially, if he had chosen otherwise. Brianna was an adult and no longer needed them. Besides, if she wanted to, she would have been welcome to come as well.

Lisa could no longer stick to that plan. Frank was in jail, presumably for defending her, and Lewis may be dead. She could not reach Brianna, and her past, as far as she knew, was public knowledge. Why did Frank have to go and do something so chivalrous now? She loved him and would always love him, but she did not want to *want him.* She had, in time, grown used to the emotional distance and had anticipated her ability to make a clean break, if necessary. She was certain now that it was unlikely she would be able to do so. *Ugh!* Lisa was irritated with the turn of events. She had to admit she was feeling some type of way about everything. Feeling some type of way about Frank. If nothing else, one thing was certain; she needed to see him. She made a few phone calls and got ready for her trip downtown.

Chapter 27

Michelle landed in the Dallas/Fort Worth airport and took a taxi to the Hilton Anatole, as instructed. She was more than a little rattled, and if she was not aware of her temperamental state, her snapping at the poor cabdriver was very telling. Poor guy threw her bags out of the cab and drove off without even getting his tip. Michelle didn't care; she only wanted to get into her room. Armand had reserved her an executive suite. She walked into the massive space and was immediately grateful. The bellhop dropped her bags by the door. Michelle took a moment to enjoy the beautiful downtown view before wandering into the master bedroom and collapsing onto the bed.

She was about to fall asleep when she felt her thigh vibrating. "Michelle, have you landed?"

"I get the notion that you know I have."

"I'm on my way over there."

Michelle felt tense all over. Armand's tone did not bode well for her . . . too businesslike. He was never business with her. Sleep was no longer an option. She needed to wake up. After locating the complimentary coffeepot, Michelle brewed and poured herself a cup. She considered adding a little something from the minibar to calm her nerves but decided against it. This was not the time for her to experiment with alcohol. The strong, black java was exactly the stiff drink she needed to get her juices flowing.

Michelle wondered if Brianna was okay . . . if she was hurt. She hated this. The ordeal was awful, but it was the mystery, the not knowing, that drove Michelle insane. Part of her motivation for becoming a private investigator was due to her discomfort with the unknown. She was always researching and uncovering some truth. Even with all the riddles she solved for other people over the years, she didn't know the first place to look to find Brianna. A lot of good her PI skills were to her now.

Michelle heard a knock at the door. It was Armand. She got up to let him in. As soon the door closed behind him, he wrapped Michelle up in a big hug right there, in the doorway. He didn't realize how much he had missed her until that very moment. She buried her face in his chest and dizzied herself with his scent. She felt her body temperature rise. He picked her up and carried her into the bedroom. Though he desired to have her, he resisted. He laid her down on the bed and took his place behind her. The scene was familiar.

She pulled his leg toward the front of her body until it rested perfectly between her legs. She felt the moisture from his lips on the nape of her neck and the chill of each breath he exhaled. She wanted him in spite of herself. It felt wrong to crave the release his love would bring her. The gentle massage he could offer her body. How could she make love when her sister was missing? Somehow, thoughts of Brianna did little to curb her carnal urges. She craved penetration.

Armand wanted her too. To savor the warmth of her feminine design around his member, to fill the room with her beautiful music. He wanted nothing more than to give her pleasure, realizing the probable pain his news was sure to bring later; instead, relishing the feel of her soft body next to his. The scent of the Chanel No. 5 that Michelle wore faithfully just for him; the curves of her small fingers interlaced with his. Though the feel of her soft round buttocks against his groin was nearly too much, Armand managed to restrain his growth. He focused on the flawlessness of her complexion. The silky feel of her hair against his face. She was truly beautiful. Armand was grateful that she was safe and in his arms. He would tell her about her dad, but he wanted to hold her a little bit longer, to extend this peaceful moment for as long as he could. He pulled her closer into his body and held her firmly. Michelle was relaxed; her breathing slow and steady. Armand was anxious; if he did not tell her now, he might not ever do it.

"Michelle, I need to tell you something."

"What is it?" she murmured, half-asleep.

"Everything is going to be okay. I need you to believe that."

Armand's foreboding was creeping Michelle out. The news she had been dreading since his phone call was on its way to her ears, and she wasn't sure if she could handle one more piece of bad news. Her body tensed up. Armand felt it too. He ran his hand from the top of her shoulder, down the length of her arm, and back in a gentle caress.

His shoulders slumped, bracing for the impact that his news would bring. "There is no easy way to say this, so, I am just going to say it . . . your dad is . . . He's gone, babe."

Michelle did not respond. For a moment he thought perhaps she did not hear him.

"Michelle, your dad—"

"I heard you. I heard you. Explain." Michelle was trying not to panic. This was the perfect time to exercise the caution she seldom did. She would not jump to any conclusions, especially not *that one*. The one that buried her father in a grave six feet underground. Never to be seen, hugged, or heard again. No, she wasn't exactly upset with her father; disappointed, but not ready to say her last good-bye. She would not.

"The coroner came to your house. Your mother watched from the doorway. The ambulance rode out of your driveway quiet, no sirens. Your father has not been seen for days."

"Stop talking." Michelle did not want to hear any more. "I'm sorry . . ." Her voice was breaking. Her body shook as she began to fight the sobs overtaking her. "I'm sorry . . . I'm sorry."

Armand did not know if those apologies were for him, but he did not need them. "Michelle, it's okay; breathe. I'm here. I got you."

He shifted his weight to the leg draped over her lower torso and braced himself for what he felt was coming. Right on cue, Michelle started kicking, slowly at first, and then, uncontrollably, throwing her body around, but Armand held his grip. He would not let go. She went crazy, swinging her arms and legs wildly. Twisting, turning . . . trying to run. Run away from Armand. Away from his words. Away from the pain sweeping over her, that seemed to fill her lungs and cut off her air supply. A life-altering, inescapable pain.

A bloodcurdling scream pierced through the air so loudly, it stopped her cold. It was deafening, so chalked with pain, that it made a few seconds feel like an eternity. As quickly as it began, it ended, beginning again, only this time, it seemed to have been traveling toward her from a distance far off; a high-pitched squeal, blooming into a full-throttled yell. It took her a moment to realize it was coming from her. Michelle was afraid and turned her face toward Armand just enough to give him a full view of the confusion and hurt anchored in the gleam of her wide eyes.

The look in her eyes scared Armand. Not the look itself. The look he understood; it was not foreign to him. He recognized the distress, the agony. It was not her disposition that frightened him but the moment itself, the implication. Michelle had become his world. Their love was something of fantasy had it not been for all the malleable truth he lined it with, and he wanted nothing more than to protect her. As he lay there, staring into her eyes, absorbing her brokenness, he understood in the most profound way that he could not. He could not take her hurt away, and it terrified him. He didn't know how to comfort her. Could not find the words to ease her burden, so he remained silent, hoping that his embrace would communicate more than his love. That it would offer itself as evidence to the raw, unadulterated fact that he was absolutely unwilling to let her carry this pain alone.

Michelle did not want to feel anything. Her mind sifted through her memory and her dreams in no particular order. The room spun in circles around her, and she closed her eyes to pull her sister close. She reached her this time. She fought the good fight and saved Brianna. She was safe. Michelle's family was intact. Her father alive and well; a faithful, loving man. Her parents birthed and raised her; they shared DNA, life lessons, and their love; it was good; unchanged. Michelle was Mrs. LaCroix, an award-winning journalist.

Lights were flashing. Her world was black and white. She was young, eight years old. There were tears on her face, but they were not hers; they were her mother's. Transferred from her swollen cheeks as she sat in her mother's lap nestled in her breasts. She was singing a beautiful song, but it made Michelle sad. She didn't want her mommy to cry. To the tune of "Twinkle Twinkle Little Star," she sang, "My lost little girl, wherever you are, just know I love you, forever my star."

The song confused her, but she didn't ask any questions. She never did. Whenever her mother cried like this . . . Michelle would sit in her lap, as close as she could, to remind her mommy that she wasn't lost, that she didn't have to cry. Fast-forward ten years. Michelle was graduating. Diploma in hand, she scanned the crowd and found her mother. Although she's happy to see her, that wasn't who she was looking for. Michelle's heart was broken, but she pretended it wasn't. She smiled and posed for pictures. She imagined her daddy was in the crowd. She did not tell her mother how disappointed she was with his absence; she never did.

More flashing lights. Michelle was in and out of consciousness. Overcome with grief. The room was filled with her screams, deep guttural groans. With each vision, each dream, each sound, Michelle released her hurt. She permitted herself to do as she never did: to love, relate, and release.

Chapter 28

Lisa was nervous about her visit with Frank. She didn't know what she would say to him or if he wanted to see her. The ride there was long and uneventful. Too long. She nearly chickened out. Fortunately, her curiosity was stronger than her panic. The taxi pulled up to the jail, and Lisa headed toward the entrance. She could not believe that Frank Mason was incarcerated. The brown brick building seemed to loom in front of her. The view of the beautiful glass buildings of downtown Dallas, which seemed close enough to touch, made the tall, ten-story building even more intimidating and that much more painful. Lisa had managed to avoid the stripes, but she had heard plenty of horror stories from other girls. This was as close as she ever wanted to be. She was not comfortable in the least bit but was determined to speak with Frank. Besides, her agitation was irrational. They couldn't keep her inside . . . Could they? Of course not.

Lisa walked inside and was almost immediately turned away. Frank was not allowed to see visitors, and she was told she would need to come back either Tuesday or Friday between 7:00 p.m. and 9:00 p.m. She was disappointed and angry that she could not see her husband. She would have to put her questions on ice for another two days. At least Frank had put her on the list; she took that as confirmation that he would be willing to talk with her. A small but important silver lining in her storm cloud.

As she stood outside Lew Sterrett waiting for her taxi, she contemplated what her next move would be. She was fairly certain Lewis was dead, pending her own visual confirmation. If it was true, there wasn't really any reason for her to leave. Though the idea of starting over fresh somewhere was still very appealing, her decision would depend largely on what Frank had to say to her. She still had been unable to reach Brianna, and she was pretty sure Brianna was ignoring her. She was certain this situation was upsetting for her, and she wanted to let her daughter know that she was available.

Lisa had been reluctant to acknowledge the river that had come to rest between her and Brianna. Brianna had always been a daddy's girl, and Lisa had failed to nurture her fragile relationship with Brianna as she got older. The hard truth was that her relationship with her daughter worsened, as had her relationship with her husband. She had been so distracted by her marital issues and pursuit of her personal happiness that she hadn't noticed the distance between them. When she did, it was simply too late. Brianna didn't want anything to do with her. Though she never dared to utter the words, Lisa could sense it. Lisa had been unable, and at times, unwilling, to do the work to repair it. Brianna didn't really need her. She was intelligent and driven. She had made all the right decisions, and Lisa wasn't worried about her.

Brianna had her dad, and that seemed to be enough. Things had changed. Lisa didn't know what would happen to Frank, and she wanted to let Brianna know that she would be there if she needed her. It was more important now than before that Brianna knows that she was not alone. Brianna had not returned one of Lisa's calls in the last several months before that day she spoke with her in the hospital. Lisa was glad to hear from her even if she was only calling because she could not reach her dad. Lisa could have pressed the issue, but on some level, she felt deserving of the treatment. Even though Brianna could not have known all that Lisa had done, *she* was painfully aware.

The ride back to the hotel was quick. Lisa's mind continued to wander. She even missed Charlie a bit. She was angry that she had been duped, but she wanted her all the same. She pondered a bit more and realized that maybe it wasn't Charlie she wanted. Maybe she just wanted somebody. Anybody. Charlie had always been available. Easy. Convenient. Lisa was not sure if she was really capable of truly giving her whole heart to someone. Not sure if she was crazy enough to do that. The potential for pain drastically increased with that kind of transfer, and Lisa was intelligent enough to keep at least a part of herself *to herself*. That was how she reasoned anyway. She was not being selfish; she was being protective. If she didn't look out for herself . . . who would?

Chapter 29

It hurt to breathe. Brianna cringed with every breath. Her chest was sore and probably bruised. Her vision was blurry, and she couldn't move. Her 140 pounds felt like 300. She was no longer tied up, but her freedom did not free her. After what seemed like endless failed attempts to lift her hands, she resolved to lie there quietly. She was lying on top of something but could not fully tell what it was. It was soft, but not as thick as a mattress and not as firm as a cot. She guessed it was probably a few blankets clumped together with a sheet covering them. She was still fully clothed except for her shoes. She could not tell how long she had been sleeping or how long it had been since her walk on the beach. A few days maybe, she figured. She was having a hard time remembering. Drugged probably. She couldn't seem to wake up.

She thought of Michelle and how worried she must be. She was glad Michelle hadn't made it to her; grateful the men had let Michelle be. Knowing Michelle was out there gave her hope, something to attach her faith to. Ironically, the person who she's known the least amount of time was closest to her and would witness the most horrific time in her life. Brianna had to hope that Michelle could find her; she had to. There was absolutely nothing else for her to do.

Being hopeless felt like a slow death, and she wasn't dying. She was lost and believed that she would be found again. Something else encouraged her, though;

something more than an ideal. It pulled her away from her thoughts and into the cold room where she lay: a scent. She braced herself for the pain and took another deep breath, recognizing the smell: Djarum cigarettes. It was the same kind that Javan smoked.

She hadn't thought of Javan until that moment. Memories flooded her mind. If she had any tears left, she imagined she might have cried. Some part of her resented her decision to resist Javan's affection. For a second, she pictured him missing her, looking and searching frantically. He and Michelle, both together, trying to get to her, to rescue her from the middle of nowhere.

A few rooms away, in another part of the house, the Marx Brothers were having a very different type of conversation. They recently learned of Frank's incarceration and, perhaps more importantly, Lewis's death. Their situation had changed drastically. Their reputation had carried them through the years, but they weren't the big bad dangerous Marx Brothers everyone believed them to be anymore. They were street relics, an urban legend, masquerading as tough guys. In truth, they needed the money.

"Damn, man, he's cold. What good is the girl to us now?"

"Calm down. You're stressing me; let me think. We'll figure this shit out."

"Can't bargain with a chalk outline, Mike."

John shuffled back and forth in the room, wearing a hole in the floor. He was a heavy guy with a hothead. His temper was legendary, and Mike was trying his best to manage it. "I think we should get rid of her."

The girl was supposed to be leverage. Lewis was no stranger and was into them for close to thirty thousand. He had put in some work for them back in the day, a young and thirsty hustler, always raving about his girl and his daughter, proud that he was about to be a daddy. He didn't do anything major, only some little nickel-and-dime stuff, getting his feet wet with the art of the hustle.

"There may be another way, John. Just let me think. Shit."

One day, out of the blue, Lewis split; disappeared with their money. The Marx Brothers looked everywhere for him, But the streets were silent. When he emerged again, they could not touch him. It seemed almost overnight he had become even more connected than they were, too connected for them to try to breathe in his direction. Anybody with the mayor's number on speed dial was out of their pay grade. Lewis had married up and shut them out. So, the Marx Brothers fell back, burying their insult and disdain until it could be rebirthed again. It was only a matter of time before the universe would offer a chance to get even. It was the nature of the beast, the law of the universe, and they had been patient.

Frank Mason found them in the same manner he found his wife, through word of mouth. They were a little suspicious at first, but the money was right and on time, every time. They did the surveillance work he requested. Months went by before they realized who it was they were actually watching and could barely believe their luck. Their arrangement with Frank had been in place for the last four years or so. Initially, they were mainly watching Lewis, but Frank made it obvious he was more interested in his daughter.

Frank wanting to keep tabs on Lewis, for whatever reason, made sense to them. They had their own reasons for doing so, but they didn't see the importance of knowing his daughter's whereabouts. It seemed strange to them but watching her had been the catalyst for their vengeance. Mike primarily kept eyes on Lewis and John took the girl. They remembered how much Lewis would rave about his baby girl and could only imagine, given her beauty, that his adoration had grown over the years. Mike was the engineer, and it seemed simple enough: snatch the girl and force Lewis's hand. The way they figured it, he would do anything to protect her.

It wasn't about the money, although they gladly accepted it; it was the principle. Lewis had embarrassed them, and they were anxious to return the favor. He played them and made them look weak, and he simply could not get away with that. They wanted to make him grovel and beg for his life; to break him. In order to pull this off, they needed more intimate information. Things someone could only know if they were close to the family.

They figured the easiest way to get in would be through the girl. They had propositioned a few guys before selecting Armand. They had seen him around the way, and he was popular with the ladies. He was exactly what they were looking for: attractive enough to grab her attention and amenable enough to follow instructions without question. Armand was an important part of their plan. They were pleased that he agreed to do it and didn't think anything of his eagerness. They were giving him a fairly substantial amount of cash to do something any man would do for free.

Armand had done great work for them. Things had gone even better than expected; the two meshed so well that he ended up moving in with her. The Marx Brothers knew it was only a matter of time before they learned of something that they could use. A vulnerability they could exploit with Lewis, but months went by, and Armand's knowledge seemed to have reached a plateau. They had been able to get some good information, but not exactly what they wanted. Nothing that they could use and Mike *suspected* Armand had fallen in love with the girl. John was *convinced* he had, despite the many women he had running in and out of that apartment. None of them compared to *her*.

All they had to go on was that the girl had a strained relationship with her father. She had no pictures of him, aside from one when she was still a small child. He would call her often, but she did not accept many of his phone calls. Lewis had never visited her at her home, but these things were not a deterrent. Even if Lewis's daughter wanted nothing to do with him, they concluded that he would still not want any harm to come to her. They had plenty of information on her but not nearly enough on Lewis, which was the sole purpose for Armand's relationship with the woman.

Mike wanted to give Armand a little more time to give them something—anything. He liked the kid, but time was running out, and they needed to make a move. Lewis was losing control a bit.

Through the years, Lewis had the same routine. First, he'd run around his neighborhood every morning, like clockwork. Next, he'd make his rounds with the women in his life, and there was an ample supply of them scattered throughout the city in various upscale hotels. One day he made at least five stops. The Marx Brothers weren't sure what all he was doing with them, but whatever it was . . . must have paid Lewis well. The man did not do anything else with his time; it simply had to be his hustle.

Once, Mike saw a chink in Lewis's armor: he witnessed a blowup between Lewis and one of his women at a hotel. It was the first time Mike had seen Lewis lose his cool. He also got word that one of Lewis's women was running with another woman. Lewis's world seemed to be spiraling out of control. Mike didn't know how much longer Lewis was going to be able to keep it together, and an unpredictable Lewis would complicate things significantly. They had to turn it up a notch to speed things along; Mike had personally pushed Armand for more information, and he had not given him anything.

Over the last several days, Mike had not been able to reach Armand at all. Mike decided it was best they go ahead and make their move. Her going out of town cemented the decision. Fortunately, one of John's old contacts at the airport was able to get her destination when she checked in her luggage. Mike and John simply took a later flight out, made the grab, and used a friend's private plane on the return trip. It all seemed simple to execute, but nothing had gone according to plan. Several things had gone terribly wrong.

First, there was Florence Griffith-Joyner on the beach. She took them by surprise; they were certain their target was alone. They had seen her twice since they had arrived, and although she had been dressed in two different outfits, she was alone the entire time they tracked her. Mike did not want or have the time to dispose of a body, so they were forced to leave the other girl, running the risk of a potential witness. She didn't get close enough to make an identification, but she saw what happened and could have alerted the authorities. He thought it strange that she had not. He had been monitoring various news outlets and had not heard anything about a kidnapping or even anyone being reported missing. Maybe the other girl realized she was mistaken. His recollection sharpened, noticing that their captive responded to her voice. Now that Mike thought about it . . . Flo-Jo called her something else . . . Bria, Rianna, Brianna, or something like that.

Leaving her there was a huge gamble that had paid off so far. Now, with Lewis dead, their plan right along with him, it was no longer a question of how could they use the girl, but how could they get rid of her. Mike did not want to hurt her. His issue was not with her but with her father. There was no way he could convince John just to let her walk away; she was too much of a liability. He needed more time to figure this out, and he didn't have it. John could only be contained for so long, and he was already upset. He needed Armand to contact him. Mike didn't fully understand why he valued the girl's life so much. Maybe he softened in his old age, but whatever the reason was, he wanted her to survive this, and he wanted to get out too. Maybe if they could still get something out of it . . . he could keep the girl alive.

Chapter 30

After Armand gave Michelle the news about her dad, they spent a few more days in the hotel. She needed the time, and Armand loved her enough to insist. He insisted that she lay in his arms and cry until she couldn't anymore. Insisted that he be allowed to carefully and lovingly massage the tension out of her body. Insisted that she release any notion that any of this was her fault. Her heart was heavy, her body run-down, but she felt strong.

Michelle spoke with her mom after she composed herself a bit, preparing to lend her mom what little strength she had . . . only to find her mother in a surprisingly cheerful mood. Michelle had thought perhaps her mom was in denial and had dismissed it, but now that she was home, she knew she had been wrong. It had been awhile since Michelle had been to her parents' house; months, in fact. The energy was awkward.

Michelle had expected a somber, ominous atmosphere at her parents' home, but it was actually relatively light. Her mother did not appear to be in any pain at all, but Michelle figured she was only trying to put up a brave front for her; she always had. It was definitely weird being there, knowing her father would never walk through the halls again, compounded by her not having to sneak in through the back door during the night to avoid any eyes that may be watching. Her life was growing more and more bizarre by the minute.

"Michelle . . . Michelle . . . Will you come here a minute? I need to talk to you."

Michelle was grateful that her mom was dealing with her loss so well, but her chipper demeanor was unnerving. She was worried that if her mom did not find a way to accept it and properly grieve, she might lose her mind.

"Coming, Mom!" Michelle climbed down out of her bed and walked into the kitchen where she could hear her mom clanking dishes around.

"Do you want breakfast, *Number One?*" Sophie called Michelle Number One for as long as she could remember. Sophie had told her it was because she wanted Michelle to know that no matter what, she would always be her priority. Michelle thought of Brianna and wondered if that was the truth.

"Sure, Mom. Are you doing okay? I'm worried about you."

Sophie stopped what she was doing and looked at her daughter. "I'm fine."

"Mom, are you sure? I haven't seen you cry or anything. You need to grieve."

"I'll be okay. I have had awhile to sit with this change. I am grieving, dear. It might not look like it, but I am, okay?"

"Will you miss him? It feels strange being here knowing he's never coming back."

Sophie walked from the stove to the island where Michelle sat on a stool and wrapped her arms around her. "Of course, I'll miss him. I loved him, but when it's our time to go . . . It's just our time. We cannot change it."

"I know, but it seems so sudden, doesn't it? I didn't even know Dad was sick."

"He's been sick for a while. We thought he was doing better, but I guess his heart just gave out."

"What did they say happened exactly?"

"Essentially, he suffocated. He couldn't get enough oxygen to his lungs. They tried to explain it to me, but I . . . I was in a daze. I don't remember beyond that."

Michelle did not understand why her parents would not tell her about the condition of her father's health, especially if it was a matter of life and death, but it didn't matter now. "Well, I am here, Mom. If you need anything, I'm here."

"I know, sweetheart, and that's what I wanted to speak with you about."

"Okay, what is it? What do you need?"

"I need for you to leave after the funeral."

"Excuse me? I had planned to stay here and help you."

"I know, but I won't be here. I think I need to get away for a few days. I've already booked a flight, and I'll be leaving in a week."

Michelle was shocked. Her mom had never gone anywhere, but she understood if she needed to leave now. She had only been at the house one night, and she could hardly stand it. "Where are you going?"

Sophie wasn't sure if she wanted to tell Michelle her destination. The truth was, her friend in the coroner's office suggested she leave for a while and let things settle down. Although there had not been any questions raised in regards to Lewis's sudden death, she wanted to be out of reach in case there were. Michelle did not need to be in the middle of any of this. Sophie needed to protect her; she could not tell her where she was going. "I think I'm heading to my parents' house for a while."

Michelle flinched like she'd been stuck with a knife. Sophie was just full of surprises today. "Your parents? You mean, my grandparents? You have never even mentioned them before. I didn't even know they were alive."

"We have not spoken in years. I think it's a good time to try to mend that relationship. There's nothing more important than family, and life is too short. Your father's passing has helped me to see that."

"That's good, Mom. Maybe I can meet them one day?"

"I hope so. If things go well." Sophie felt a little guilty about lying to Michelle, and even more so about going to her parents' house. It actually was not a bad idea. Maybe at some point, she really should go and try to repair things.

"Good. That would be nice. So, you don't need me to stay after the funeral?"

"I'm positive. Of course, you can come back and help with dinner, but there's no need to stay beyond that, really."

"If that's what you want, I'm fine with it. I have a few things I need to tend to, anyway. If you change your mind at any point, let me know."

"I will. Now let's eat breakfast. I'm starving."

Chapter 31

Frank had a feeling he was going to prison, but he was not sure he cared. He felt sick inside. How could he have been so blind all these years? He had been so busy trying to keep the nature of Brianna's adoption a secret that he had not been paying any attention to his wife's condition. No wonder she spent so much time away from home. She was married to a man who took absolutely no interest in her as a woman. He was ashamed of himself.

How could things have gotten so far out of hand? He was not a bad person. Sure, at first, he was just trying to meet the requirements in order to get the money from his trust, but he loved Lisa and Brianna; they were his world. He was angry with Lisa for losing the money, but more so because he did not know how to keep things in place without it. He could not pay the Marx Brothers, and it was probably a matter of time before Brianna would find out the truth. She would certainly hate him, and she would have every right to do so.

He had not had any visitors yet. Not even a lawyer, but he put Lisa and Brianna on the list, just in case. Jacob was his only friend, but that friendship was over. Frank was still angry, and if he saw Jacob, he would beat his ass all over again. Some part of him wanted to speak with his old friend, the man that he once loved like a brother. He wanted to know how he was capable of doing something so heinous. He would never have guessed that he could do that, and even now, it was difficult for him to believe. He heard that Jacob was still in the hospital but no longer in ICU. He was glad for that. Jacob's continuing improvement ensured that there could be no murder charge.

Jail was not his favorite place, but there was something about the isolation that gave him peace, or at least, it helped him to find it. There were so many things he needed to address, to correct, and he had no idea where to start. From his cell, he did not have to make any decisions. Everything was decided for him; it made it easier for him to deal with everything. It simplified his reality. Frank needed to be honest with the women he loved. He was not looking forward to it, but he'd do it. He was not concerned with getting out of jail, acquiring a lawyer, or anything of the like. That part of the process was inevitable. He was prioritizing. Focused, finally, on the things his money could not fix. No amount of money could repair the broken relationships in his life. He would have to do the work. He only wondered who would be first.

Chapter 32

The ride to the funeral seemed painfully long. Michelle held her mother's hand while they sat in the backseat of the Escalade limousine, riding in silence. She was dressed in a slender black dress with a cut just below her knees; her hair pulled back into a ponytail. She wore a large pair of black Jackie O sunglasses over her eyes, a look intentioned to disguise her; she did not want to be easily recognized.

Sophie looked exceptionally beautiful and was dressed similarly. She was grateful to have Michelle so close. This proved to be more difficult than she had anticipated. Even though her life with Lewis had been tumultuous, she would miss him for the rare moments when he made her feel loved, special. The rest she was glad to say good-bye to. The limo came to a stop, and the driver got out and opened their door. Sophie took a deep breath and stepped out of the vehicle. She took Michelle's hand and walked carefully to the area where her husband, Lewis, would be laid to rest.

With each step, she felt the contents of her stomach threatening to interrupt the service as she drew nearer to her seat in front of the casket. Her legs trembled, and she was convinced her knees would buckle if she didn't sit quickly. She scanned the crowd and did not recognize many of the people there. Once she sat with Michelle on her right-hand side, she felt better. Lewis looked handsome lying there; the arrangement was really beautiful.

Sophie would certainly miss him. She felt her decision to have the ceremony at the burial site was fitting. The weather was a mirror of him: cold, yet appropriately sunny, with a slight overcast of cloud cover.

She did not know many of Lewis's friends, but she shared the arrangements with the few she did. Perhaps they were responsible for the large gathering. Sophie had to admit she was more than a bit surprised by the turnout; she had no clue Lewis was so popular. Not as surprising, though, were the number of women in attendance. The photographs flashed through her mind and a few of the women there she recognized. If Michelle had not been beside her, she might have made a scene. Their presence was beyond disrespectful, and she was no longer the type of woman to accept it. For Michelle, she would not address them; for Michelle, she would permit their insolence for the moment . . . and deal with them later.

She shook her head and wiped her eyes. She needed to focus. Be present. Michelle was stoic. She hardly cried at all, but Sophie felt her pain. She held her mother's hand so tightly that if she had any color in it, she'd have lost it. Poor Michelle. Sophie could only imagine how painful this was for her. Without warning, Sophie started to feel something she had not felt over the last week. Something she expected to swarm her while she watched Lewis take his last breaths . . . guilt. She felt remorse over her decision to free herself, realizing the act cost her daughter her father.

The part of the ceremony where people viewed the body commenced as the last rows took their turn. This process always seemed a bit odd to Sophie. She understood that on some level it confirmed that the person was, indeed, deceased, but she always thought it better to consider the perished as absent and to remember them as they lived. Nevertheless, the procession moved fairly quickly. Faceless women, men, of various ages. Some cried hysterically, while others scoffed over his body, but there was one whose frame had been so prominent in the pictures that Sophie recognized her by it alone, one that lingered a touch longer than the rest and claimed Sophie's attention. From her seat, Sophie saw her hands on Lewis's face.

"The nerve of this *bitch*." Although she tried to remain discreet, Sophie's blood was boiling.

Michelle shook her mother's hand softly. Although she had barely spoken above a whisper, Michelle heard her words clearly. She noticed the tension in her mother's body growing. She thought her mother might jump up and maul this woman while she paid her last respects to her father. Michelle could not see what the woman was doing from behind her shades, but whatever it was, it upset her mother greatly. The woman stood too long for her comfort, and as she turned, she glanced their direction, Michelle recognized her immediately. Time froze. *Lisa?* It was Lisa! She definitely did not want her mother confronting her *here*. She rubbed her mother's arm in an effort to calm her down. Lisa was completely out of line, but Michelle could not afford to have *that conversation* here. Michelle literally held her mother in place while Lisa walked away and off funeral grounds. Michelle would deal with Lisa *personally*.

The funeral went smoothly, and that near crisis with Lisa was averted. Michelle was heated, though. She understood why Bria thought her capable of what she did. Who lusts after someone's husband at a funeral? Her mother's state of mind was questionable, and that did not help matters. She was not sure if something was still going on between Lisa and her father, but after Lisa's public display of affection at the funeral, Michelle was all but positive. She may as well have tongued him down right there. Michelle shook her head to erase the image.

She was getting the few things she brought with her together and preparing to leave her mother's house. She did not have her car, so either Armand needed to come and get her or she'd have to call a taxi.

"Armand, any word about Brianna?"

There was no way Armand could tell Michelle what he knew without implicating himself. If she smelled smoke, she would definitely keep looking until she found the fire. It was better to keep his answers vague. "Yes . . . and no."

"What? What does that mean?"

"She is still alive, but I'm not sure where she is yet."

"Do you think she's hurt?"

Armand was evasive, and Michelle did not like it. "No, I don't think so."

"Do you know *anything?*"

Armand chided himself for not being a little more forthcoming. He was too short with her, and adding to her stress level was the very last thing he wanted to do. He tried to reassure her and convince himself of his next answer. "I'll handle it."

"I know, but I just feel weird not doing anything."

"Michelle, you *are* doing something. You're staying safe and out of sight. They think they have you. I don't know what would happen if they find out they don't."

Michelle was not simply going to sit on her hands. If she could not help find Brianna, she could at least finish their work. They still didn't know who their parents were or why they had been separated.

"Listen, I want to go see Frank, Brianna's dad."

"In Lew Sterrett? Michelle, did you hear *anything* I just told you?"

"I know, but I need to do this. Besides, no one will be looking for me there."

Michelle was not taking no for an answer. She would take a car if Armand did not take her.

"Michelle, I don't like it."

"Look, nothing happened at the funeral, right? It went fine. Besides, it's the jail. Who would possibly hurt me there?"

"Michelle . . . that is *not* the point."

"Armand, I was not asking you. I'm going."

Michelle's stubbornness drove Armand crazy. He wasn't changing her mind. He had no choice but to let her go. "Fine, woman."

Michelle chuckled at that, knowing she'd won.

"How are you going to get in there?"

"Well . . . I'm going to pretend I'm Brianna."

This time, it was Armand's turn to laugh. "You're going to *what?*"

"I'll pretend I'm Brianna. I'll use her license."

Armand stopped laughing. "Oh yeah? How are you going to trick her dad, though?"

"I don't know, but I need to speak with him and find out what he does know. Since I can't help find Brianna, I can still try to find our birth parents. There are simply too many coincidences for no one to know nothing. Somebody has some answers. I just need to pose the correct question to the right person."

"Well, as always, be careful."

"Wait, what are you doing? You're not about to hang up, are you?"

"I was, why?"

"I need you to come get me from my mom's house."

"Michelle . . . Why didn't you say that in the first place?"

"I wanted to know about Brianna. It doesn't matter, Armand. Come get me . . . pretty please?"

"I promise. You make me crazy, but I love you anyway. Be there in twenty."

Michelle threw her phone on the bed and went looking for her mom. "Mom? Mom, where are you?"

"I'm in the den."

Michelle made her way to the den. She had a few questions for her mom before she left. "Hey, Mom, my ride is coming to get me, but I wanted to check in before I left."

"It's been long enough. I told you I didn't need you to stay."

Sophie loved having Michelle home, but her presence was sending her on an emotional roller coaster, and she didn't know how much longer she could last before she spilled her guts.

Michelle frowned. "Mom, it's only been two days since the funeral." She did not fail to note the fact that her mother was less than thrilled about her being there. She thought she would be happy that she wanted to stay. She was always asking her to come by, but now that she was here, Sophie acted as if she couldn't wait for her to leave. People grieved differently, and Michelle had never lost anyone so close. Maybe her mother just needed to cry alone.

"I know, but I'm fine. The sooner I can regain some sense of normalcy, the easier things will be for me."

"I know. I have a quick question, though. I learned a few things about Dad and . . . Well, it has me thinking."

"You can ask me anything, you know that."

"Am I adopted?"

"Michelle, you have already asked me that, and I told you no then, and the answer has not changed. No, you are *not* adopted. What makes you ask that?"

"I know Dad liked to, uh . . . move around."

"What does that have to do with you? You are my daughter. It is true your father, unfortunately, took certain liberties, but that has nothing to do with you. He is your father, and I am your mother. Understood?"

Michelle was not satisfied with that answer. It would have brought her comfort hearing the conviction and certainty with which her mother spoke had it not been lacking very important details. The answer did not explain Brianna's absence nor her presence. Michelle could not question further, though; she would get nowhere and only frustrate herself in the process. She got her stubborn resolve from her mother. Unless Michelle had something extra to add, she was not going to get a different answer regardless of how many different ways she posed the question.

"Yes, ma'am, I understand. Thank you, Mom."

Sophie cringed. She wanted to tell Michelle the whole truth, but she didn't know how. She simply could not do it. She told herself it was better this way; that Michelle never knows about her sister since she could never be with her. Sophie had no clue where she was or if she was alive and well. She hoped, though. She sure hoped she was. "So, who is coming to get you?"

"Armand."

"Armand. Am I finally going to meet this young man?"

Michelle considered it. It had been two years, but with everything going on, maybe now was not the best time. "Not today, but soon enough."

"I'll give you this week, but I want to meet him before I leave, *Number One*."

Michelle heard Armand's car in the driveway. She needed to beat him to the door if she wanted to delay their meeting. She got up and walked to where her mom sat, hugged her, and kissed her forehead. "Yes, ma'am. I've got to get my bags. Love you."

"I love you, too."

Chapter 33

Mike was still waiting to hear from Armand. It had been nearly a week, and John was growing more impatient by the day. Their prisoner was not talking, but she had eaten the food he offered. Of course, he had to convince her that it wasn't poisonous or anything by eating a little piece himself. He didn't fully understand why he was so invested in saving her. This was not the first time they had to deal with a situation like this, and the previous solution worked well for them. They were never called in for questioning, but he did not want to hurt her. Something would not let him. He could not even consider it an option. He picked up the phone to call his brother Javan.

Although Javan was younger than he, Mike looked up to him. Javan had made all the right decisions and was gunning for partner at his architectural firm. Mike needed some sound advice, and he couldn't think of anyone better to speak with.

"Mike, how are you, bruh?"

"I'm good, but I need to holla at'chu. Got a minute?"

"For you, of course. What's good?"

"I got a little situation with John."

"You and John always have something going, man. I thought you were trying to fall back. He's loose."

"Still ridin' that way, but, uh . . . This was unfinished business."

"Mike, I know you and John are close like brothers, man. I was always jealous of his position, but understand that what I'm saying is not on a jealousy tip. That man is not your brother. He's got more than a few screws missing. Only a matter of time before that train derails."

"Say, Javan . . . Listen, man, I know how you feel about John, all right, but can you focus for a second?"

"I *am* focused. I know that whatever this is . . . was *his* idea and don't bother trying to convince me otherwise."

"Javan, it was *my* idea. My plan, and now it's busted, and I need to fix it before John does."

"Was this why he was so amped up the other day when I came by?"

"Yeah, it was, but, look—"

"Nah, Mike. Why didn't you say anything when I was over there?"

"I needed some time to think. You're my little brother. Think I like coming to you with my bullshit?"

Javan was already giving him a hard time. Mike could only imagine what he would do once he got the full story. "We're family. Are you going to give me any details?"

"Not on the line, just come by later. John will be ghost, and we can chop it up."

"I'll see you then."

Mike wasn't happy with getting Javan involved in any way, but he was desperate. John was going off the deep end. He didn't want Mike feeding her. Mike felt a little better knowing that he might be a little closer to finding a solution. He got up to check on Michelle.

They were in a newly remodeled four-bedroom house off Rosewood in South Dallas. It wasn't bad for what it was, and it was pretty roomy. She was in the back room on the far side. He opened the door, and she looked up at him from where she sat on the floor. Her eyes were full of questions but absent of the perturbation that had been so prevalent before.

"Do you need anything?"

She shook her head no.

"These hands," Mike held up his hands for Brianna to view, turning them for effect, "ain't for roughin' up females. That's not me."

Brianna stared at him. She did not know whether she should believe him. He had been the nicer of two captors, but he had taken her away from everything she knew. "What do you want from me?"

Mike never missed a beat. "Your pops owes some cash from back in the day."

Brianna let the words stew. "So, I'm a bargaining chip?"

"Not anymore."

"So, what am I?"

"That's not important. He was into us for the cash, but not anymore."

"Was? What do you mean was?"

"Your pops can't pay."

"What, what are you talking about?"

Mike realized his mistake, but it was too late to pull it back. The sting had reached her valentine; the spike in her pulse showed in her eyes. He stumbled over his words, hesitant to be the one giving her this news.

"I mean, yeah . . . He died." Mike could not tell her that she missed his funeral; it seemed cruel.

"I don't understand. He was just . . . I just . . ." Brianna started crying uncontrollably, sputtering inaudible words.

Mike decided to let her be and give her a chance to calm down. Brianna could not believe it. How could her dad be dead? He was just in jail. Did someone kill him in jail? What was happening? She held her arms and rocked back and forth on the pallet. This could not be true; it couldn't be. She needed to get out of there, but she didn't even know where she was. Mike said he wanted to help her. Maybe she would take him up on his offer. What did she have to lose?

Mike didn't want to be the bearer of bad news. He had no intentions of telling her at all, but it slipped out. Hopefully, the news would encourage some cooperation from her. He needed to know everything Armand had failed to tell them. It was her only shot at walking out alive. He could fight John, but he'd rather not. John was his friend and had been for as long as he could remember. He saved his ass so many times he lost count; he didn't want to cross him like that. Hopefully, Javan could lend some insight. When he checked his cell again, there was a text message from Armand, asking him to call him. Mike dialed, anxious to hear what Armand had to say. For his sake, he'd better have some answers.

Chapter 34

It was Tuesday, and Michelle was waiting to see Frank. She endured the uncomfortable frisk, wand search, and passed through the metal detector. If it took all of that to get in for a few minutes, she could only hope her exit would not be as complicated. With only Brianna's driver's license in hand, she followed the guard into a room that looked to be about four feet wide with hard cement walls and listened to the big metal door slam shut behind her. She took her seat in front of the shatterproof glass and mentally introduced herself to Frank, her sister's father.

Frank was happy to see Brianna, thankful that she was well. When he was told he had a visitor, he felt a little anxious, but once he saw it was her, his nervousness fled. He grabbed the old-school black phone and motioned for her to do the same. His smile was so bright, it almost made her forget where they were . . . almost. It had been such a long time since he had seen Brianna last. He hadn't realized how much he had truly missed her. She was a sight for sore eyes.

"Brianna—"

Michelle shook her head. She hadn't intended to, but it was done. This was not how she wanted this meeting to go, but she went with it.

Frank scrunched his face in confusion, not understanding. "Brianna, baby girl?"

Michelle shook her head once again. It was all she could manage to do at the moment. It was happening almost involuntarily. She kept shaking her head until she saw the change in his eyes, confirmation that her truth had registered.

"You're her *sister?*" Frank was numb. What were the odds? How could this even be possible? "Where did you come from? I don't understand."

Michelle fought back her tears, trying to maintain her composure. She wasn't sure how the next words would sound coming out of her mouth, but she had to know what he knew. "We found each other. Brianna . . . Brianna couldn't be here, but I'm here in her . . . place. We need answers, and I hope you can help us."

Frank could not believe his eyes. The voice did not belong to Brianna, but her face . . . They were identical. She was beautiful, just like his daughter, and he could not lie to her. Besides, his actions had hurt her as well.

"What is your name?"

"Michelle. My name is Michelle."

"Michelle, I am so sorry for what I did. I love Brianna, and I raised her the best I could. I gave her everything I had. I hope you'll let her know that."

"We need to know the truth. Please."

"The truth will be difficult to hear and painful to speak. You deserve to know it. I . . . I purchased Brianna when she was a baby."

The air left Michelle's lungs, and she strained to fill them again. Was Brianna *purchased?* Like a damn tote bag? This man was sick.

"A woman was in a bad way, and she needed the money. I needed a baby."

Michelle kept her cool, turned off her emotions, and stayed the course. She could not afford to get swept up in her emotions now. She was finally getting the answers she needed.

"I gave her $5 million, and she gave me her child. Well, *one* of them, obviously. She didn't have a name for her yet; she just called her number two."

Michelle's heart sank. Tears streamed from her eyes. Her sister was sold and bought like an accessory. No one deserved to be treated that way. What type of person would do such a thing?

Frank did not fare any better. He felt as if he might pass out any minute, but he knew he needed to get this out. He saw the pain he was causing her, and even though Michelle was not his daughter, he loved her like she was.

"I am so sorry, Michelle. I did not mean to hurt anyone, but I know I did. I own that."

"How could you do that? How could you take my sister from me?" Michelle's rage rose to the surface. "All these years, I thought I was an only child. She thought she was too, but you knew differently. You knew the truth! You kept us apart! Why?"

"I have my reasons, but you would never consider them valid, and I could not ask you to. I love Brianna, and the last thing I ever wanted to do was hurt her, but if the truth got out about how I adopted her . . . She could have been taken away from me. I would have lost everything I loved. So I figured as long as no one ever knew . . . Who would it hurt?"

"You selfish bastard! It hurt *us!* You changed *our* reality forever. We were intended to share this life together, but your desires came first. You ripped us apart. Ignorance is *not* bliss; it's simply ignorance. I deserved to have her in my life, and she deserved to have me. You had no right!"

"I am sorry—"

"I don't want to hear it. Where did you take her? Where were we? Was I there?" Michelle was crying now.

"The hospital. Took her from the hospital."

"From whom? Who is my mother? My father?"

"I don't know."

The guard came to the door. Their thirty minutes were up, but Michelle was not ready to leave. She pleaded with the guard for more time, screaming at Frank in desperation. "Who are our parents? Frank, answer me!"

Frank sat in silence. His face was sullen, dismayed. He couldn't tell her. He wouldn't. That information he would save for Brianna.

"Wait, Frank . . . Frank!" Michelle grabbed at the door as the guard escorted her out of the room and toward the exit.

Chapter 35

Brianna was heartbroken over the loss of her father. She hadn't even gotten a chance to speak with him. She wished that she could at least talk to her mom, Michelle, or someone to confirm Mike's story. For now, she had no choice really but to believe him. She didn't know how it would benefit him to mislead her, but she held out hope that maybe he was mistaken. John had come in earlier to intimidate her, brandishing a 9 mm and promising to beat her, shoot her, or some combination thereof. She learned early on that it's best to remain quiet. Every interaction with him had been violent. John was mean, scary, the kind of stuff nightmares were made of. Mike, on the other hand, was not as frightening. He had a quiet demeanor, firm but gentle. She wanted to trust him, or maybe she needed to. She needed something to grab on to.

There were no windows in her room. No decorative items or furniture of any kind. The walls were wood panel, and the floor was carpeted. The door was barred from the outside, and she believed that she could count how many pieces of Sheetrock were in the ceiling. She had been walking around the room for several hours, trying to think of anything she may have missed that could help her, or help Mike. She heard the door slam, and she knew John was gone. Each night he left around the same time and stayed gone until morning.

Mike would usually come in to feed her while John was away. She could not help but feel a twinge of disdain at her new normal. Had she been with them *that* long? The door opened, and Mike walked in with her tray of food, the same ham sandwich with mustard, lettuce, tomatoes, and pickles, the same baked Lay's potato chips with a glass of V8 Juice. He set the tray down near the door, left, and closed the door behind him. After enough time had passed for her to retrieve the tray, he reentered the room. Brianna was a bit surprised and uncomfortable with the change. She was not sure what it meant.

"Chill, ma, I ain't goin' to hurt you."

Mike's statements were robotic, devoid of emotion, and Brianna couldn't tell if he was serious or not. She didn't know what Mike wanted to speak with her about, but she was prepared to help him if she could.

"Look, someone is comin' through. Keep quiet. Shit get real bad, real fast, otherwise. I'm tryin' to help you out. Fuck me, and I'll let John loose on ya ass."

Brianna understood, and she nodded in agreement. She continued eating and did not verbally respond. She thought of screaming, yelling for help, but the truth was that she didn't know who this person was that Mike's expecting. He could be even worse than John. Mike had not hurt her, and, given the circumstances, he had taken pretty good care of her. She would not say anything. She decided that silence would be best.

"I'll be back later to get that tray."

Mike left the room and prepared for Javan's arrival. Javan had called and said he'd be there any minute. Mike had not decided if he would tell him the whole truth. There were pros and cons to both. Mike heard Javan's Benz pull up in the driveway and shook his head. He had told Javan about driving that ride in the neighborhood. It attracted too much attention they did not want or need. He opened the front door and waved him inside.

"Are you fuckin' serious, J? What the fuck did I tell ya ass 'bout that damn car?"

"Look, I paid for that car, and I'll drive it if I choose to. Tonight, I chose to. It's that simple."

"But you *knew* you were comin' through, though. That shit attracts unwanted mufackin' attention, J. I don't need that bullshit."

"Get off it, bruh . . . I'm here now. Talk."

"Pushin' it, bruh."

"Now, what could you not tell me over the phone?"

Javan and Mike each took a seat in one of the four rusted metal fold up chairs that made up the living-room furniture. The bare cement floor creaked as each sat down, causing the chairs to scrape across its surface. Mike blew out some air as he explained his issue. "This guy was into us for close to thirty large. Old debt, but we saw an opportunity to collect and had to take it."

"Okay . . . So what happened?"

"Well, we snatched up this girl—"

"You did *what?* Wait a minute. No, you *didn't.*"

"Look, it was stupid. But we got his seed. We were goin' to hold her until he broke us off. Nothin' major. He got the dough . . . but—"

"I cannot believe I'm hearing this. Are you fucking kidding me, bruh? What the fuck, man?"

Mike figured Javan would trip a little, but it's not like he had never had any trouble. Mike knew about the bones in his closet, and he really didn't have any room to judge him. He may as well tell him everything. "The dude died, now I'm stuck wit' her."

"John?"

"He got a tote for her."

"Damn it."

"That was neva the plan, though."

"Shit. I cannot believe you got me over here in the middle of your shit, Mike!"

"I know, but, shit, come on. I remember your *situation*. How did you get out? I need a way out."

"A way out? Is she here?" Javan got up and started walking through the house. "Where is she?" He ignored the insinuation. That was a moment in his past, and honestly, he didn't know the answer anyway.

"Wait, Javan. Hold up."

Brianna could hear voices. Distant at first, but they got louder and louder. She could hear Mike saying something, and the other she couldn't make out.

"Where is she? Which room, Mike?" Javan was yelling now, annoyed that his brother had got him mixed up in this mess. He was not leaving this girl at John's mercy. He didn't trust him.

Chill bumps covered Brianna's arms and legs. The hairs stood up all over her body. Her heart started beating faster. She *knew* that voice. She knew it. Brianna ran to the door and began beating on it and screaming frantically. "Javan? Javan!"

"Brianna?" Javan could not believe it. What was Brianna doing here? He turned to his brother, his eyes accusatory. "What is Brianna doing here, Mike?"

Mike was confused. He didn't know who Brianna was. "I don't know who Brianna is . . . the girl in there is Michelle."

"Which room is she in, Mike? Brianna! Bria!"

"Javan, I'm in here! I'm in here! Javan!"

"I'm coming, Bria. Just hold on, babe."

Javan turned again to his brother. "Open this damn door, Mike. Open it right now!"

Mike was not sure what he should do, but he had seen that look in his brother's eye before. He twisted the tiny metallic knob: twice to the left stopping on thirty-five, then to the right, landing on sixteen, then three times to the left, pausing on ten, listened for the click, removed it, and pushed the metal bar to the side. Javan thrust open the door, and Brianna collapsed into his arms, crying uncontrollably.

"You found me! I cannot believe you found me!"

Mike fell back against the wall, bewildered by yet another turn of events. This was not Michelle? How could they have fucked this up? Who was this girl? "Say, yo' name is Michelle . . . J . . . hol' up. Yo' name is Michelle, right?"

Javan interceded for Brianna. He did not want his brother talking to her. "Don't talk to her, bruh; just don't say shit."

Mike continued to plead his case. "Javan, you're my brother, I didn't know. We better than that. Come—"

The steel Mike saw in his brother's eyes stopped him cold; then Javan continued to console Brianna. "Are you hurt, baby? Are you okay?"

Brianna stopped crying and looked at Javan. Did he just say brother? Suddenly, she no longer felt so lucky. How did Javan find her? How did he even know she was missing? Michelle did not know Javan to tell him. No one knew about Javan. He had been her little secret.

"Javan, how do you know Mike? How did you find me? I don't understand." Brianna began backing away from Javan, her arms outstretched in front of her. She was shaking and overcome with distress. "Were you in on this? Are you working together?"

"Bria, baby . . . Wait, hold on . . . Let me explain. I didn't know you were here. Mike is my big brother. He called me over here to talk to me about something, all right?"

Brianna was still backpedaling, not completely convinced. It just seemed too good to be true.

"We are not working together, okay? Mike, tell her, man."

"Br-i-an-na . . ." Mike stated hesitantly. "He's straight."

"See, babe? Now let me take you out of here. Come here. It's me, Bria."

"Javan, I can't let you do that, man."

"What are you talking about? Mike, this isn't just some girl, man. I love her, and I'm not leaving here without her. Bria . . . Bria . . . Come here."

Brianna wanted to believe Javan, but how could she be sure?

"Look at me, woman. Have I ever lied to you about anything? I need you to trust me right now. I know it looks bad. Just trust me. Come here."

Brianna looked at Javan, standing in the doorway, arms open, begging her to join him. Her legs moved without her permission. She was in his arms before she could object. He pulled her through the hallway that she saw for the first time.

"Javan, man, wait. You can't just walk up out of here. Whatchu think this is? I could be lookin' at twenty-five, easy."

Javan dithered and considered the severity of his brother's words. He could not ask Brianna to keep quiet about this. It was horrible what his brother had done. Brianna could have been seriously hurt, and that thought alone made Javan want to fuck his brother up himself. "I don't want you losing daylight in a cell, bruh, but I'm not leaving here without her. John could be back any minute; she's not safe here."

"Javan, I don't know who you think she is, man, but her name is not Brianna. It's Michelle."

Brianna looked at Mike but did not say anything. She did not correct him. If he thought she was Michelle, so be it. They must have intended to grab Michelle, and she was not going to tell him that Michelle was still out there.

No, she would just have to trust that Javan could figure this out.

"Mike, I don't care who you think she is . . . whatever you want to call her . . . Brianna or Michelle. Consider her gone, bruh. She's coming with me."

Mike looked helplessly at his brother. He knew better than to try to stop him. He did not know how he would explain this to John. Javan could see the stress lines on his brother's face, but it was of no concern to him. Mike would have to figure it out.

"I'll take her somewhere safe. We won't go to the cops for now. I won't tell you where we'll be, but I'll be accessible by phone."

"Nah, man, that ain't happenin'." Mike had expected some advice—not a damn rescue effort.

"Let me help you with this. You cannot control John, and the last thing I'm sure you want is a dead body on your hands."

Mike trusted his brother but not this girl. He hadn't wanted to believe it, but John was right. The only way to stay free was to silence her—permanently.

"Javan . . . I hear you . . . but—"

"Mike, I am *not* asking you!"

Mike looked at Brianna and knew he couldn't harm her. If he had to do time, he earned it, but he was done with this part of his life, ready to put it to bed for good. Besides, he had a move left, and he didn't need her for it.

"I'm telling you. I'm leaving with her right now. Bria, let's go. Just hold on to me."

They were standing in the front room, almost to the door. Some part of Mike was still trying to keep them from leaving. It may have been silly, but he couldn't shake the guilt from betraying John. He would definitely not be cool with this, but Javan was right. He did not want John to body her or for anything bad to happen to her. This may be the only way.

"I'll call you later, Mike. John is crazy, and I advise you to leave too."

Javan took Brianna out of the house, placed her in the car, and drove away. Mike stood in the doorway, dumbfounded. The girl would have her life, but he was not sure how much longer he would have his. He only had one card left to play, and he hoped it kept him in the game.

Chapter 36

"I cannot believe she would look at me and lie, Armand."
Michelle was fuming. She called Armand as soon as
she stepped one foot outside the jail and demanded
that he take her back to her mom's. As far as she was
concerned, he could not get there fast enough!

"Michelle, you don't know anything yet, okay? Just
hold off until you ask her."

"I am so furious! I just . . . It's the only thing that makes
sense."

Michelle had given Sophie every opportunity to come
clean about everything, and she had not taken any of
them. Michelle wondered if she would still deny it with
so much evidence stacked against her.

"So, Frank told you that he bought your sister? From
whom? Maybe it was the doctor's doing?"

"I don't think so. It had to be her. I wish it weren't."

Michelle's stomach was a swarm of butterflies, and she
was sweating enough to fill a kiddie pool. She would take
no pleasure in the conversation she was about to have
with the woman who had raised her. She only hoped she
would be as happy on the other end of the rabbit hole
once her mother came clean . . . *if* she came clean, as
Alice was.

"You can come in. She wants to meet you anyway. No
time like the present."

"Michelle, you're upset. Are you sure about this?"

Michelle gave Armand a look that let him know that he need not speak another word. They pulled up to the house, and Michelle jumped out of the car, bolting inside before Armand could take the car out of gear. He was not far behind her.

"Mom! Mom, I need to talk with you."

"*Number One,* is that you, love?"

Her mother's nickname for her used to elicit feelings of joy and made her feel loved, special, but hearing it now simply pissed her off. "Funny you should say that . . . Number One."

Sophie was perplexed by Michelle's angry disposition. "Is something wrong, Michelle?"

Michelle stormed into the living room where Sophie was seated, flipping through some pictures. "We need to talk."

Sophie noticed Armand standing behind Michelle. "Is this Armand? Did you finally bring the young man by to meet me?"

Michelle looked at Armand, who tried to disappear into the living-room wall. The heat she felt about everything resonated through her being. "This visit isn't about him, Mom."

Michelle's statement garnered Sophie's undivided attention. She tried to get ahead of the potential trouble that resided in her daughter's stare. "Michelle, I don't know what is going on, but you need to change your tone."

"Trust me, my tone is the *least* of your worries."

"I am your mother, and you will *not* speak to me in this way."

"Are you my mother? Are you *sure?*"

"Michelle, what is this nonsense? Yes, I am your mother. You're my *Number One.*" Sophie chuckled halfheartedly, feeling uneasy with this line of questioning.

"Why do you call me that?"

Michelle's question seemed innocent, but her manner had deeper implications. She was fishing for something, and Sophie wanted her to get to the point or drop it altogether. She tried to keep her attitude light, hoping that it would lighten the tension that slowly engulfed the room. "Michelle, what is this about?"

"Mom, this is about the $5 million you gave me after I graduated from college."

Sophie's heart began to flutter, and her hands shook nervously. She told herself to relax; she had nothing to fret over. Michelle did not know anything. How could she? The only other person that knew . . . took that to the grave with him.

"Yes, it was a gift from your father and me," Sophie stated, confident that her answer would end these questions. She looked at Michelle softly, ushering a soft plea for her to accept what she offered, but Michelle was not having it.

"It's interesting . . . I talked to Dad, and he did not know anything about it. He didn't say anything, but when I thanked him for it, I could see the surprise in his eyes."

Sophie's stomach churned in angst. This could not be happening. She sent a silent prayer for something . . . anything to end it. "I didn't tell your father everything, Mich—"

"Where did you get the money, Mom?" Michelle interrupted her, refusing to indulge one more lie. Embedded in the fury growing beneath her brown eyes, her heart was breaking. Why wouldn't her mother tell her the truth?

"My savings. I had been saving it since you were born."

Michelle shook her head to keep from crying, wiping the beginnings of tears from her eyes with the back of her wrists. "Don't you mean since *we* were born, Mom?" Would she still pretend that Brianna didn't exist? The game was over, and Michelle would not let her continue playing.

Sophie could not hide the shock on her face. She stood up and instantly fell back into the chair. Her legs could not hold her. She felt her head swimming. Panic took over, coursing through her limbs and blanketing her thoughts. "Michelle . . . how did you—"

"I found her, Mom. The daughter you sold like a piece of jewelry—my sister!" Unable to hold them back any longer, Michelle's tears stained her cheeks as they fell from her eyes.

"Michelle . . . You don't understand." Sophie felt defeated. She never wanted to hurt anyone, least of all her daughter.

"What is there to understand? What is with you people? Will one of you stop making excuses and own it?" First Frank wants sympathy, and now her mom?

"Michelle, you have every right to be angry, but please, let me explain." Sophie thought that if she could get Michelle to hear her side, that things would be okay. Michelle would understand, and all would be forgiven. Naturally, she did what she had to do.

"Explain *what*, Mom? Didn't you love her? What right did you have to take my twin?" Michelle felt more anguish at this moment than she had at any other point in her life. Brianna was not only her sister but her twin. Their connection was not only a matter of familial ties but something more, something deeper. They shared the same womb and entered into the world together—only to be ripped apart by people charged to protect them. It was almost too much for Michelle to stomach.

"I know . . . I was afraid. I didn't know what else to do."

Sophie did not know how to speak her truth. How could she tell Michelle that she did not know if she had loved her? That she had pondered, planned, and poised herself to love one child, not two. That it was not only easy to give that baby away, but it brought her comfort and relief? She felt very little, if any, emotional attachment to a child she had only known about for a few minutes.

"So, you gave me that blood money to live on?" Michelle felt sick. This was simply not fair.

"Michelle, sit down, please." Sophie searched for the words to make things right, to soften the harshness of what she did. "I need you to—"

"Are you insane?"

"Michelle, sit down! Please. Just . . . just . . . sit down."

"I don't know who you are anymore. What kind of mother are you?"

Hearing that question triggered something in Sophie. She had done the best she could do at the time. She would be the first to admit her mistake, but she was not about to let anyone, including Michelle, make her feel guilty about it. "What kind of mother am I? Michelle . . . You are young. What do *you* know about this world? What hard days have *you* seen? Don't you dare stand there and judge me."

"I know that I would never sell my daughter for money," Michelle spat.

Those words, "sell my daughter," pierced Sophie's soul. The weight of her choice cemented her place as an active participant in what had to be one of the worst possible things a mother could ever do to her children. She did not only separate them, but she chose between them. "Sit down."

Michelle sat down on the couch farthest from her mother.

Sophie tried to find the words the best way she knew how. "You have no idea what I went through with your father before you were born. I am only sharing this with you now in hopes that you will have a better understanding of what happened."

Michelle doubted there was anything her mother could say that would change how she felt, but she forced her mind open to listen.

"I was young, in love, and very naïve. I thought I could handle being away from my family. I thought I was ready to start a family with your father. Maybe I was, but he was not, and it was not easy for us. I didn't even know about—"

"My sister . . ." Michelle finished her sentence. She wanted to remind her mother of who the child was. She was not some stranger or some other mother's daughter. She was *her* daughter.

"Her . . . until I delivered. It all happened so quickly. We made the exchange; then she was gone. I did not even know the man's name. I had planned to take the money and leave with you."

Michelle was not satisfied, but she could see that, for the first time, her mother was being completely honest. Still, there was no excuse for what she had done. "Where was Dad? Did he know?"

"No, your father was not there, and he did not know. Anyway, once we got home, I realized that I had made a huge mistake, and I could not leave without your sister. So, I stayed. We stayed, and I hoped to see her but never did."

"Touching." Michelle's mind was all over the place, and her response was more of a knee-jerk reaction, devoid of emotion.

"That is the truth, Michelle. It is the truth, regardless of whether you agree."

"You just don't get it, do you? Okay, let's say I believe you. What do you think is supposed to happen now? What do you want me to do with what you have told me? How am I to live with it?"

Sophie could not tell her what to do. She could only hope that it would allow Michelle to forgive her one day. "I am sorry. I have regretted what I've done, every day, but it could not be undone. I could not change anything. I thought of her every day . . . every single day."

"You made a decision out of hurt, causing several others to hurt too." Michelle looked at her mother, and it was like she was seeing her for the first time. Her mascara left patches of blackness on her face as evidence of the pain she failed to shed. Below her gentle blue eyes were pockets that exceeded the depths of the Grand Canyon, carrying in them a lifetime of heartaches, joy, and indifference. Her mother had always been a woman with a quiet strength. It was a quality that Michelle always admired about her, and on some level, envied. But *this* woman was broken and needed to be healed, to be helped, loved.

"That song you used to sing to me about the lost little girl was about her."

Sophie nodded in agreement.

"I never understood why you were so sad. I felt like I wasn't enough. That I wasn't the little girl you had expected. I would sit in your lap, and you'd just cry. It was terrible."

It was the first time Michelle had ever said it aloud. She had not even told Armand, and she could not bring herself to look up at him, but she could feel him watching. He wanted to comfort her, but this was between her and her mother. He could not, and would not, interfere.

Sophie did not think she could feel any worse until that moment. "Michelle . . . I have always been proud of you. I love you. You have exceeded all my expectations. You saved my life, baby." Sophie spoke slowly to allow her heart to wrap around Michelle. She loved her and hated that she ever made her feel that way.

Michelle's eyes were swollen red and burning. She hated all of this. For a moment the two, mother and daughter, let the silence clear the air. A lot had been said, and it would not be fixed overnight.

"Where is she? How did you find her?" Sophie broke the quiet with her questions in the same way the question itself had cracked the silence in her mind . . . abruptly.

Armand, who had made himself scarce while they hashed it out, suddenly became visible again. Michelle kept her eyes on him as she responded. "She was kidnapped. Armand is helping me to get her back."

Armand cleared his throat. Michelle answered the question in his eyes with a shrug of her shoulders. She was tired of all the secrecy. No more lies.

"Some people were following me, and we think they grabbed her by mistake." Michelle felt numb as memories of Brianna flooded her mind. She missed her and prayed she was all right.

Sophie was immediately alarmed. Her body tensed, and she searched Michelle's face for an answer. This girl did not tell her anything. "Dear God, Michelle, are you in danger?"

"I don't know. I don't think so."

"Does she hate me?" Sophie felt it might have been the wrong question to ask, but it was the first question that popped into her mind.

Michelle rolled her eyes, annoyed with her mother's selfishness. This was not about her or about how Brianna may feel about her. Her concern should have been for Brianna's safety. Of course, true to form, when it was Brianna's life on the line, Sophie, yet again, made it about her own emotional state.

"She probably will, Mom. I almost hate you, and you kept me."

That hurt. Sophie did not know how to respond to that. Michelle was being hateful, but she deserved it. Undeterred, she continued to press for information. "What's her name?"

"Brianna. Her name is Brianna."

Sophie had found some comfort over the years in the idea her daughter had been better off. She did not want anything to happen to her before she ever got a chance to hold her and apologize. She mused over the name. "Brianna . . . That's beautiful."

She turned to Armand, "Do you have any idea where she is?"

"Yes, ma'am, I'm doing everything I can. Michelle, we need to get going."

Michelle got up to leave. "I don't understand how you could do it."

"Michelle—"

"You looked me in my eyes and lied to me like it was nothing." She was ready to go. She needed some fresh air and some space from her mom.

"I never lied to you," Sophie countered.

"Each second that passed by without telling me . . . counts as a lie."

"That's not fair, Michelle. Circumstances didn't allow for that . . . There was never an appropriate time. I wanted to; believe me, I did."

"Bottom line . . . If you wanted to, you would have. Who is my father, by the way?"

"Lewis is . . . was your father."

With that, Michelle left without saying another word. Sophie cried and prayed that her daughters could forgive her.

Chapter 37

Lisa felt liberated. Lewis was dead, and there was no chance that Frank would ever learn of her past. Lewis's wife looked very familiar, but she couldn't remember where she might have seen her. She was not overly concerned, though; that part of her life was finally over. She could move on with a clean slate and didn't have to leave Dallas. She tried calling Brianna again, but she still didn't answer. Number two on her list of things to do was to repair that relationship.

She might not be Brianna's biological mother, but she was still her mom. She wished she would pick up or text or something. Brianna was simply being stubborn. Nobody's perfect, although Brianna liked to think her father was. Lisa had been in the hotel since the funeral. She even missed visiting day with Frank yesterday, so she would have to wait until Friday. It was a beautiful day outside. Walking weather. She decided to take a stroll.

As soon as she stepped outside, she was made aware of her error. She mistook the Texas sunshine for a warm day, but it was freezing outside. Maybe she could walk around the hotel instead. She still had not seen the majority of it. She wandered around the expansive first floor of the building. There were various statues, restaurants, cute little boutiques, and other artistic pieces throughout the hotel. Lisa enjoyed herself throughout her stroll. She did not make a purchase, but everything seemed to feel different now that her situation with Lewis was finally over. Quite literally, her reality had changed.

She was headed back to her room when she thought she saw a familiar face. It couldn't be. What were the odds? Though she was resistant to believe it, the more she stared, she realized that it was true. Brianna was at the hotel.

"Brianna! Brianna!"

Michelle heard someone screaming Brianna's name. Excitedly, she turned and looked wildly for her sister. After she didn't see her, she realized the person might have been calling to her. She stopped to locate the feminine voice. She scanned the sea of people walking around and found Lisa. *Lisa?* What was *she* doing here? She motioned with her hand for Armand to keep walking, watching him board the elevator and head up to the suite. She waited as Lisa walked toward her. Michelle did not want to talk to Lisa in such a public place; she needed some privacy. Lisa extended her arms for a hug, but Michelle declined the contact.

"Brianna . . . Do you want to go somewhere to talk?"

Michelle nodded, in order to not speak and give herself away yet, and Lisa proceeded to lead her to *her* room. Lisa's room was on the second floor and, thankfully, did not take long to reach. Michelle became increasingly upset with each passing minute. She thought of how disrespectful Lisa had been to her family at her dad's funeral, and how rude she had been to her mother and felt she might explode. She was tired of all the lies and secrets. Enough was enough. Brianna did not like her, and now Michelle had her own reasons for disliking her. Someone needed to check this woman.

"Brianna, how are you? I've been trying to reach you."

Michelle did not respond.

"Brianna, do you hear me? I'm talking to you."

Still nothing. Lisa sighed in frustration. Her daughter was even less cooperative than she anticipated. If they were going to mend their relationship, it would take some effort on her part too. "Look, I know you don't like me very much right now, but I love you. I'm trying here, but you've got to meet me halfway, Bria. No one is perfect."

"Kiss my ass." Michelle could barely believe she'd said it herself. Oh well, it was out there now, so she figured she might as well run with it.

Lisa was shocked at her daughter's sudden callousness. "*Excuse me?* Who do you think you're talking to? You may be upset, but you will *not* speak to your mother that way."

"You know, that is the second time I have heard that in the past two days. Both of you claim to be my mother, but one of you has been playing make-believe. I think we know which one of you that is."

Lisa was flabbergasted. What in the hell had gotten into her daughter? "Brianna, what are you talking about?"

Michelle started laughing. An uncomfortable, pain-filled laugh. Her heart was broken, and her hurt ran deep. This laugh was the only thing holding her together. "All of you—you're a bunch of liars . . . every last one of you."

"Brianna, I don't know what your father has told you but—"

"My father is dead! He has not told me anything."

Lisa looked at Brianna curiously. Brianna was clearly unstable and needed some help. She reached for her phone to call 911. Brianna was freaking her out. Michelle grabbed her phone before she could get to it.

"Brianna, calm down. Everything will be okay."

"I don't know about that."

Michelle was not in the mood to play games, but she found Lisa's facial expressions mildly entertaining. Either she did not know about her existence, or she was going for the Oscar for Best Supporting Actress in Drama.

Lisa was adamant on having the upper hand on the conversation. "Your father is not dead. He's in jail, but he's very much alive."

"No . . . *My* father is dead. I saw you at his funeral. My mother saw you standing over him. You touched him like you had a right to do so. The nerve. You are a real piece of work."

Lisa put her hands on her head and looked wide-eyed at Brianna. This girl had clearly lost her mind. The only funeral she had attended in years was for Lewis, but surely this could not be who Brianna was talking about. Why would she think Lewis was her father, and who was the mother she was referring to? "What are you talking about, Brianna? What's gotten into you?"

"Please, stop calling me that. Clearly, I am *not* Brianna."

Now, Lisa was convinced that Brianna had truly lost her mind. She realized that she would be having a hard time dealing with her father's incarceration, but this was a bit much. She seemed to have created a whole other reality.

"Brianna . . . listen—"

"I am *not* Brianna! My name is Michelle. Michelle Lewis."

Lisa did not understand. Michelle saw the confusion in her eyes, so she took a different approach, burying the proverbial hatchet squarely across her forehead. "My father's name was Leonard Lewis. I believe you and the rest of his whores called him Lewis."

No, this was simply not possible—or was it? She and Lewis never discussed their families. "Did you just call me a whore?"

"I am Brianna's twin sister . . . her *identical* twin sister. I guess your husband did not share the details of the *adoption* with you. Please, allow me."

Lisa plopped down on the bed and tried to wrap her mind around the news Michelle dropped in her lap. Frank never said anything about a twin.

"Frank, your husband, in name only, gave *our* mother a lump sum of cash and took Brianna right out of the hospital room."

Lisa suffered from the shock of the allegations . . . except they were no longer allegations. Michelle was living proof of her husband's deception. Frank could not do that. She wanted to believe that he couldn't. She had accused him of it, but she didn't think that he was actually capable of doing something so inhumane. No wonder he reacted so violently when she had said that . . . She had struck a nerve.

"Okay . . . Michelle? This is a lot to take in at once. I'm sorry, I need a minute."

"You can think on your own time. I need answers now. I think twenty-two years was enough time for you to get this mess sorted out, and you failed. All of you failed. So, no, I'm not giving you one more minute."

"Who do you think you are talking to like that?" Brianna was one thing. She was her daughter, whom she had raised and loved. This . . . Michelle . . . was a woman. Sister or not, Lisa was not going to be disrespected.

"I'm talking to *you!* Trust me . . . This is *not* what you want. You're the woman Bria has called Mom, and that is the *only* reason I have not *gone there* with you. To me, you're nothing but a lying, disrespectful, high-class whore, and I would want nothing more than to mop the floor with that long, black hair of yours. You fucked my father, knowing he was a married man . . . Oh, and that shameful display you put on at the funeral? You are fortunate that I didn't just handle you in the lobby. If you step to me . . . step correct. My dad was not the only one in the family with a mean streak."

Lisa was not afraid, but she thought it better to let this slide. Michelle was obviously and rightfully upset. "Let's just talk, okay? We're both emotional right now."

"What was going on between you and my dad?"

"Nothing that concerns you." Lisa did not want to dig that back up. Only two people knew about the arrangement, and one of them was dead. She was in no hurry to add someone to that exclusive list. "It was a money thing. I paid him to keep a secret for me."

"Oh, so, you fucked him for free and paid for his silence."

"I guess. If you want to put it in those terms."

"If there is some other way to put it . . . please enlighten me." Michelle was baiting Lisa, trying to provoke her to say one thing out of line.

"I don't like your tone." Lisa was trying to be nice to this girl, but she was pushing it.

"Did you ever once ask Lewis about his family? Did he ever mention us?"

Lisa did not like the conversation in the least bit, and she did not want to answer any more questions. "This conversation is over. I don't owe you anything; I don't even know you."

"I am the daughter of the man you were sleeping with."

"Lewis and I . . . That's old. We have not been together for a while. It was a long time ago."

"It was not long enough." Michelle invaded her space a bit and stepped toward her.

Lisa stood as she saw Michelle start to approach. She was not trying to fight this girl, but she was not going to let her get the upper hand. "Michelle, I'm sorry, but I think you may have the wrong idea here."

"I am sure you do, but I saw pictures of you two together." Lisa may not have known about Michelle, but she was definitely messing with Lewis. Michelle was not going to let her weasel her way out of that one.

"What pictures? Does someone have pictures? Did Brianna see them?" Had someone had been following her? What in the hell was going on?

"We saw them together. My dad wasn't the only person you were caught on candid camera with, either."

Charlie had to be the other person. Brianna knows? She had tried so desperately to keep her past in the past that she had neglected to take care of her present. Now it was coming back to bite her. She had been careless.

Well, now, it was Lisa who wanted to get answers. "Where did you get them?"

"Someone sent them to your house. Brianna thinks that Frank saw them before he was hospitalized."

Frank did not see those pictures. He certainly would have mentioned them to her during the argument, but he did not say a word. He only asked about the money.

Michelle saw Lisa flinch, determined to stick the knife in further, she said, "We know about the money too. We don't know where it is . . . but we know you took it. So, you're an adulterer as well as a thief."

Lisa folded her arms across her chest, no longer interested in this exchange. "You don't know anything about me, little girl. Leave this room. I think we've talked enough."

"Fine. I can't stomach another minute alone with you anyway. You're a wretched woman, and Brianna deserved better than you."

Michelle left, slamming the door behind her. Lisa sat on the bed trying to wrap her head around what she had learned. Was Brianna a twin? She could not believe it. Frank had known all these years. Her heart ached for Brianna and the betrayal she must be feeling. In the midst of the melee, she neglected to ask Michelle about her. She might not have told her anyway, though. She tried calling Brianna again. Still no answer. She couldn't talk to Frank for another couple of days, and Brianna was still MIA.

She called the only other person she could think of. The only other person she knew loved her.

"What is it, Lisa?"

"Charlie . . . You answered." Lisa had mixed feelings. She was elated to hear Charlie's voice but still upset about what she had done.

"I almost didn't. What can I do for you?" Charlie knew she was being harsh, but she had to be. Her heart was ready to jump through the phone and right into Lisa's hand.

"Why did you just leave like that?"

"I needed to leave and get myself together."

"How are you? I've missed you."

"Have you, Lisa? Has your husband missed me too?" Charlie knew what this was about. Lisa needed something from her. All she ever did was take from her.

"Was that necessary?"

Charlie was screaming internally. Loud, boisterous screams. Lisa was impossible. She had been nothing more than a *fun time*.

"*We* weren't in your future. *We* were only in mine."

What was going on today? It started off so promising and was going in a completely different direction now. A 180-degree turn. First, she gets verbally attacked by Brianna's twin, and now, Charlie? Maybe leaving wasn't such a bad idea after all.

"I need you."

"I need me more."

"Just come by so we can talk, Charlie. In your letter . . . you said that you at least owed me that, right?"

Charlie wanted to see Lisa, but she was not sure if she was strong enough yet. Lisa took a lot out of her emotionally, and this conversation was already draining her. Besides, there were things she was not prepared to share with Lisa. It was better that she does not see her until she was.

"I know I said that and we will talk, but not today, Lisa. I need to go."

"Charlie, wait—"

"Good-bye, Lisa."

"My daughter is missing!" Lisa didn't think Charlie cared, but she was willing to try anything to extend the conversation.

"Excuse me? What are you talking about?"

"Brianna. I haven't heard from her, and I'm worried. I just needed someone to talk to."

"Lisa, I don't have time for this."

Charlie disconnected the call. Lisa lay on the bed staring at the phone. Unbelievable. That conversation had not helped her at all. Charlie had some nerve. She wasn't innocent, and Lisa had the dirt but chose not to throw it at her. Too bad she did not return the favor. She decided not to engage in any more conversations for a while. This was too much. She needed a stiff drink and a hot shower. She decided to start with the shower.

Chapter 38

Javan eased off the gas and allowed his black beauty to roll to a stop in the driveway of his six-month-old, three-story, red brick home. He leased it soon after he and Brianna began dating, pegging it as the perfect starter home for the family he anticipated they'd have. He glanced at the passenger seat where Brianna lay, lost in blissful sleep. Eyes fixated on hers, careful not to wake her, he stepped out of the car. Three long strides brought him to the front door. He pulled out his key to unlock the door when he felt a light tap on his shoulder.

His heart crashed into his rib cage, and he spun around with his fists clenched. Allen, Texas, was a good hour or so from the city, and Mike didn't know about it.

"Whoa!" Noticing Javan's hammer pulled back, poised to strike, the man backpedaled with his hands raised high in the air, quick to identify himself. "It's me, Mr. Harris. I thought you might need some help or something."

Javan did not relax completely, though his expression softened a bit.

"Doctor Baxter, what are you doing out here?" Javan eyed his limited edition Michael Kors timepiece. "It's nearly 3:00 a.m."

Doctor Baxter stood even with Javan at a solid six foot two. His deep set, pea-green eyes complimented his full head of low-cut, dark brown hair. He flashed Javan his best smile, displaying a full set of the best porcelain money could buy and dimples deep enough to swim in.

"I know it's late. I was getting in myself from the hospital, and I thought maybe you were having car trouble or something. I didn't mean to startle you. Just trying to do my neighborly duty."

Typically, he would be in bed at this hour, but he was on call at Texas Health Presbyterian Hospital this week. Peter Baxter was one of the few OB/GYNs with a specialty in maternal-fetal medicine recognized by the American Osteopathic Board of Obstetrics and Gynecology, and since getting the accreditation, he spent a lot of time at the hospital.

"Thank you, I'm fine."

Peter got the notion that Javan was ready for him to leave, but he had cause for concern.

"That lady in your car? She doesn't look to be in great shape. I'd like to give her a once-over if you don't mind."

Javan wanted to be left alone. Brianna was still sleeping, and he needed to get a few things in order before he took her into the house. "I think she's fine, Doctor Baxter, but thank you."

Peter insisted. "Please, I am an obstetrician, and I would like to take a look at her. It won't take long." Peter had to think quickly. He could see that Javan was still hesitant, although he did not fully understand why. "It's part of the oath I took when I became a doctor. I cannot, in good conscience, walk away from her like that. If something is wrong and I did nothing . . . You see where I'm going with this?"

"Fine, but I'll need to be present."

"That's great! Just let me run and grab my medical bag; I'll be right back."

Peter sprinted across the street to his house. Javan unlocked the door and walked inside. The moon's light reflected off of the wood floors as it poured in through the open doorway, the big, bay windows, and the skylight in the center of the large foyer. He walked briskly down the short hall, to the left, and down a few steps and entered into his "special place." It was the most coveted room in all the house. He couldn't stop the smile widening in his spirit as he stood looking at all its beauty. This space always gave him a sense of calm and hope. He couldn't wait to share it with Brianna. He took in one last look and closed the door. He didn't want to run the risk of Brianna seeing it before he was ready. It had to be perfect. He had one more thing to check; then he could bring Brianna inside, into her home.

"Ah! Who are you? Get away from me! Don't touch me!"

Brianna kicked the strange man out of the car door, slammed it shut, and locked all four doors with lightning speed. She looked around, bewildered, uncertain of where she was or how she came to be there.

He had not meant to wake her, but, jeez, the kick was unnecessary. Her screams pierced his ears; instinctively he leaned forward to comfort her. That turned out to be a big mistake, and his swelling lips were proof of that. Peter was certain he knew her from somewhere. He was horrible with names, but he seldom forgot a face, and hers did not belong to a stranger.

Brianna stared at the man she caught studying her face under the streetlight. Who was he? From where he sat on the ground she could see no muscles to speak of. He was dressed too well for a murderer, rapist, or burglar. It must be something else. How did she leave the house? Whose car is this? She opened the glove compartment and rummaged through the various papers looking for something that would tell her. She picked up an old insurance card: Micah J. Harrison?

"Javan! Javan! Where are you?"

Doctor Baxter motioned with his arms for the woman to calm down.

"I'm a doctor." He pulled out his badge to show her, to no avail. "My name is Dr. Peter Baxter." Peter gave up and sat back down on the lawn. He was practically yelling at the top of his lungs trying to speak over her, and it wasn't working. Only a matter of time before other neighbors ventured out to see what the ruckus was about.

Javan charged toward the front door and found Doctor Baxter sitting in the yard a few feet from his car. His body stiffened at the sight of him alone with Brianna. Something wasn't right. Doctor Baxter seemed too familiar with Brianna . . . too eager.

"*Oh my Gawd! Javan!*" Brianna spotted him in the doorway. Why in the hell was he just standing there? "*Javan!*"

He rushed to Brianna's door but couldn't open it. For a second, Brianna's locking it had slipped her mind. She leaned over and unlocked the passenger door, choosing to remain seated on the driver's side. Her eyes darted between the two men accusingly. Where had Javan brought her?

"It's OK, Bria. This is Doctor Baxter. He's just going to check you out and make sure you're good." He shot a disapproving look at the physician. "I thought I told you I needed to be present."

Doctor Baxter looked sheepishly at Javan. How was he supposed to know she would flip out like this? He'd been practicing medicine for ten years, and not once had a patient woke up swinging. "I haven't started or anything like that. I was simply trying to figure out if I could wake her."

Doctor Baxter tried to sound convincing, realizing that what he told Javan wasn't entirely true. He was trying to place her face in his past, but he didn't need Javan to know that yet.

"And she woke to some strange man prodding her? What did you expect?"

Realizing Javan had a point, Doctor Baxter lifted his 170 pounds from the ground, trying to calm the situation. "I am very sorry, miss, I did not intend to frighten you. If you don't mind, I would still like to do a quick physical exam and run a few tests. Of course, I think I may need to see a doctor myself after that kick."

Brianna managed a light chuckle and nodded, conceding to the exam. Javan helped her to get out of the car and carried her into the house with Peter following closely behind them. He shuffled into the living room and placed Brianna gently on the couch.

Doctor Baxter surveyed Brianna's body. He took his hands and felt along her arms and legs. He could feel tension but no broken bones. Brianna winced a little from his touch but didn't speak. Opening his medical bag, he asked a barrage of questions.

"Bria, is it?"

"Brianna. Brianna Mason."

Peter did not recognize the name at all, but her eyes, nose, and high cheekbones reminded him of someone. The answer taunted him. "Ms. Mason . . ."

"Brianna is fine."

"Very well, then, Brianna. I see that you have some soreness? Do you mind sharing what happened? Have you been in an accident recently?"

Javan cleared his throat. "Ahem."

Doctor Baxter briefly turned his attention to Javan, puzzled a bit by his interruption.

"Sorry. Something in my throat." Javan tried to adjust, coughing a few times for effect, to sell Doctor Baxter on his explanation.

The physician did not believe that for a minute. Something was going on here. He turned back to Brianna trying to detect anything that she may not be able to say aloud. He silently wished he had not consented to Javan being there. It started to make sense. Her bruises and the way she attacked him. All were clear signs of abuse.

Javan forced his eyes to circle the room. He knew he couldn't ask Brianna to keep quiet about what happened, but he hoped she would not say anything to Doctor Baxter. He didn't want his brother in trouble over this. He looked away from Brianna.

"No, I have not been in an accident." Brianna figured Javan did not want her outing his brother, but in earnest, she did not feel like explaining the whole ordeal. She barely understood what happened herself.

"It's been a rough few days for her," Javan offered.

"I see." Doctor Baxter met Brianna's eyes and spoke intently. "Physically, you seem fine. You are, however, exhibiting classic signs of post-traumatic stress. Are you sure you don't want to talk about it? I am not a psychologist, but I can recommend someone."

Brianna thought about telling him. He seemed genuinely concerned, and there was something about the way he looked at her. She got the impression that he knew her, loved her even.

Javan rubbed his clammy hands together. Beads of sweat covered his forehead as he awaited Brianna's response. There would be nothing he could do for his brother if Doctor Baxter took the information to the authorities. Nothing short of advising him to run.

"I'll . . . I'll take that referral if you don't mind. I just don't want to hash it out tonight."

Doctor Baxter sighed in frustration. This too was typical of victims of abuse. He gave her his business card and scribbled the psychologist's name and number on the back.

"Contact me if you need anything." He drew out his words, emphasizing each one. "The referral information is on the back. Please contact her. She's really good, and I know she can help."

"Thank you, Doctor Baxter. I appreciate this. I am sorry I kicked you. I didn't know."

"It's okay. I shouldn't have been so close. You were only defending yourself." Doctor Baxter felt Javan's eyes on him, but he kept his eyes on Brianna.

"Yes, thank you, Doctor Baxter. *We* appreciate it. Good thing you *happened* to be out." Javan forced a smile.

"I suppose it was." Doctor Baxter stood and gave Javan a firm handshake. "You be sure to take good care of her. I would hate for anything to happen to her."

If Javan didn't know any better, he would have sworn Doctor Baxter was threatening him. "Naturally."

Doctor Baxter bent down once more and spoke with Brianna. "Call me. All right? I insist. I would like to do a follow-up. Come by my office. We'll run some lab work and confirm that everything is as it seems."

"Sure, I'll do that."

He squeezed Brianna's hand. "Good. I'll see you soon."

Doctor Baxter nodded to Javan, grabbed his bag, and left. He would be keeping tabs on this young lady. The situation did not sit well with him, and once he had a chance to calm down and think, Doctor Baxter finally realized who the young woman reminded him of. It had been at least twenty years, but her beautiful blue eyes stirred his heart as if she were still his. The timetable was about right. This woman looked to be between twenty and twenty-five years old. This could be her daughter. The only kink in his theory was the last name, Mason. The name she should carry was Freemont. He held tight to the strand of hair he had taken from Brianna. A DNA test would put his questions to rest. If this was her daughter, she could be the key to him finding her . . . the only woman he had ever loved. She disappeared without saying a word to him and had taken his heart along with her. This may be his chance to get her back . . . for good.

Javan ran Brianna a warm bath. He could barely contain himself while he bathed her. The sight of her nakedness was enough to send him over the edge. Her skin was as soft as cotton, and the lavender bath beads he put in the water . . . made the scene picture-perfect. He took the sponge he purchased from Bed, Bath, and Beyond and gently scrubbed her caramel covering from her neck to her toes. He took his time and paid special attention to her bruises. When he finished washing her body, he washed her hair. Her long, beautiful tresses had been mangled and matted from neglect.

Brianna dropped her guard completely and enjoyed the feel of his hands in her mane. She felt the tension leaving her body as the tips of his fingers fondled her temple and the strawberry-scented candles lured her to peace. Javan had never done this for her before, and it was exactly what she needed. The bath concluded, he draped a white terry cloth robe over her and carried her into the master bedroom.

"I'll take care of you, Bria. Don't worry about anything. Just relax."

Brianna wondered what Javan had in store for her. The bath was just right and would be a nice ending to the night. Sleep was calling out to her. She felt like a small girl in his arms and rested her head on his shoulder. It was a short walk from the bathroom to the bedroom. Brianna opened her eyes to see that candles littered the room. Strawberry and Peach Mango Blossom scents danced beneath her nose, creating a frenzy. She was pleasantly surprised.

"This is beautiful. When did you do this?"

Javan could not hide his joy. His eyes beamed with pride. He had aimed to impress her, and it seemed to have worked. Aside from that near calamity with Doctor Baxter, everything was going according to plan.

"I told you. Don't worry about anything. Not tonight. Not anymore."

He placed Brianna on the bed and retrieved the "goodie basket" he had put together containing body oils, powders, lotions, pearls, a dime bag of that sticky, an assortment of perfumes, and a few music discs. Brianna's eyes widened, and she gave him a look that posed a question with a hint of mischief. He smiled innocently and shrugged his shoulders.

"Take off the robe and lie down."

Brianna dutifully complied. She scooted back a few inches and spread her legs, giving Javan an unobstructed view of her Brazilian front. He licked his lips hungrily and rubbed his neck with the back of his hand. Brianna was such a damn tease, but tonight, he would not be the one left with the badass blues.

"On your stomach, please. Don't make this any harder . . ." He shook his leg, drawing her attention to his package, and shifted his wand to the side. ". . . then it already is."

The candlelight freestyled a ballet number across Brianna's smooth caramel surface. Javan stood frozen, momentarily forgetting his mission, completely captivated by the show. He took the lotion, his personal concoction, and began to moisten every inch of skin. He did not leave one part of her lovely body dry. Honey filled his lungs and intensified his primal urges. Pain rippled through him as his engorged member strained against his briefs. He fought his need to end things quickly and put himself out of his misery. Brianna deserved everything he was giving her. Deserved to be catered to in this way.

She had not given him the opportunity before, and he was not going to blow it. He had to woo her before he could love her again. He would not take advantage of her vulnerable state. She had to know that she was safe with him, that he would protect her. Things had to play out in the way he had always envisioned them. Their last conversation was not lost on him. She had ended things, and he intended to change her mind about him.

Brianna was experiencing a new high. The sensual massage Javan lavished on her set her body ablaze; the wet warmth between her legs spoke volumes. She was not sure how much more she could take. The idea of adding a little pleasure to her pain was almost too tempting to pass up. Every kink, every knot, was released by the magic of his hands. Brianna was floating, and nothing could bring her down.

"Hmmm . . . this . . . feels . . . amazing." Brianna ushered the words out between breaths, trying to maintain her composure as her feminine design found itself at the mercy of Javan's artistic endeavors. She was putty in his hands as he kneaded her muscles slowly and deliberately. His large hands palmed her ample bottom and sent her libido into overdrive. He worked his way from the small of her back, down to the sensitive soles of her feet, moving back up her legs to the source of her pain. Javan enjoyed watching her squirm so much that he almost hated to stop the train.

He leaned in and whispered in his rich baritone voice, trying to complete her trip into bliss. "Ms. Mason, you should be able to rest easy now."

Brianna took a deep breath and expelled the sexual tension that had been smoldering over the last half hour. "That was your plan all along, huh? Butter me up, and then put me back in the fridge?" Brianna could handle Javan ending their sexual tryst prematurely and recuperated quickly.

Javan laughed, kissing her forehead. "Of course not, but you've had a long night, and it's already late."

"I guess." Brianna could not believe it. Javan pulled one of her moves on her. She shook her head at the torturous teasing. Dammit.

"Aren't you tired?" he asked, amused with her irritation.

"After that? Not really."

Still nude, she crawled under the down cover and savored the king-size, feather-top mattress. It was a far cry from the pile of blankets on the floor she had previously been sleeping on. She got comfortable and resumed her inquisition. "Javan, where are we?"

"I started leasing this house a little while ago. Don't worry; we'll have plenty of time for a tour. For now, get some rest."

"Can I use your phone? I need to make a few phone calls. Let my sis . . . my friend Michelle know that I'm all right."

Javan's loyalties were divided, and she didn't want to share with him who Michelle really was or that she had witnessed the whole thing. She found it a little odd that Javan didn't inquire about the confusion back at his brother's spot; she had anticipated him asking who Michelle was, but it didn't come up . . . at least, not yet.

"That can wait until tomorrow. It's late, woman. Go to sleep. I'm here. You're safe now." He kissed her forehead a second time and exited the room.

Overall, Brianna was grateful to Javan, to God, the universe, and whoever else sent him to his brother's spot. Alone with her thoughts . . . She revisited the events that had transpired over the last week. She thought about her father's passing. Her freedom was bittersweet. She wished she could talk with him, see him one last time. She missed him already. Before long, dreamland welcomed her, and she was fast asleep.

***

Javan retreated to his special room to relax and clear his mind. He was too excited to sleep. He finally had Brianna all to himself. He would never have thought that his shiftless, no-account, big brother would have been the one to make it possible. He had waited a long time for a chance to show Bria how deeply he loved her. Fate had put his plan into motion; now it was only a matter of time.

He glanced around the room and marveled at his photographs, a collage of the half year they had spent together. There were many, mostly candid shots of an unsuspecting Brianna, but some of them pictured both of them. Javan walked to his fireplace and stared at the painting hanging above it. It had been his favorite picture. Brianna was lying in her bed, giving Javan a dreamy look, one hand beneath the pillow that held her head, the other draped at her side with a pillow between her legs. One of the few that Brianna had posed for. Each time he looked at it, he swore she was looking back at him.

He left the room, locking the door behind him. The red sky bled through the curtains that shaded the windows on either side of the front door. As he reached the very top of the small set of steps, more of the morning's sun shone through, announcing the new day. He wandered back into the bedroom where Brianna slept. He stripped naked and crawled into the bed beside her. It took all of his strength to suppress the urge to wake her with his growing erection. His appetite could not be satisfied. Many nights he had laid beside her and touched himself into fulfillment, but he would not do that. This morning, he would wrestle with his longing. He would endure the ache.

Chapter 39

The confrontation with Michelle had her frazzled. How could Frank have kept something like that from her? Lisa would have never thought him capable of such a thing. Her nerves were frayed, and after learning of Frank's secret, she decided to follow through with her plan to leave town. A change of scenery would enable her to think clearly. She had one stop to make before heading out. The bank.

"I need to make a withdrawal, please."

The teller took the bank card along with the state-issued identification card Lisa placed on the marble counter and stepped away to confirm her account status. Lisa regretted having to do this, but Frank left her no choice. She sighed with sadness. Some things simply aren't meant to last.o

"Thank you, Ms. Porter. How much did you need to withdraw?"

"All of it. Please."

The teller gasped. "Ma'am, are you certain? That's over $8 million."

Lisa's expression grew stern. The teller realized her error. "I apologize, Ms. Porter, I did not mean to sound unprofessional. I wanted to be clear that this is, indeed, your intention."

"I understand. Yes, all of it."

"Of course. Please have a seat in the waiting area. This type of transaction requires managerial approval. Can I get you anything while you wait?"

"No, thank you."

"Very well, then. I'll notify you once the transaction has been authorized."

Lisa waltzed over to the waiting area and settled into one of the chairs closest to the window. Preston was busy for this time of the morning, but she enjoyed watching the high-end cars roll up and down the street. She was only a few minutes away from joining that elite class. Tolleson Private Bank had housed her stash for years. She chose them for their discretion. Plus she had a friend behind the scenes.

"Excuse me, Ms. Porter."

Lisa turned away from the window to see the teller standing just beyond her reach. The formalities were no longer necessary. No ears could listen in, and Lisa could see nearly the entire floor from where she sat.

"Nicole?" Lisa asked, lifting an already high arching, freshly trimmed brow.

"Lisa, I know I said that I would take care of this for you, especially since you took Lewis off my hands. I mean . . . I know I owe you from way back, but—"

Nicole unwittingly entered into a minefield. Her life as a dancer was short-lived thanks to Lisa. A few months in, Lisa offered her this deal, and she jumped on it.

"Just spit it out, Nicole."

"The manager is asking a lot of questions. I don't think we have this kind of cash on hand."

"How is that possible? We talked about this earlier this week. That was the whole point of my coming here. The entire reason for your presence here," Lisa spewed through clenched teeth.

"Lisa, I'm not trying to screw you, but you need another way. This isn't looking good."

Lisa was angry enough to spit fire, but she needed to keep calm. Nicole was a simple bitch. She had to handle her delicately, or she could ruin everything. "What are you suggesting?"

"He hasn't rejected the request, but I think if maybe you asked for a smaller amount, he'd sign off on it."

Lisa couldn't tell if Nicole was telling the truth or not. She had played the loyalty card after Lisa landed her this job and got her out of the strip club. She never seemed like the greedy type, but with money, it was safer not to trust anyone. Unfortunately for Lisa, she didn't have a choice in the matter. She would have to take her at her word.

"Fine. Give me ten thousand in cash; I'll be by later with routing information so that we can transfer the rest."

Nicole nodded, but her eyes revealed her fear. She had heard about Lisa and was convinced that there was a "but" coming.

Lisa didn't disappoint. "But . . . If you're lying, and I am *one penny short* of what I should have, that situation with Lewis . . . it was awhile ago, but I'm sure you remember how he had you permanently on your knees fattening his pockets?"

"No need to go there, Lisa. We all did what we had to do, and I got my cut."

"Oh really?" Lisa chortled wickedly. "The gangbang . . . was that *your* idea too? Did you get your *cut* of that? Lewis did."

Lisa watched as the horror crowded Nicole's frail features, recalling one of the worst nights of her life. Nicole had come to her in tears, begging for her help. She was on the verge of ending it all that night, but Lisa agreed to assist her . . . for a nominal fee, of course. Nicole's lips began to tremble, and Lisa knew, at that moment, she had her. Still, she had to drive the point home.

"Didn't stop with just you, though, did he? Who was next . . . your little sister? Did you ever find her, by the way?"

Nicole remained silent. Lisa did not mind. Her words were not necessary. Nicole's face told her everything she needed to know.

"I hate to bring up all of this ancient . . . trash . . . but I promise you, if you cross me, that mess will seem like a damn kiddie ride at Six Flags compared to what *I'll* do to you."

Nicole wiped her damp eyes with the sleeve of her blouse. She would have Lisa's money, even if she had to steal it.

Chapter 40

Brianna awoke to find Javan, nude, and in the bed with her. She was not bothered by it, though; it was not the first time. It did not matter how frequently they were together . . . He always wanted more. She used to wonder what he did while she slept but had never bothered to ask. Javan was ruggedly handsome and chunky in all the right places. She briefly considered waking him, but her stomach won the toss. *Vajayjay* would have to wait her turn.

Brianna quietly slipped out of bed and found the kitchen. She was starving. Fortunately, Javan had enough food to feed a small community. The microwave display read 1:45 p.m. Brianna found the remote to the television that hung from the ceiling over the island and turned it on. She turned it to CNN. Catching up on the news made her feel like she was behind the times. She kept the volume low so that she would not wake Javan.

The kitchen was fairly large, and everything had its place. Brianna was a clean woman, but Javan was almost methodical in his placement of things. Everything was categorized and labeled. Dinnerware versus lunch or breakfast utensils, etc. He even had a map, dictating where everything was. Brianna was slightly taken aback by his attention to detail; it seemed a little obsessive, but it did help her to find everything she needed without any issues. She loved to cook and could have gone to culinary school but failed to see the benefits. There wasn't anything she could learn that she didn't already know.

In no time at all, she whipped up some gourmet-style scrambled eggs, pancakes, bacon, and hash browns, topping it off with a few fruit slices, a glass of orange juice, and a glass of milk. While she ate, she caught up with the latest events, then decided to look for a phone so she could call Michelle and let her know she was safe. The house was even more beautiful in the daylight. It had a Greco-Roman motif. Each of the three hallways on the first floor was filled with paintings from that era; it was like walking through the halls of a museum. Out of the five rooms she had managed to find, she had not seen one telephone, computer, or anything that she could use.

Javan woke up, and she could hear him rummaging around above her. She cut her adventuring short and took the stairs up to see him. The entire second floor of the house was the master bedroom, complete with two walk-in closets, a Jacuzzi-style bath, and sitting area. She noticed a picture of the two of them on the nightstand, beside the bed; it was cute, but she couldn't recall having posed for it. She picked it up for closer inspection. She remembered the outfit, but she was almost positive she had not been with Javan at the time the picture was taken.

Javan walked up behind her and kissed her neck. "Morning, beautiful."

"Morning, Javan."

"Do you remember when we took that picture that day at the arboretum? It was such a nice day out. We had been walking all day, and you stopped a random passerby and asked them to take the picture." Javan laughed softly at the thought. "You said you wanted to capture the moment."

Brianna did not know what he was talking about. They had never even been to the arboretum, and she certainly was not the sentimental type. She did not remember this day at all. Javan had to be imagining things. The picture had to be photo shopped or something.

"How are you feeling, babe?"

"I'm feeling much better, thanks."

Javan took the picture from Brianna's hands and placed it back on the nightstand. Turning Brianna around to face him, he planted a soft kiss on her lips.

"I am glad you're feeling better. You're safe now."

"Me too. I just don't understand why. I cannot figure it out. What did they want with me?"

"It wasn't about you."

Brianna looked at him with her eyebrows raised waiting for the rest, but Javan had no intention of continuing the conversation. He felt her eyes tunneling a hole into his mind, but he kept his mouth closed. "That does not make sense to me. None of this makes any sense at all."

"Well, it's over now. You have me, and I have you, and that's all that matters."

Brianna did not like the insinuation. She was grateful to him, but she was no closer to wanting a relationship now than she was before, and his proclamation was somewhat creeping her out. No need to upset him, though. She would let him have his moment.

"Thank you for taking me out of there. The odds of your finding me were not high, but you did. I am extremely appreciative of that."

"So am I, beautiful. I have always dreamed of being your hero, but to actually do it . . . That was a gift from the universe to me."

Brianna smiled and gave him a light peck on his lips. Maybe she could be in a relationship with him. He was a good guy and had saved her life. Javan let her go and walked to his closet to get dressed.

"The other closet has a few clothes in there if you want to put something else on. I think the clothes are about your size."

Brianna followed Javan' finger the few yards to the spare closet.

"And don't worry, they haven't been worn or anything."

A *few* clothes was an understatement. The near bedroom-sized closet was filled to capacity, and everything in it was not only her exact size but matched her style as well. It was like she was looking into her closet at home, and many of the items still had the price tags. "So, most of these are new?"

Javan did not respond. She figured he didn't hear her, so she selected a V-neck purple tee and denim Capris, dressed, and stepped out to find Javan waiting, still in his robe.

"Nice. I'm glad you found something."

"Thank you. They fit perfectly. Where did you get these? Did they belong to some special lady? Someone you haven't told me about, perhaps?" she joked.

"Never. Those are all for you, Bria. All for you."

Brianna caught the message behind his words. He had not been with anyone else. He had done all of this just for her, but she wasn't ready to address that. "You're not dressed?"

"Come here."

Javan had one thing on his mind. Phase two of his plan was in full effect.

"What is it?"

Even as the question passed her lips, her legs moved without an answer. His words wrapped around her and pulled her into his open arms. The instant she felt his lips grace hers, her heart began to stage a resistance. The passion he displayed was met with indifference. Something had changed in him, in her. This was no ordinary kiss. She felt the powers of the universe being passed from him to her in that kiss. Perhaps she was still soaring from earlier that morning, or maybe it was the copious amounts of attention he had lavished on her recently, but whatever the case, it was unlike anything they had shared before and felt too close to the real thing.

Javan searched for her soul, trying to convince her to let him in, pleading for an entry into that divine space. He grabbed her shoulders and drew her closer. Her body grew limp as the inferno consumed her. She stopped thinking, forcing her inhibitions into submission as the electricity between her legs surged. She thrust one hand into the folds of his robe and twirled her fingers in his chest hairs; the other grabbed hold of his gentle giant and slowly stroked him to life, eliciting a series of moans. The feel of her delicate fingers on his skin nearly did him in. Months had passed without her touch. Javan devoured her breasts like a fiend on a binge. He savored the taste of her large chocolate mounds on his tongue.

Brianna felt her vajayjay throb with each lick, crying for attention. Javan did not disappoint. With one hand, he unbuttoned her Capris, slid his hand inside them, and used vajayjay's flute to play a song that turned Brianna's legs to jelly. Her body shook as continuous waves of ecstasy washed over her. Her walls tightened around his fingers, guiding him to her sweet spot as he plunged them in and out of her love cave. Brianna screamed with delight. Javan assaulted her pearl until he felt her body convulse and his fingers dripping with her gratitude.

"Javan . . ."

She didn't need to say more. He knew. He snatched her Capris off and thrust himself deep into her wetness, into vajayjay.

"*Ja . . . Ja . . . Jaavvaaannn! Oh my . . . Gawd . . . yes . . .*"

Javan dug inside her feminine walls. She felt amazing. He felt that perfect peace calling to him with each dive, but he wasn't ready. He rolled on his back, surrendering his body to Brianna, putting her in a position of power. She was in her element. Her eyes rolled with pleasure as she rode him like it was what she was born to do. He stared at her beautiful design, allowing himself to be distracted by her rhythm, the feel of her juices coating his thighs. The tight feel of her vajayjay around his magic stick. The tricks she performed.

"Damn, Bria. Shit. Oh shit."

That perfect peace calling to him again. He never could last that long with Brianna. But he wanted this time to be different. He wanted to tattoo his name in it, give her something to think about. He grabbed her hips and began pumping feverishly.

Brianna cried out and fell forward on his chest. She could feel his hands all over her buttocks. Slapping, grabbing, massaging. He was in so deep she felt him in her chest. She knew she would come soon. She felt it rising. An inevitable wave of heat destined to scorch them both. She took her tongue and lightly licked the tip of his earlobe, wrote her name in his neck, then sucked it to make it permanent. Javan, without losing stride, sat up and moved to the edge of the bed. He took Brianna in his hands and turned her into his own personal yo-yo, bouncing her up and down on his love jones.

"Javan! Damn . . . Fuck . . . Ahhhhh . . ."

He quickly stood up and bent Brianna over the bed. He did not want to make her feel good. He aimed to make her crazy. He admired his work from behind for a few minutes, then nudged her forward until she lay flat on the bed. Javan covered her glistening wet body with his own, still filling her vajayjay with his *good love*. Brianna was climbing that mountaintop again. He could feel each grip she took on her way up.

"It's mine. It's mine, baby."

"It's yours, Javan . . . Gawd . . . It's yours."

He was giving her everything he had. All of him. Cementing his place in her life; in her world. Pushing himself into her future. Pushing her into oblivion.

"*Don't stop. Javanss . . . Gawd . . . Please don't stop.*"

"*Come on, baby . . . Give it to me.*"

"*I'm cooomin' . . . baby . . . Gawd . . .*"

Their bodies moved in unison, both reaching for that extraordinary inescapable flash of bliss. It felt right. Organic. Together, they arrived at that special space reserved for lovers. They were spent, their bodies weak from their lovemaking. Javan looked at Brianna. He loved this woman. Finally, she was all his. He thought about calling his brother and thanking him. His wife was home. His wife was home.

Brianna felt resolved. She was not happy, but she felt an absence. The absence of the weight of the emotional torment that had colored her days for the past several weeks. For the first time in a long while, she felt some small measure of peace. Her entire life had been an invention. She had been kidnapped, rescued, and rendered fatherless. Nothing would ever be the same for her again. But at this moment . . . at this precise moment in time . . . Brianna could release these things and just be.

"I love you, Brianna."

There it was again. That L-word. Brianna left her end silent. She did care a lot about Javan, but she did not know if she could call it love. He had crawled into a place in her heart and stirred something deep within her. Though it was something no one else had managed to do, she was not ready to anchor him there . . . or maybe she just didn't know how.

Javan was not bothered by her loss for words. He did not need her to say anything. He was still high off the love she showered him with moments ago and held on to what he perceived to be the physical expression of their love. She had never let him go in naked before. Why would she if she didn't love him?

"I was thinking . . ." She tarried as the words really hit home. "I am really glad you found me, Javan." Tears gathered in her eyes as her emotions boiled over.

"My brother told me he had someone there, and I got so angry. I couldn't believe it. I knew I wasn't leaving there without her."

Javan's words were genuine. He spoke softly, but they pierced Brianna's surface like barbed wire on an open thigh, cutting deep into her open wounds as she relived her nightmare.

"When I realized you were . . . her . . ." Javan turned to catch a glimpse of a fresh set of tears falling down Brianna's sullen face; it perfectly mirrored what he felt, "I felt my soul splinter. I freaked out. I could have killed my brother."

Brianna dried her eyes and restructured her thoughts, still wanting some clarity about things. "It seems like everything happened so fast. I was walking along the beach, and the next thing I knew, I wasn't."

"How long were you there?"

Brianna shrugged her shoulders and turned to face him. "I don't know. A week maybe? I don't know."

"I know what my brother is capable of, but I never thought any harm would come to you."

"I never knew you had a brother, Javan."

"You never wanted to discuss our families."

"True, but I thought you would have at least mentioned him."

"He's kinda the black sheep of the family. Always in trouble. We are not that close."

"Guess it was pretty lucky for me that you two spoke last night, then, huh?"

"We both were. John is loco. He had to have Mike rattled in order for him to call me."

"John was never nice to me. Mike was . . . different."

"I want you to know that we are two very different people."

Brianna smiled at Javan to allay his misgivings. His brother was not even newsworthy compared to everything she had learned about her mom over the last couple of weeks. It was messed up what Mike had done to her, but at least he had shown some concern for her well-being. "He could have really hurt me."

"But he didn't."

"No, he didn't."

It was not lost on her that Javan had not taken her to the police station or even mentioned calling the police. She understood. She could never imagine turning Michelle in no matter what she had done. "By the way . . . Can I use your cell phone now? I need to call my family and let them know I'm okay. I'm sure they're worried about me."

Javan did not want her calling anyone right now. Nothing to remind her of what's happening outside of that house. He didn't want anything pulling her mind away from him. "Listen, you don't need to make any calls right now. Let's get dressed and watch a movie in the theater room. Afterward, I'll let you call whomever you'd like."

"Someone dear to me is probably worried sick about me, Javan. I would like to let her know I'm safe."

"After the movie, all right? After the movie."

Brianna did not want to wait, but she did not have a choice. Javan was not giving her his phone. She didn't want Michelle still stressing about her safety. This was the third time he had insisted she put off calling. She found it a bit peculiar but temporarily pushed her skepticism to the side.

"I'm anxious for you to see the movie I selected."

"I guess I'll have to wait then."

"It won't be long," Javan promised.

Brianna hoped it wouldn't be.

Chapter 41

Frank had been expecting her. He had so much he needed to say. He pressed his hand against the Plexiglas, and she did the same. His heart was beating in his chest. He felt like a little kid again. She always had that effect on him.

"Franklin . . . How are you? Sorry I haven't been to see you, but I'm sure you understand."

Frank understood. He was happy to see her at all, given the circumstances.

"What took you so long? You enjoy keeping me waiting?"

She laughed. "Never that. Had some personal business to take care of."

"I see . . . and what of our business?"

Frank knew that she had not kept up her end of their bargain. He only wanted to see if she would be honest about it.

"I thought *our business* concluded when *we* began."

"*We* were incidental and as much as I enjoy you . . . It didn't change anything, did it?"

"It may have."

Frank had changed things for her, though she had a feeling he would never believe it. "When was the last time you slept with my wife?"

Charlie did not respond. She wanted them both.

"I thought so. The agreement was that I would allow your little tryst as long as you kept Lewis and his daughter away from my family."

She regretted having ever made that deal, but at the time, it seemed like her best option. Frank had caught her outside his home. He originally thought about calling the police, but he pestered her for information, trying to get to the bottom of things. She had told him nearly everything she knew about Lewis and her deal with him . . . how she was afraid that he might kill her if she did not follow through. He had agreed to allow the relationship with Lisa to continue uninterrupted, as long as Lisa was willing, and Lisa never had to know; it was between them. She was surprised that he knew who Lewis was and accepted his offer. *Both* offers.

She could not deny the electricity between them; the connection. It helped that they both knew Jacob too. They were tied in more ways than one. Their fling had spanned the last three months or so. She did not see him as often as she saw Lisa, but when she did . . . It was explosive. They usually only got together when Lisa was meeting with Lewis, but occasionally, Frank would sneak away for her. Franklin had a certain something, and he made their time together count.

Charlie raised an eyebrow. "Have I not done that?"

"I don't know, have you? The sister came to see me. She had Brianna's ID. Can you explain that?"

She knew it would only be a matter of time before Michelle made her way to Frank. She had intentionally left out certain pieces of information when she spoke with her to buy him some time, but there was no stopping it. When Michelle left her room that day, she studied the note awhile longer and recognized the handwriting. The note and pictures were from Jacob. He had pulled the pin from the grenade with that move, and the whole situation had become one huge ticking time bomb.

"It must be true."

"What must be true?"

"Lisa called me."

Frank shifted his gaze to the tight spirals of the phone's cord. He didn't like discussing Lisa with her. The situation was already complicated enough. "And? I nearly killed a man defending her honor, and she has not even bothered to come and see me. I heard she did manage to show up at Lewis's funeral, though."

Charlie ignored his comment. He could go on and on about Lewis, and she did not want to hear it today. However, she wanted to address the situation with Jacob. "What happened, Franklin? I've been sitting with Jacob every day. The wire in his jaws has kept him from sharing the details, so I'm asking you. Why did you attack him?"

"I had not planned on it. Jacob and I have had our issues, but I had never been so angry in my life. I felt the rage. It took over me. I blacked out."

"What happened?"

"I found out Lisa had been giving me doctored bank statements."

"No way."

Frank took a deep breath and wished it were a lie. "Millions are missing. We were leaving the hospital, and I questioned her about it. It got heated quickly, really out of hand. Then, out of nowhere, she told me . . ."

Frank did not even want to say it out loud. The thought still made him queasy. Still made him angry.

"She told you what? And what does that money have to do with Jacob?" Charlie wanted answers. Jacob was one of the few people Charlie could call a friend, and Frank nearly killed him.

Frank fought through the images swarming his mind, looking for words to finish his thought.

"Frank . . . come on . . . told you what?"

"She said that bastard raped her!"

Frank was getting heated all over again. He took his fist and hit the glass. The guard rushed to the door, but Charlie waved him off.

"Calm down before this short visit is reduced even more so."

"I'll tell you what . . . I'd beat his ass all over again."

She shook her head. This was wrong. Lisa had not known Jacob. She was sure of it.

"When? How?"

"When they were in a foster home together."

She gasped and nearly fell out of the chair. This was terrible.

"Franklin, that can't be true."

"What? What are you talking about? She described it to me in detail. How he befriended her, and then came in the middle of the night . . . ripped her clothes . . . and . . . and . . ." Frank stopped himself. He couldn't bring himself to say it. Tears fell from his eyes as he mentally rehashed the horrid tale.

"No, Franklin, no, that could not have happened." Charlie was adamant and brought Frank's gaze up from his lap, through the glass, and held it in her unwavering stare. His strong cheekbones and square jaw hinted at his disbelief, but his eyes revealed a softening resolve.

"Yes, it did! Why would she lie about something like that?" Frank felt his anger rising again. She had to be mistaken. Lisa would not do that.

"I don't know, Franklin! But she did. Jacob was *never* in a foster home."

"Do you mean that I'm sitting in here for nothing?"

She stammered over her words. "I mean . . . Lisa was raped, but it was not Jacob. It was her father. I don't know how many times it happened, but I saw for myself the last time it did."

"What do you mean you saw it?"

"I was . . . in a house across the street. I had a clear view from my bedroom window."

Frank did not know how to feel. Lisa lied to him. Typical. He had wrongly let his emotions blind him.

Charlie held her hands up in mock protest. "I'm not making excuses for her, but I'm sure she had a good reason."

Frank scoffed. He couldn't believe it; he didn't want to hear this. "Are you really defending her, after everything you've told me?"

"Things have changed, Franklin."

She didn't know what reason Lisa could have for doing this, but she was not going to rush to judgment. Her hands were dirty enough.

"Have they? She is still noticeably absent."

"Brianna is missing."

"What? What do you mean she's missing?"

"That's why Lisa called me. She needed to talk. I thought she was lying, but if Michelle showed up here with Brianna's ID . . . It makes sense."

Frank started breathing heavily, shaking his head in disbelief. He had only been a little late with the payment. Why would they have taken her without even trying to contact him? Surely they know where he is. He had tried to get word out to them, but he didn't know what he was doing. He must have failed miserably. "That explains why Bria hasn't been to see me. I should have known something was wrong. I think I know who has her, but I need to get out of here. Get me a lawyer."

"I think I should tell Lisa and let her handle this for you. I really shouldn't—"

Frank was getting frustrated. She would be available and down for whatever otherwise, but when it's something this serious . . . she puts it off on Lisa? "Why not? This is my daughter's life."

"I need to think about *our* child too."

"Huh? What are you talking about?"

"I'm pregnant."

Frank's heart stopped.

Chapter 42

Brianna wished she was dreaming, but she was painfully aware that it was real. The theater had seating for about ten people, and Javan had filled every seat. Blowup dolls completely dressed and named, all present to view the short. Brianna laughed to mask the discomfort she felt. This was some weird mess. She recognized some of the dummies, dressed as a few characters from different iconic pop culture television shows and movies. Upon closer inspection, she realized they were all couples: Lucy & Ricky, Clair & Cliff, Bones & Booth, and even Dwayne & Whitley! He could not be serious!

Javan let her know on the way down that it was an original film. He hired a few students from the University of North Texas's film department to help him do it. Brianna was no longer uneasy. She was flat-out scared.

"Javan, what are these dummies doing in here?" Bria laughed nervously.

"I don't like watching movies alone." He laughed. "They don't talk or anything."

The film started innocently enough. It was a cute love story, and she was rather enjoying it. It was pretty funny, and then . . . Something cut her laughter short. A scene that was eerily familiar, and so were the next few scenes, including the day at the arboretum that Javan had described, and it was not long before Brianna realized she was the female lead! She nearly jumped up out of her seat, knocking Dwayne to the floor. She looked at Javan, who had a smile a mile wide plastered across his face.

Everything Brianna and Javan had ever done had been captured in the film and plenty of things they had not. The first time they met in the parking garage at work. The shameless rump session they had in the elevator shortly after. More recently, the mandatory staff meeting that was a ruse to get Brianna alone, even the massage she received last night was included! Bria started hyperventilating. This was not happening. Just when she felt it couldn't get any worse . . . They married.

The whole thing was absurd. Brianna lost her cool. "Javan, what is this?"

"Do you like your surprise? I made it just for you, babe."

"I don't know what to think . . . When did you do this?"

"A little while ago. You like it?"

"It's . . . something."

"*Excuse me?*" Javan had not expected this type of reaction. He wanted her to be pleased; thrilled. He put a lot of thought and a moderate financial stake into this short. And he did it all to impress her.

"I mean . . . It's just so shocking. So . . . creative. I'm speechless." Brianna really was speechless. She could not think of one single word or phrase to describe what she was thinking. This was *not* normal. Between the fake photo upstairs, the dummies, the denied phone calls, and the end of the movie, Brianna was beyond disturbed.

"Javan, why did you do this?"

"Isn't it obvious? I love you. I want to be with you, Brianna. I was afraid to say it before, but now I'm ready to profess it in front of these other great couples. I love you!"

There's that L-word again. This was not what she needed. Javan had lost his mind. What in the hell was he talking about? "What other couples are you talking about? I know you're not talking about these dummies?"

To her dismay, he motioned to the dolls. Brianna shook her head. This was *not* happening.

Javan thought Brianna would think the dummies were cute, a sweet gesture. Perhaps they had been a bad idea. "Look, forget the dummies. I love you. I'm pouring out my heart here. Don't you love me?"

She couldn't lie to him. He always saw through it, but she was sure her truth would hurt him. She had to choose her words very carefully. "Javan, I love you too, but . . ."

"There's no but . . . I want you."

"You're not thinking clearly. I'm not good for you. Not good for anyone."

"But I saved you! Brianna, what more do I have to do?"

His impatience was shining like a new pair of diamond earrings. What more did he have to do before he would be good enough for her?

"It's not you . . . It's me. You know intimacy is not a strong suit of mine. I love you, but this is a bit too soon. Don't you agree?"

Javan took her hand in his and spoke lovingly to her. She needed to understand. "I never wanted this space between us, but I got a lot of love for you, Bria, and never wanted to pressure you into anything you didn't want. The moment I realized I was in love with you . . . I decided to love you from where I was in whatever manner you'd allow."

Brianna thought she might hyperventilate. This was too much.

"I have been more than patient with you, Brianna. I dealt with the ridiculous rules, the curfew, the whole nine."

"You have been patient, and I appreciate that about you." Brianna felt awful. She avoided his love to protect herself but hadn't really considered how the distance affected him. She didn't fully appreciate his humanity. She stood up and slowly started backing out of the short aisle. "You have been the perfect gentleman. Really, you have, and I love you for that. I even thought of you when I was lying on the floor at your brother's. I hoped you would come and save me."

"And I did."

"Yes, you did. That was pretty amazing. You were amazing." Brianna tight roped the line between the truth and the version Javan wanted to hear.

He had not been looking at Brianna as she spoke and most of her words escaped his hearing. No longer actively listening, he replayed her words in his head, *you were amazing*. Brianna continued talking as she made her way to the door taking advantage of his being distracted. "I was so relieved when I heard your voice."

"You were?"

"Of course! I had been so scared and all alone."

Javan whipped his head around and stared at Brianna with *crazy* etched into his eyes. Rattled by his sudden movement, Brianna lost a few vertical inches, nearly falling into the door frame.

Confusion cluttered his mind for a moment as he tried to determine why Brianna would leave without him. She had walked to the door without saying a word to him about it. Shrugging off the questions in his mind, he walked to where she was standing.

"You'll never be alone again. Ever." Javan meant every word. He spent his life looking for someone to love him and someone to love. His parents had disposed of him, and his brother only loved him when it was convenient, but Brianna was different. Being with her gave him life.

She backed slowly into the hallway. "What . . . What do you mean?"

"We'll have each other."

He quickly closed the space between them. The momentum carried the two of them into the hall. Javan was on fire, and he felt a tingling sensation all over his body. His breaths were ragged. He placed his hand around her throat, leaning into her, whispering into her ear. "I can't get enough of you." He slid his tongue into her ear and began to suck it lightly. He drew a line from her ear down her neck and stopped just atop her shoulder. "I have waited so long for this. To have you here. Just like this."

"Javan, please. Don't do this right now." Brianna was afraid. Javan had never been so rough with her. Certainly never choked her. The universe had to be messing with her. This was a test; it just had to be. She had to think of something quickly.

"What's wrong, Bria?"

"I'm just not in the mood."

Javan was not deterred in the least bit. Brianna always teased him.

"Why?" he asked as he gently covered her neck with kisses.

"Come on, Javan. You said I could call my family after the movie."

Javan still did not want her talking to anyone. He expected to be rewarded for his romantic gesture. How many guys create a short film for their women? Brianna was spoiled and unappreciative, but he loved her. Besides, what harm would one phone call do?

"All right, Brianna. Be quick, though. I have a lot planned for us today."

Brianna was relieved. She hoped her suspicions were wrong, but she would send up a flare just in case. Michelle was still her best chance. It took a few tries, but she finally remembered Michelle's number. The first time she called, she didn't get an answer. She immediately hung up and tried again.

"Michelle . . ."

"Brianna . . . Oh my goodness. Bria? Are you okay? Where are you? I'm coming to get you."

"Hey, sis, I love you too. I missed you so much."

Something was wrong, and Michelle could hear it in Brianna's voice. She was not answering her questions. Brianna did not say she was safe. Michelle was happy to hear from Brianna and thought that meant she had somehow gotten away, but she could tell her sister was still in trouble. She just needed to figure out where she was.

"I hear you. Where are you, sis? Give me something."

"My friend, Javan . . . You remember him, Javan Harris? That's him . . . he came and got me."

"Brianna, is he standing there?"

"Yes, and I think I'll stay here for a few days."

"Are you in danger still? Is he connected to the guys that took you?"

"Well, it's a nice, big, beautiful home. Took awhile to get here, but I feel free; there is definitely a relationship here. Reminds me of us."

"They're twins?"

"No, nothing like that, but there are some major similarities."

Javan stood a little way down the hall waiting for Brianna. She knew he was listening to the conversation. She tried to keep it simple. Fortunately, Michelle caught her subtleties.

"Bria, are they brothers?"

"That's the one! Exactly, and so you know I am in good hands."

"I cannot believe this. I am so sorry this happened, sis, but I will find you."

Brianna was on the verge of tears, but she had to hold herself together. She laughed, hard and loud to scare the tears away.

"I love you too and look forward to seeing you in a few days or so."

Reluctantly, Brianna disconnected the call. She took a deep breath and composed herself. She had dated Javan for nearly half a year, but she realized that she did not know anything about him. Something was off about Javan; his energy was weird. "Thank you! She's relieved that I'm safe. You're her hero."

Javan beamed with pride. "It was nothing."

Brianna wanted to run out of the house, but she did not know where she was, and she did not want to make the situation worse. She was growing increasingly uncomfortable. She had to trust that Michelle would find her. It's hard to feel safe when you're still fighting to get home. If they had a long day ahead of them, she shuddered to think of what else he had planned for her.

Chapter 43

Brianna was no longer with the Marx Brothers, but she was still not out of trouble. Someone related to one of them, a brother, had her. Michelle shook Armand awake.

"Babe, wake up. Wake up. Brianna called."

"What? Did she get away?" Armand was exhausted after a long night with Michelle, but news of Brianna's phone call gave him the boost his system needed.

"She is not with the Marx Brothers anymore, but wherever she is . . . She doesn't feel safe there. Do any of the brothers have any other relatives, a brother maybe?"

"Not that I know of. I mean . . . Mike might, but I'm not sure."

"Well, she is with someone named Javan Harris, and I think he might be bad news."

"What makes you think that? How did she get there?"

"It's hard to explain. She just didn't sound like herself." Michelle vacillated briefly as she wrangled her emotions. She was antsy and frustrated with Armand's questions. "Talking in code . . . We need to find her!"

"I didn't speak with her. I need to know what you know."

"You know everything I know."

"Okay, well, this may be a good thing. She might be easier to get with just him in the way. I'll find out what I can. Did she say anything about where she is?"

"Only that it's a big house, and it took awhile to get there. I'm not sure how much help that'll be."

"Well, you never know, babe. Let me get up, shower, and see what I can find out."

"Okay, I'm going to take a taxi to my mom's. I don't like the way I left the other day. I have never talked to her that way before, and we need to talk it out."

"All right, babe, just be careful."

"I will. Hit me on my cell when you find out something."

Michelle left the hotel suite and headed for her mom's. She was not worried about running into Lisa. In fact, she was hoping she would. She still had a few talking points to go over with her. However, she made it downstairs and into a taxi without incident.

Armand thought about what Michelle told him; the information was bittersweet. Had Brianna still been with the Marx Brothers, he could use his familiarity with them to his advantage. Even though he did not know exactly where they had hidden her, after two years of working with them, he at least knew their habits, but this Javan Harris character was alien to him. It would have only been a matter of time before Armand would have figured out where they were. He pulled out his phone and saw that he had another missed call from Mike. There was no harm in calling him since Brianna was no longer there.

"Mike, it's Armand."

"Dude, where have you been? Shit is all fucked up right now."

"I'm sorry, I had some personal business. Family stuff. I had to leave town. No reception in that part of New Orleans."

"Whatever. You had a job to do, and you failed."

"What are you talking about, Mike? I got you the girl, didn't I?"

"You fucked up."

"Told you where she would be."

"Yes, but you didn't tell us that she wasn't alone!"

"I told you to grab her from the beach. I'm no genius, but you grabbed her from a vacation spot. Are those beaches ever empty? Besides, I gave you the time and everything."

The information he had passed along had been useful. He thought that Armand had lost his way for a minute, but he came through strong in the end. Mike could not deny him that. "True, but something went wrong. The girl got away."

"What do you mean?"

"Look, I was a little nervous about John. I didn't want to hurt the girl, you know that, but after John found out Lewis was dead . . . she became a loose end."

Armand assumed that it would be John that would cause an issue. He also knew Mike would keep her safe. It was wrong to gamble with Brianna's life, but he had to protect Michelle. She was his priority.

"Well, where is she?"

"My brother took her."

So, it was Mike's brother. Mike's brother, Javan Harris, had taken Brianna. Now Armand needed to figure out how and why.

"Your brother? How did that happen?"

"Like I said, I was nervous about John. I didn't know if I'd be able to control him too much longer . . . So I called my bro over, to get some advice. He's a smart dude. Plus, he's kind of been in a situation similar to this awhile back."

"Cool, that sounds straight."

"Well, he got here and started wilding out. Walking through the house screaming and shit. Then the weirdest shit happened."

"What?"

"Michelle recognized his voice or something and started yelling his name! I couldn't believe it; then he turned to me and asked me why some girl named Brianna was there. I told him I didn't know Brianna. He insisted that the girl was Brianna, and he took her."

Armand's mouth went dry, and he started choking.

"You all right, Armand?" Mike sounded concerned.

"Yeah." Armand talked through his coughing fit. "Wow. Who is Brianna?"

"I don't fucking know. I didn't at least. Then, I got to thinking. That girl running down the beach . . . Maybe *she* was Michelle."

"What are you talking about, Mike?"

"The girl we snatched . . . She responded when my brother called her Brianna."

Armand played it cool. No need to panic. He needed to reassure Mike that they had grabbed Michelle. He didn't need them looking for her.

"Mike, did she ever say she was not Michelle?"

"No, but come on . . . That was just too much of a coincidence."

"Look, if I were confined and someone was trying to save me . . . I'd be whoever they wanted me to be. She was probably just pretending because she saw a way out."

"Maybe you're right."

"I mean, you said it yourself, John wanted to kill her, right? I'm sure she knew that."

"True . . . I'm getting too old for this shit."

"So, what's the deal with your brother? You think he'll talk?"

"Nah . . . He ain't goin' to say nothin'. I've seen that look in his eyes, and honestly, shorty might have been better off here with John's crazy ass."

"What do you mean?"

"Look, Armand, I like you, and that's the only reason I'm telling you this. My plan is shit, and I'm tired of all this. I'm being square with you. John is violent, but my brother? My brother is a different type of crazy. He's my little brother, and I love him, but some females . . . haven't fared so well with him."

"I don't understand."

"If you care about that girl like I think you do . . . You need to go get her."

"What are you going to do about the money?"

"Fuck it. Lewis is dead anyway. I think I'm going to leave for a while. John hasn't been back since he left yesterday."

"Are you worried about him?"

"Nah . . . I'm actually relieved. He would not be happy about the girl being gone. I'm going to leave before he gets back from wherever he is. It's time for us to split anyway."

"Where is your brother?"

"I don't know, and even if I did, I wouldn't tell you. That's my brother. You'll have to figure it out. Be easy, youngin'."

John was never coming back. Armand had taken care of him personally last night while Michelle was sleeping. It was a precaution in case he couldn't find their physical location. John had an itch he had to scratch daily. He was a slave to the pipe. Every day at the same time, he went to the spot for his juice. Last night, Armand was waiting for him when he came out. Armand was not a killer, but it did not take much to incapacitate John. He tried to get the location of the house from him, but John rebuffed him. Two moves and it was over.

He went home and slept like a baby. Figured he had plenty of time to find Brianna with John out of the picture. Michelle had put him back on a timeline. Now he needed to find everything he could about Javan Harris. He showered quickly and sat down on the couch to make a few phone calls. Armand, like Lewis, had learned a lot from his tutelage with the Marx Brothers. He had been well versed in how to work connections and had gained a respectable number of friends just for being linked with them. His steadily increasing street IQ coupled with his attractiveness got him into some pretty exclusive circles. A few of those friends owed him a favor or two, and he had a feeling he would be cashing in on them pretty soon.

He pulled out his laptop and Googled Javan Harris. The Javan Harris that fit the description recently won a city contract to oversee the construction of a new hotel. The address to his house and a condo leased to him was also listed in the search result. Armand wrote the addresses down and decided to start there first. Hopefully, Brianna would be in one of them, but given the time Michelle told him it took to get there . . . He knew it was not likely. He would check both because it was better to have a definite no than a probable yes.

Chapter 44

Michelle sat across from her mother in the living room. She had been there for the better part of an hour, and they still had not exchanged any words. She had not been able to speak, literally. She did not know what to say. She was pretty sure her mother wanted an apology for the way she had spoken to her, but Michelle did not want to give her one. Someone needed to break the ice in the room.

"Mom, are you going to talk to me?"

"If I say no, then, what will you do?"

"I don't know. Leave, I guess."

It was a stupid question. Michelle was her daughter. Of course, she was going to speak with her.

"Tsk-tsk. Michelle, you are as stubborn as your father."

"You've been telling me that since I was a small girl."

Sophie laughed. Smiled a sad smile. "I'm glad you came back. I was not certain you would."

"I was not either, to be honest."

"Well . . . thank you."

Michelle did not respond. What was she supposed to say?

"Any news about your sister?"

"We're working on it. I talked with her today."

"How did she sound?"

"Afraid but strong."

"I hope Armand can find her. I do love her."

"I guess love hurts."

"Michelle, I'm sorry. I know I hurt you both. It was not my intention." Sophie's heart was bleeding. She hadn't meant to hurt anyone. She was only trying to save herself. She hadn't expected, nor wanted, any of this to happen.

"Mom . . . I have spent the last month wondering if you were even my mother. I cannot tell you how betrayed I felt. There are no words for it."

"I was going to tell you; I just did not know how."

"We met at a restaurant, and I thought I was losing my mind when I saw her walk in. We just sat there for the longest time, staring in disbelief. It was unreal."

"Why didn't you come to me, Michelle?"

"What would you have said, Mom? We decided not to ask any of you anything, seeing as though, for all we knew, you had been lying to us our entire lives. We didn't know who to trust."

All of this saddened Sophie. She thought it had worked out well for everyone. "So, where are Brianna's parents?"

"Funny you should ask that. The man that raised her . . . He's sitting in jail right now, and her mom . . . Well, she was the woman at the funeral that upset you."

Sophie knew exactly whom Michelle was referring to. "Oh, I see."

"She didn't know. She knows now."

Sophie furrowed her eyebrows, a silent inquiry. Michelle decided to respond to that query. "I told her. It was not a very pleasant exchange."

Sophie was certain it was not. Michelle had a temper like her father's. The other day was one of the few times she had seen it. "Things didn't go so well with us, either, did it?"

"It went as well as could be expected, given the circumstances."

"I don't think so."

"Trust me; it could have gone a lot worse. I could have gone my entire life and never known Brianna, and you would have let me."

"That's not true, Michelle."

"Isn't it, Mom? Sure, it is. Let's not do this."

"This?"

"This pointless argument. There's nothing you can say that will excuse it. Nothing you can say that will change how I feel about it."

"I don't want to change your mind, Michelle. I want you to understand."

"It's not going to happen. Let it go."

"Michelle Kaye Lewis, I understand you are upset, but you still need to be respectful. I am not perfect. I have made mistakes and giving your sister away was one of my biggest."

"Really? Have you done something worse? Do I even want to know what it is?"

Sophie bit her lip. This was going to be harder than she thought. Michelle was no longer angry; sadness filled her eyes. Her heart was hurting.

"I just never expected anything like this from you. With Dad . . . I could see that coming but not you. We shared everything, but something this important . . . you withheld."

"All I can ask is that you forgive me, Michelle. Please?"

"I'm trying, but I need some time."

"That's fair."

Michelle knew she would eventually forgive her mother, but she did not know how long it would take or how to begin that process. Time would tell.

"Did you ever tell Dad?"

"Not when it mattered. He was never around anyway, so I doubt it would have made a difference."

Silence ballooned and settled back between them, each lost in their own thoughts. Trying to come to terms with the fact that their relationship would never be what it was; trying to decide if that was for the best or not. Michelle's phone vibrated and disrupted the muted chords.

"Hello?"

"Michelle, I struck out at the addresses I found on record for Javan. I need a favor, and you're not going to like it."

"Anything if it will help Bria."

"I need you to ask your mom to use her contacts to see if Javan has any properties registered to him that might not be public knowledge."

"My mom does not have any contacts, Armand. I have never even known her to talk to anyone besides my dad."

Sophie gave Michelle her undivided attention when she heard her name. Her interest was piqued. She was eager to help Brianna in any way she could, to redeem herself some.

"Just trust me on this, Michelle and ask her. We need to know. It's easier to deal with a definite no—"

"Than a probable yes, I know. Hold on a second."

Michelle did not know what Armand knew about her mother that she did not. She trusted his judgment, however, and if he insisted, she would ask, even if it was a waste of time.

"Is that Armand?"

"Yes."

"News about Brianna?" Sophie was anxious. She had been wrought with worry since Michelle told her she had been taken.

Michelle exhaled, slightly frustrated with her mother's interruptions.

"We think we know who has her. Some guy named Javan Harris has her. We need to get her, but we need a list of any property he owns that might not be listed publicly. Armand seems to think you can help with that."

"Yes, I can."

Michelle wished she could say that she was surprised, but the truth was, she didn't know what to expect anymore. There was so much she didn't know.

"Armand, she said she'll help. Just keep doing what you can, and I'll call you back."

Sophie grabbed the phone and her address book. She scrolled through the names until she found the one she thought would be most useful. "I need the name."

"Javan Harris."

"Be right back."

Sophie walked into another room to make the phone call. She wanted privacy. The less Michelle knew, for the time being, the better. Michelle was already upset, and she didn't want to risk making things worse. Her curiosity got the best of her, and she followed behind her mother and listened out of sight.

"Mr. Sterling, how are you doing? Yes, sir, this is Richard's daughter, Sophia. It has been awhile. I'm fine, sir, I was wondering if I could bother you for a small favor. Nothing too serious, but I'm trying to buy some land from a local, and I think he left off some properties on this listing. If I gave you a name, could you verify that the list he provided is accurate? No? Are you certain you can't do this for me, Mr. Sterling? I realize it isn't protocol, but I would hate for your lovely wife, Elizabeth, to learn of your little arrangement with your secretary over a little legal technicality. I mean, no one wants that, right? Oh, you can? I hope it's not too much trouble. That's just great, thank you so much. The name is Javan Harris. Yes, that's right, Javan Harris. When can I expect it? Fifteen minutes is perfect, sir. Thank you so much, Mr. Sterling. I'll be sure to let my father know how good you were to help me."

Michelle tiptoed quickly back into the living room and waited for her mom. She wondered who this Mr. Sterling was, but more importantly, when her mom took to blackmailing people. She guessed her parents weren't so different after all. She started to wonder what else her mom had lied about it. She did it so effortlessly. How could a reasonable person possibly trust anyone like that? Who *is* this woman?

She picked up her phone and dialed the number Brianna had called from. No answer. She hoped she was okay. Michelle's exterior was calm, but inside, she was a ball of nerves. Finishing the task of discovering who their parents were was a necessary distraction for her, but now that she had uncovered the truth, she was left with empty hands. Hands that could do nothing at all to help her sister. She tried to relax her mind.

She thought of her father, his laugh and the little wisdom he had shared with her over the years. She had not stopped long enough in her life to appreciate it very much, or him, for that matter, but she had to admit they had gotten her to this point. *Live today as if you intended to be here.* She remembered vividly when he said those words to her. He showed up late to her college graduation party. The guests were leaving and against her mother's wishes, she was helping her clean up.

He had tried to speak with her, but she had refused him. She was angry. Hurt. He had missed so many important snapshots in her life; in her mind, he was no longer a part of it. He had chosen not to be, but for an instant, at his persistence, she let him in. He clasped his arms around her, swallowing her whole, and whispered how much he loved her. He filled her heart with his pride and adoration. She was his baby girl, and there was nothing he would not do for her. Part of her believed him because she desperately wanted it to be true, but the part of her that resisted, that held on to every space left vacant by his disregard, was less than impressed with his wordplay.

It was the last time Michelle was vulnerable to her father. She wanted the last feeling he gave her to be that one, what she was feeling at that precise moment. Protected, loved, treasured. Neither of them knew that when he released her, he would never hold her again. Now, she was sitting in the living room, in a chair she had seen him occupy whenever he was home. It was still hard to accept that he would never do it again. But Michelle felt something other than grief. She felt robbed. She would never get a chance to mend her relationship with her father. The opportunity had been taken from her. She wanted to blame someone. Her dad was young. His death was premature; she should have had more time. That is why she chose to at least speak with her mom. Life was too short.

Sophie came back into the room, handing the list to her daughter. "I got the listing for the properties. I hope it helps."

"I hope so too."

Michelle called Armand and gave him three additional addresses: one for a condo in North Richland Hills, a house in Fort Worth, and a house in Allen. One of them had to be where Javan has Brianna. It just had to be.

Chapter 45

Brianna was pinned to the wall under his weight, choking as his grip increased. She pulled on his fingers, grabbing at his arms, trying to break free, but he only strengthened his hold on her.

"Don't fight it, Brianna. I know how you like it." He clasped his hands together and pulled her up off the ground until her eyes met his. He could see the alarm in her eyes as she fought to breathe. "Bria, you intoxicate me. You're making me do this. Why? This was not a part of the plan."

Brianna could not respond. She tried to shake her head in protest, but his grasp was so tight, she could barely move. She was slowly losing consciousness. She managed a weak "please" before she passed out.

Javan released Brianna and let her fall gently to the floor. He stood over her marveling at her beautiful figure. He resisted the urge to take himself into his hand at the sight of her sleeping. He could feel his passion surging through him, his loins awake and thriving. *Damn it, Brianna.* She went and fucked everything up. Javan was upset with the turn of events. She was not supposed to react that way.

He had everything planned perfectly. After the movie, he prepared lunch for her. Nothing but the best. He even serenaded her while he cooked. Javan had a voice comparable to Maxwell. The kind of voice that could make sound waves orgasm. He did not like singing and on some level was embarrassed by his ability. He didn't consider it a talent or a gift but a vice. He hated it and the bastard he figured passed it along to him. To him, it was a weakness; it made him seem soft. Javan rarely sang for anyone, and this was the first time he had done so for Brianna. Today was supposed to be special, and he wanted it to be perfect. He knew she'd be impressed, and he was right.

She seemed kind of tense after that scene in the hallway following the movie. He knew it had been a mistake to let her make the phone call. She had seemed anxious ever since, and he needed her to calm down. He thought a little music would do the trick. He sang John Legend's, "All of Me," and she loved it. It seemed appropriate to Javan. The lyrics described him and Brianna perfectly. He could not lose with her.

Today, he wanted to make it official between them. Things were going about as well as he expected. The music had softened her defenses, and she had been drawn nearer to him again; that little distance he felt previously was dissipating. He had taken her on a tour of the house. She saw the nursery for their future children, his library, her home office, complete with a few of her favorite things, his weight room, a game room, and the in-ground pool in the backyard. He could tell that she was surprised with some of the rooms, particularly the nursery, but for the most, she took it all in stride and seemed fairly impressed.

Javan was feeling optimistic. Brianna had even commented on the length of time it must have taken him to put everything together, considering all the details he included. For instance, he had the same paintings that hung in her office at work on the walls in the office he created for her. The nursery looked like it had been professionally decorated and was suited to welcome

either a baby boy or girl. He had put a lot of thought into
it. He was pleased with their progress until they got to
the last room of the tour. It was time . . . *the big reveal.*
He intentionally left it for the end.

He placed a blindfold over her eyes, after much pleading and reassuring, leading her carefully downstairs to
the living room and opened the big French doors. He
brought her into the center of the room, retrieved his gift
from its hiding place, and took his place in front of her.
Once in position, he asked her to remove the blindfold,
and Brianna did as instructed. She opened her eyes to
what must have seemed like a million different pictures
of her in various poses. Javan was not prepared for the
horror that quickly framed itself in her face.

She was everywhere but had not posed for one single
picture. Javan had to call her name to get her attention.
There he was, on bended knee, ring in hand, preparing to
pose the most improbable question. "Brianna, I love you,
and I hope I have shown you that."

She looked at him wide-eyed, confusion and panic
lodged themselves in her throat. She hadn't wanted to
stay, but she could not get her legs to move.

"Will you marry me? I love you." Javan knew the
answer. He stood and slid the ring on her finger, beaming
and gushing with pride. His journey was complete. He
felt like he had climbed Mount Everest . . . and in the
next second, Brianna threw him from the peak. Sent his
heart crashing to the bottom, draining his blood supply,
taking his life. She did not say anything at first. She just
stood there in muted shock, unable to speak. Her eyes
darted all around the room. Bouncing between the pictures, the ring, and Javan. He thought perhaps she was
overwhelmed by the moment, too filled with excitement
to say anything.

When he felt he could no longer bear the torture . . . It happened. Brianna broke her silence. "Are you fucking crazy? What? What is this? Where did you get these pictures? What is this place?"

He stood in disbelief as she walked around in circles, frantic and disturbed by what surrounded her. She stopped walking and looked at Javan, still standing in the middle of the room, in the same place she left him before she unleashed her rant.

He did not understand what was happening. The pictures were beautiful and allowed him to be close to her when she had kept him away. She should be happy. The man she loved just proposed to her. They were getting married.

"Brianna, stop behaving like this. We are getting married. This room is but a small measure of how deeply I adore you. Don't you understand? I love you." Javan felt things going south. His plan was unraveling quickly. He did not like it. He did not like that one bit.

Brianna responded without thinking. Javan had gone too far, and she reacted instinctively. He had lost it. This was a nightmare. She didn't know what he could have been thinking. Perhaps she should have wondered, though. She should have considered his feelings before she said what she said. Before she let those words run from her mouth and into that space where his heart had been.

"I will *never* marry you! Are you out of your mind? I don't even think I know you. You're psychotic!" Brianna had tried to run up the stairs and toward the front door, but Javan was faster. Bigger. He had sprinter's legs and easily caught her. Brianna did not make it easy. She fought him. Punched. Kicked. Even bit him. Nothing worked. It only served to exacerbate his anger. They ended up against the wall with his hands around her neck. After all of this, he wanted nothing more than to make love to her. She rejected and discarded him, but he desired her. He hated how weak she made him feel. He felt some of that power return to him as he choked her, surging and electrifying his senses as her body went limp, yielding itself to him.

He did not stop. He had become someone else. Her losing consciousness was not enough. She needed to be punished for her behavior. She embarrassed him by not shouting a resounding and elated "Yes!" to his marriage proposal. They should have been celebrating their union, but Brianna had ruined it. He had put in ample amounts of his valuable time, preparing for this moment. Everything was perfect for her, but she—just like the others—was another spoiled rich kid who needed to be taught a lesson.

Brianna was not the first woman to capture Javan's heart, but he was determined that she would be the last. He hoped she would be different. Some part of him still did. She was fortunate that he had learned not to react hastily. Had this happened a couple of years ago, things might have gone very differently. Carla was not so lucky. Her body was never found, and the accused, Micah Javan Harrison, disappeared. There should have been a state-wide manhunt, but someone with a higher status, more weight than the lowly homicide detective assigned to the case, stopped the investigation cold. With no evidence of a crime, no leads, and no suspect, they could not pursue it. It was like neither he, nor Carla, ever existed, and he had not been seen again . . . until now.

Brianna had unwittingly served as the catalyst for a dynamic change. Though it had not been the first time that such a change had occurred, it was the first time in a while. Javan had tried to love her, but she rejected him. Brianna did not appreciate his niceties and had taken him for granted. He had managed his anger all these years, but Brianna's actions had forced him to put those techniques away. He could no longer be the "nice guy" with her. He was not accepting no for an answer. He knew from the first time he saw her that she was special.

He experienced urges he had long since forgotten, and he knew it was only a matter of time before she would be his. If only she had expressed her love aptly. If she had not been so damn disrespectful. Javan could not allow that. If Brianna wanted to act like the other bitches before her, then, so be it. That was exactly how he would treat her. Brianna had crossed the line. There was no going back after that. Javan would make her pay for how emasculated he felt in her presence. He had been silent about her ridiculous rules and had put up with her nonsense with little protest, choosing to deal with the pain and discomfort inflicted by her selfishness because he cared so deeply for her. He had considered it all a means to an end, a necessary hardship that ultimately would result in the family he desired.

Javan had loved many women, including Carla. Each of them was beautiful, successful, and wealthy. They were his type. Javan felt like he had something to prove, and these women could help in some way, but it never worked. He was always left more broken than before. They left him in pieces, and he was forced to pull himself together again. New state. New city. New people. Javan would enjoy his fresh start and refrain from engaging with the opposite sex, but inevitably, there would be one woman that he could not disregard. One that would invade his mind and possess him.

Most ended amicably as far as that went, but Carla was different. She had torn him open in a way that no woman had before her. Javan decided he would not let it get that far with Brianna. He had done even more for Brianna than he had for Carla. He had dedicated an entire house to this woman. Javan was so desperate for love, trying to replace the mother he never had, to impress the father that had taken a laser to his life trying to cover him up like a bad tattoo.

Mike was his brother, and he loved him, but they had not been raised together. Their father was a proud man, and his image was of the utmost importance. There was no possible way he would allow his friends at the country club know that he had fathered a child with his maid. Instead of embracing Javan as his son, he sent him away. Mike always kept in touch with him, though, and lent him whatever he had.

Javan blamed his dad for how Mike had turned out. He could have been a lawyer or a doctor. He had a brilliant mind and was on the right track, but something changed him. Javan guessed that their father had screwed his brother out of his future the same way he had screwed him out of his. Javan worked hard to get where he was and decided years ago that he would have everything his father had—even if he had to take it from him.

He had traveled a bit and accomplished more. Finally, he made it back to Dallas and was ready to complete his life. He needed Brianna to finish the picture, and she had turned him down cold. Javan was in pain, and he needed to neutralize the situation, to convince Brianna that they were better together. Once he had her by his side, he knew he could confront his dad and lay claim to what was rightfully his. Mike had decided to accept his exile, but Javan would not. He didn't feel he had enough to go at him, not without Brianna. She complemented him perfectly. He needed her. She was designed for him, and if he couldn't have her . . . no one would.

He had taken her to a room not too far from the living room and sequestered her. It was not a bedroom, but it

was nice enough. It would do. Javan did not want her
to be too uncomfortable. He considered her his wife as
long as she wore his ring; the superglue he lined it with
was meant to all but guarantee that this would always be
true. He needed to make sure that she would appreciate
everything he had to offer first. Once he was satisfied that
she had learned her lesson, then they could resume their
lives together. Not a moment sooner, though.

Javan wasn't certain about what he wanted to do with
her yet. He looked at his watch. Some time had passed.
Perhaps a conversation was in order. He needed to see
what state of mind she was in. He had been sitting in *her
office,* tendering his resignation. He would not be returning to work anytime soon, and if he failed to change her
mind, he imagined he'd have to move again. He made
his way through the house to the room Brianna was in,
unlocked the door, and stood just inside.

Brianna was sitting in the far left corner of the room
rocking and cradling her legs. She stopped moving when
she heard the door. She looked at Javan in complete
disbelief. How could she have been so foolish? This man
was a complete stranger. Even his posture was different.

"What in the fuck are you looking at?"

Brianna kept her mouth closed, but she could not look
away. She stared at the man she had made love to just
hours before and did not recognize him. Javan had never
before spoken to her in this way, and he had certainly
never put his hands on her. How did she miss the signs?

"I asked a question."

"Nothing."

Javan walked to where she sat, squatted, and put his
face directly in front of hers, so close that their noses
were touching. Brianna shook with fear; she could feel
her teeth chattering.

"Don't fucking lie to me. I hate that shit. Last chance.
Now, what in the fuck are you looking at?"

"I . . . you. I was looking at you."

"Apologize."

"Huh?"

"Did I stutter? Apologize."

"I . . . I'm so . . . sorry." Brianna whimpered. She had never been so afraid in her life. She didn't think anything could have been worse than being dragged off the beach, but she was wrong. *This* was worse.

"Stupid bitch. Do you even know why you're apologizing?"

Brianna shook her head no. She had no idea what was happening. She just wanted it to stop.

"What in the fuck did I see in you?"

Brianna was lost. The situation was overwhelming her senses. She did not know if she wanted to vomit, sleep, cry, or laugh. Javan shook his head, completely disgusted with this pathetic version of Brianna. Could he have misread her over the last few months? He expected a little more fight from her. She seemed to be folding right in front of his eyes. It hurt him a little to see her like that, but bitches gotta learn.

"I love you. You know that? Why are you behaving like a bitch? Do you want me to treat you like one?"

"Who are you?" Brianna couldn't believe what she was seeing and hearing.

"It's me, love, your husband." Javan flashed her a devilish grin. "I haven't gone anywhere."

"Why are you doing this, Javan?"

Javan sprang to his feet. "*You* did this, Brianna! I didn't want this. I wanted to marry you and give you access to the best of everything, but you didn't want that." He motioned to the house and everything in it with his arms as he spoke.

"I'm sorry."

"You ran from me! I had to chase you, just like I've been chasing you ever since I met you! Sports isn't your thing. Why do you keep running from me?"

"I was afraid."

"Afraid? I love you, woman. I couldn't let you leave."

Brianna wanted to run again, but she knew it would be a futile attempt. Javan was between her and the door. He must have picked the only room in the house without windows to stick her in.

"I don't understand, Javan. If you love me, how could you do this to me?"

"I am not *doing* this. *You* brought this on yourself. *You're* making me do this to you."

Brianna wanted to speak, but her lips refused her. Probably it was better that way. She didn't know what to say. This was insane.

"See, I know you, Brianna. You think I can't see the shit you hide, but I do. I don't like it."

Brianna was starting to panic. She looked at his feet. They seemed to glide across the floor as he walked back and forth. Javan kept talking, but she continued to focus on his feet. She felt her body calming a little. The pattern was soothing; it was the only thing that made sense. She could not believe what she was hearing.

"My heart is . . . fragile. Do you understand? Talk!"

Brianna looked up to find Javan staring at her.

"Bitch, do you hear me talking to your simple ass?"

"What do you want me to say?"

Javan dawdled before responding. He was not sure what he wanted her to say. He had asked but how could he believe anything that came out of her mouth now? He also did not know how he felt about her asking him anything, even if it was a valid question. But he needed answers.

"I want to know if you understand."

"Understand what?"

"Are you trying to piss me off?"

"No."

Javan was not convinced. "I think you are."

"I'm not." He was poised to step to her. Brianna raised her arms defensively and prepared to shield herself, if necessary.

He started laughing. Brianna amused him. What the fuck was she doing?

"If I want to touch you, I will. Not a damn thing you can do about it."

"I have to try." Brianna wasn't sure why she said anything at all.

Javan liked that. A little gumption finally. It was about damn time. He detested the idea of having a weak wife. "There may be hope for you yet."

"Will you let me go?"

"I'm not holding you."

Brianna rose hesitantly and walked slowly toward the door.

"I'm not holding you, but if you leave this house, no one will ever hold you again. Next time, you won't wake up."

Brianna stopped and considered his words. He was behind her, but she did not need to see his eyes to know he was serious. He would kill her. She was certain of it. She wondered if it would be worth it to try to escape. She took a few more steps toward the door but didn't venture out. She did not want to live this way, but she did not want to die, either. She had to trust that Michelle would eventually find her. She just needed to survive until then. She turned around, walked back to her corner, and took her seat.

Javan smiled, pleased with her decision. "Good. I'm glad we're finally on the same page." He walked out.

Brianna was not sure how to feel about that, but she was glad to see him go. The lock even gave her a little comfort. On some level, the lock kept her in . . . but it also kept him out.

Chapter 46

He was grateful to be out of jail. Charlie had come through for him with the lawyer and bail money. It was the least she could do after dropping that baby bomb. He could not believe he had been so careless, but he couldn't think about that now. He still had not heard from Lisa and could not reach Brianna. He had been out a few hours and had gotten little accomplished. The Marx Brothers were missing in action, and he had no physical location for them.

He wanted to speak with Jacob, but one of the conditions of his bail restricted it. He didn't know what else to do, so he figured he would go to the only place he could think of: Michelle's parents' home. Maybe Michelle could tell him something. He had to get Brianna back. He went home to get the address and was surprised to find Lisa there. She was in their bedroom packing a bag.

"Well, how's this for a surprise?"

Lisa jumped and nearly screamed. She had not expected to see Frank. In fact, she was trying to leave town and avoid any contact with anyone. A lot was going on, and she realized she did not want any part of it.

"Not nearly as surprised as I am to see you. When did you get out?"

"Does it matter?" Frank was furious with her, but he needed to ease into the conversation. He didn't want to run her off without the answers to his questions.

Lisa thought about his question. It didn't matter to her. She was tired of all the drama. Frank acted like he had done nothing wrong.

"No, I guess it doesn't."

"So, are we going to talk about what's going on between us or not?"

"I vote no."

"Lisa."

"Franklin."

Frank cringed. He hated when she called him that. "I know you lied about Jacob."

Lisa ceased her packing efforts and gave her husband her undivided attention. Maxwell began to croon "Cold" through the speakers. How appropriate, she thought as she let the chorus finish before responding to Frank's statement. *How can you be so cold? Good God the girl's gone cold* . . . That was exactly how she felt. Cold.

She did, however, have a dagger of her own to throw. "I know Brianna has a twin sister."

Frank sat down on the bed. Nothing was a shock anymore. He didn't know how Lisa found out, but at this point, it wasn't even important.

"Why did you lie?"

"Why did you?"

"I wanted to protect you."

"Protect me from what, Franklin? Hmm?"

"From any legal recourse."

"I guess Jacob helped you with that?"

He nodded. "Your turn."

"The truth was too painful to speak. Who told you?"

Lisa already knew who had told him. She had gone to visit Frank but saw her on her way in and changed her mind. Charlie knew Jacob, and, given the history between her and Frank, it only made sense that she was the one that told him. Enough was enough. She did not need either of them. They could have each other. She had what she needed from them and was ready to move on.

Frank didn't want to tell her about Charlie. He didn't want her having any more ammunition to fire at him, but something told him she knew despite the question. "A little birdie."

Lisa didn't feel like playing with Frank. She didn't even really want to talk to him. "Charlie? No need to pretend, Franklin. I saw her at Lew Sterrett."

He exhaled. That's why she had not been to see him. She knew.

"How long?"

"Excuse me?"

"How long have you known?"

"From the beginning. Really? Did you think you were that slick, Frank? Please, you are not that inventive."

"You could have told me the truth, Lisa."

"Trust is not something we have."

"Still, I could have killed him."

"Are we talking about Jacob or Lewis?"

"Both, but Jacob right now."

Lisa did feel guilty about that. "I didn't mean for that to happen. I hadn't planned to tell you anything, but it just came out . . . By then, it was too late."

"And Lewis?"

"You never asked."

"How are we supposed to move past that . . . or any of this?"

"Who said I wanted to?"

Frank was dumbfounded. He hadn't anticipated Lisa not wanting to be with him. Some part of him still wanted her. He didn't know why, given all that had happened, but he couldn't deny the twinge of pain he felt in hearing that maybe she didn't want to try to repair their marriage.

"Lisa, I know I should have told you the truth about Brianna, but we've both made mistakes."

"I don't have to listen to this."

"Yes, you do. Regardless of whether you like it, you owe me."

"Frank, you cannot be serious. I don't owe you or anybody else."

"Come on, Lisa. The affairs? The money you stole? Not to mention this big-ass, fucking lie you fed me about Jacob."

"I didn't steal anything. That was *our* money."

"Lisa, please. All right. We're down to fifty large. We had millions. Where did it go?"

"I needed it. It's gone. Just let it go."

"You are one selfish woman."

"And do you really want to pull the adultery card? I wouldn't have done anything if you hadn't starved me. What was I supposed to do? You acted like you didn't even want to be here. We made love, what, a few times out of the year? When was the last date we went on, Frank?"

"Maybe if you hadn't been spreading your legs to everyone else, I would have wanted to make love to you."

"Fuck you. I quit Lewis, but I guess Charlie neglected to mention that little detail."

"Lewis was not the only guy, and you know it."

"That is not the point."

"Like hell, it isn't! It's the *entire* point, Lisa!"

"None of that would have happened if I felt wanted here. Brianna's presence here just made me feel like a third wheel. You made me feel like an outsider in my own family!"

"Don't bring Brianna into this. This has nothing to do with her."

"It has *everything* to do with her. You changed! You didn't even discuss it with me, Frank. You just did it, and I accepted it because I had nothing else. I was your wife. Didn't you think maybe you should have run that by me first? Never let me on the team. I was nothing more than a glorified accessory."

"Lisa, I was not trying to do that. It was a split-second decision. I didn't go to the hospital intending to do that, but I thought of all that money, and so I went for it. I guess, over time, I felt guilty about it, and maybe I spoiled Brianna a bit, but that didn't mean I didn't love you. I loved you the best way I could."

"Money does not solve everything, Frank. I wanted you."

"I know that now. Just give me a chance to prove it, Lisa."

Frank wanted to know where the money went, but he didn't want to ruin any chance he'd have for reconciliation by pushing the issue. If he knew anything about Lisa, he knew she would not be leaving empty-handed. Besides, he would let it go if it meant he could keep her.

"Lisa, we have a family. Believe it or not, I did love you. We took vows. You belong to me."

"Right. *Everything* belongs to you. Even the woman I had? Just had to have her too? That's sick, Frank."

Frank did not know how to respond to that. He was pissed when he realized that the person Lisa was sleeping with was a woman. He took it as a personal insult to him as a man. On some level, his sleeping with Charlie helped him to retain some of the dignity he lost. Lisa's words hurt; forced him to deal with his hypocrisy. He had become complicit in her affair by beginning one of his own—and with the same woman, no less.

"Lisa, I was hurting, and I lashed out. It didn't mean anything."

"Of course not. It never does, does it?"

"Don't leave. Not like this. What about Brianna?"

"Brianna does not want to see me. Thanks to you, she wants nothing to do with me."

"How is that *my* fault?"

"She blames me for this sham of a marriage, and you let her. You have never taken any responsibility for your part in it, and I let you. Shame on me, I guess."

"I'm sorry. I messed up."

"I'm sorry too, Franklin. For what it's worth, I loved you."

"So, go with that. Stay here and let's work this out."

"If Brianna wants to see me, my number will be the same."

Lisa grabbed her bag and headed for the door. Frank stepped in front of her and blocked her path. He didn't want her to leave.

"Frank, please move."

"Lisa, I love you. I know you don't believe that, but I do. When I thought Jacob had hurt you . . . I lost it. I couldn't stand that. Please give me a chance."

"Frank, I just can't. I need to leave. To start over. I don't know who I am anymore, this woman. I need a change."

"But, Lisa—"

"What is there of me to love, Franklin? What do you love? Do you even *know?*"

Frank could not answer her. He didn't know. He couldn't explain why.

"Just let me go."

"But I love you. I want this." He grabbed Lisa's hands and looked into her eyes. "I don't want you to leave me, Lisa. Please don't do this."

"Franklin, we are no good for each other. We aren't. I love you too, but this isn't going to work. Look at this mess we've made."

"Where are you going?"

"I don't know yet. Some place with white sand and blue water."

Frank let her go but doing so brought on some of the worst pain he's ever felt in his life. Lisa picked up her bags and walked down the hall to the front door. Reluctantly, Frank followed behind her.

"I hope Brianna's okay. Let me know when you find her. Hope you beat the charge too."

"Wish you were sticking around to help me."

"Me too. Give Brianna my love."

"I will, and I meant what I said at the hospital, Lisa. I *will* find you."

"I know."

Lisa got into her car and drove away. Frank meant what he said. He had done a lot to hold his family together, and he was not willing to let go of it entirely. He would let her leave for now, but he would have her again. She was still his wife, but for now, his focus was on Brianna. He grabbed the address for Michelle's parents' house, hopped in the car, and headed that way.

Chapter 47

Michelle hung up from talking to Armand. He was down to the last property on the list and still had not found Brianna. She was worried but remained hopeful. Armand vowed to her that he would bring Brianna home, and she believed him. Things were still awkward between her and Sophie, but, at least, they were talking.

"Armand said he's headed to the last property."

"She has to be there, right?"

"We hope."

"Shouldn't we call the police or something?"

"Tell them what, exactly? I'm sorry, but I trust Armand to keep Brianna alive."

"I know, but this is really big, Michelle."

"Bottom line, all we have is our word. What are they going to do? I'll tell you. They'll go by and look to see if anything looks out of place. If it doesn't, they'll leave. Brianna will still be there. So, there's no point. We have no proof of anything."

"You sure seem to know a lot about this type of thing."

"Well, I don't. Armand explained it to me, and as I stated, I trust him."

"I think I'd feel more comfortable if the police were involved."

"Mom, we both know that you doing what's comfortable isn't always the best thing."

Michelle's comment cut Sophie. She knew Michelle was angry, but she didn't know how many more of these jabs she could take.

"Who is Mr. Sterling, Mom?"

Sophie did not want to discuss her past life with Michelle and did not feel the need to. Michelle was still her child. There were answers that Michelle deserved, but that was not one of them. "I took that call in another room for a reason, Michelle."

"So, we're not going to talk about how you blackmailed that man?"

"No, we're not. That is *my* business. It is *not* up for discussion."

"That's just great, Mom. Why stop keeping secrets when it's worked out so well?"

"Michelle Kaye Lewis, watch your tone. I've been patient, but you're pushing it."

Michelle rolled her eyes. She didn't care about what her mom had to say. If she did not need her help to get Brianna back, she wouldn't have stayed. She was getting upset all over again. More lies. More secrets. She decided a walk might do her some good. She could use the fresh air. She figured she'd stay outside until Armand called her back. It had to be less painful than sitting in the room any longer with her mom.

Chapter 48

Fortunately for Brianna, Javan had only verbally assaulted her. He threatened to do more, but he hadn't . . .
yet. She got the impression that he didn't want to hurt
her. The situation was beyond weird for her. She had been
trying to tell Javan that she had never meant to hurt him
and that she cared a lot about him, but he wasn't listening to her. He wanted what he wanted, and she could not
reason with him. Brianna hadn't eaten anything since the
brunch Javan had prepared several hours ago. It was now
well into the night, and she was hungry.

He did not seem to care. If she had any questions about
that, he confirmed it when he entered the room with his
plate, sat, and began to eat in front of her.

"You hungry?"

Brianna nodded her head.

"I know. This is good too. Grilled steak, salad, and
mashed potatoes covered in gravy. Really hits the spot."

"Why are you doing this?"

"Cuz you don't appreciate shit."

"You act like you don't even know me, Javan."

"Sure, I do. High class. High maintenance. Quick read."

"That's not me."

"Please! Who the fuck do you think I am? Huh?"

"I thought you loved me."

"I do, but you need to be taught how to treat a man."

"I never would have pegged you to be capable of something so cruel."

"Well, this is how you handle a bitch."

"Please, stop calling me out of my name."

"Shut up. I have barely seen you over the last few months. I had to make up some lie just to spend a few minutes with you. Who the fuck are *you?* Tamar Braxton or somebody? You ain't worth all that."

"I told you I had a lot going on. It wasn't because I didn't care."

"Fuck that. You *make* time." Javan put his fork back down on his plate. "You make time when you care!"

"I tried!"

"Fuck you! You're a damn liar, Brianna!"

"Do you talk to your mother with that mouth?"

Javan rushed at her and slapped her hard across her mouth. His plate went flying to the ground, his food scattered across the floor. "Don't ever say shit about my mother."

Brianna cried out in pain. Blood gushed from her quickly swelling lips.

Javan was furious. He couldn't believe she said that. She hadn't learned *anything*. He looked at his food spread across the floor and got even angrier. He kicked her in the stomach. Brianna grunted from the impact as his steel-toed boot crashed into her rib cage.

"Stupid bitch. Look what you did! Made me waste my food. Shit!"

This was why his previous relationships had failed to work out. Women did not know their place. Brianna was proving to be a real disappointment.

"You're crying now? Did I hurt you? I tell you what . . . Whenever I find that whore of a mother, I probably will talk to that bitch just like this. She doesn't deserve anything better. It's not like she had ever been there for me."

Brianna tried to move farther into the corner, but it hurt to move. She didn't think anything was broken, but she was pretty sure she was badly bruised.

"What did I do to you?"

"Made me love you. I wished I didn't fucking care so much. You frustrate the shit out of me. Fuck."

"Please, let me go. I'm sorry. I'll do whatever you say."

He didn't believe her, but he found some joy in hearing the words anyway. There's no way he broke her down that quickly. "I told you . . . You are free to go."

Brianna felt defeated. Tears poured from her eyes. He was not going to let her go. She was going to die there. She did the only thing she could do. She looked skyward. "God, please . . . I need some help. Please."

Javan squinted to see her in the darkness. The only light he allowed into the room was the small sliver of light that made it in from the hallway. Now he wished he would have turned on the light. He would pay good money to see the look on her face.

"God, please help me."

"He cannot help you, Brianna. No one can."

Brianna cried even harder. Her face was a palette of blood, mucus, and tears. This could not be the end for her. She had so much left she wanted to do.

"Brianna."

Brianna was broken. Her spirit was coated with a deep sadness. Why was all of this happening to her?

"Brianna, stop crying." It pained Javan to see her crying. He just wanted to love her, but she had complicated things.

Brianna kept her eyes closed and continued to pray. She didn't know what else to do. She was starting to believe Javan was going to kill her and that he was going to do it slowly. "I just want this to be over."

"Are you sure?"

Javan started to walk toward her, but he heard a noise, and it did not sound like it was coming from outside. It was quick, but he could tell it was definitely from within the house. Brianna could wait. He peeked his head out the door into the hallway but did not see anything. He walked toward the front door, in the direction that he thought the noise might have come from.

Through the frosted glass in his front door, he could make out a male figure. He clenched his fists, preparing for the worst. It was late, and he was not expecting company. He unlocked the door and slowly opened it.

"Mr. Harris."

"Doctor Baxter, what can I do for you?" Javan forced a smile for the good doctor.

"Well, as I told you earlier this week, I was on call. I just got back from the hospital and realized I hadn't heard from Brianna." Doctor Baxter waited for Javan to say something, but since he remained silent, he continued. "I told her I wanted to follow up, and I was hoping that now would be a good time."

Javan closed his eyes to hide his annoyance and kept smiling. "I completely understand. We had actually forgotten about . . . goodness . . . Anyway, she went home not too long ago. I'm afraid you missed her, but I'm sure she'll call you. You know, once things get settled."

Doctor Baxter knew Javan was lying, but he had no proof; only his gut telling him something was very wrong. He didn't bother hiding his disappointment. "Oh well, that's a shame. I guess I couldn't bother you for her contact number, or an e-mail, or something?"

"I am not comfortable giving out her personal information like that, Doctor Baxter. I figure if she wanted you to have it, she would have passed that info herself."

Doctor Baxter wanted to wipe that smug grin off his face. He kept his composure, though. "Hopefully, I will hear from her."

"Hopefully."

"By the way, I thought I saw someone on your lawn when I first pulled up, but I didn't see anything once I parked. Maybe I imagined it."

Javan didn't see any cars in the street. Doctor Baxter was just trying to scare him, and it wasn't going to work. "Looks like it. There is no one here but me."

Doctor Baxter peered into the hallway behind Javan as he closed the door, blocking his access. He did not see anything.

"Have a nice night," Javan said before closing the door.

Doctor Baxter walked home, plotting his next move. The DNA results had confirmed his suspicions. Brianna was Sophia Freemont's daughter and his bridge to a new life.

Javan went back into the house and returned to the room where he was keeping Brianna prisoner. However, Brianna was gone. He was not worried. She may have used Doctor Baxter's little intrusion to leave the room, but she had to be in the house, and she couldn't have gone far.

"I know you're in here. You can't hide," Javan laughed as he searched. This female was a trip. Where was she going to go? She was entertaining. He gave her that much credit. She kept things interesting, but there would be definite repercussions for leaving the room.

"Where are you?" Javan crept through the house, listening for her. "Brianna! You gon' pay for this shit! I don't like my time wasted, not that I had shit to do, but, still . . ."

He noticed the back door was open and smiled to himself. Of course, she went into the backyard. "We need to finish up. You said you wanted it to be over, right?"

As he reached the back door and stepped his foot out into the yard, he ran into an invisible brick wall. At least for him, that's how it felt.

Armand was waiting for him outside the door. He saw Javan's foot, surprising him with a hard left that caught him square in the jaw. Javan went flying back inside the house. He landed with a thud, confused and in shock, but he quickly scrambled to his feet. Armand was coming toward him. His mind reeled. *Who in the fuck is this?*

Javan swung and missed. Armand caught him again, this time with a right.

"Wait. Wait. Shit. Who are you?"

Armand didn't say a word. He just hit him again. And again. Javan felt like his face was on fire. His eye was swollen, and his lip was busted, but he was determined not to let this dude kick his ass. He swung wildly to create some space between him and his attacker, scooting away from him as quickly as he could.

"What do you want? Take the shit."

Armand stopped moving. Javan stood up. Armand had a few pounds on him and clearly better hands. Javan steadied himself.

"Fuck you, bitch. You caught me off guard, but I see you."

Armand was not worried about Javan's mouth. His only concern was getting Brianna out safely. Javan was in the way. Brianna was in the backyard, out of harm's way for now, but Armand would feel better if she was in his car. He didn't have time for this.

Armand ran at Javan and hit him with an uppercut. Javan felt his feet leave the tiled floor. Armand didn't even let him land. He snatched him out of the air and threw him into the hall as Javan slammed into the wall. Wasting no time, Armand picked him up again and slammed him into the opposite wall. Javan tried to stand, but Armand ran his foot into his face, breaking his nose. Javan couldn't move and was helpless as Armand kicked him repeatedly. He tasted his blood as it filled his mouth, poured from his nose, and leaked from his lips. He still couldn't find out what was on his mind: *who the fuck is this dude?*

Javan stopped moving, and Armand stood over him, satisfied that he would not pose a problem. He felt it was safe enough to walk Brianna through the house and to his car. He backpedaled out into the backyard, keeping an eye on Javan, and motioned for Brianna to join him. He noticed her hesitance. "Brianna, I know you're scared, but you need to come with me. I'll explain everything later."

Brianna still didn't move. He searched his mind for words to convince her that she could trust him. "I'm Michelle's friend. She sent me to get you. She's worried sick about you."

Brianna moved gingerly but as fast as she could to Armand's side. He still had his eyes on Javan, who was still lying in the hall motionless where Armand left him.

"I know this is scary, but you need to trust me. We're going to walk out the door. The guy that had you . . . Javan? He's lying on the floor, but he cannot hurt you. We're just going to walk past him. All right?"

Brianna nodded. "Okay."

Armand took Brianna by the hand and walked with her slightly behind him. Javan lay almost flat against the wall. As the two of them inched past him, Javan didn't flinch, never moving a muscle. They made it outside, and Armand led Brianna to his car about a block down the street.

"Stay here. I'll be right back. Lock the doors, and if you see anything—I mean anything—crank the car and leave. The keys are in the ignition."

Brianna nodded, and Armand headed back to the house. He wanted to make sure that Javan would not be a future issue. It didn't sit well with him that he didn't move when they walked past him. He was not unconscious, so Armand figured he was pretending. He didn't like loose ends, and he wanted to be certain. He made it to the house, his senses on edge, realizing the door was still open. He walked in and into the hall, but Javan was not there. Armand was afraid of that. He looked around for a few minutes but could not find him. Javan had disappeared.

"I don't know where you are, but if you can hear my voice, know this: If I see you again, I'm putting you in a body bag. Stay away from her."

He made his way back to the car, relieved to see Brianna was still waiting. "Your sister will be glad to see you."

Brianna took a deep breath and sat back in the seat, relieved to be headed home finally.

Chapter 49

Michelle did not recognize the metallic Maserati. She went back into the house to see if her mom did. Armand had told her the Marx Brothers weren't anything to lose sleep about anymore, but she was still a little rattled.

"Mom, are you expecting company?"

"No, why?"

"Someone just pulled up." Michelle pulled back the curtains far enough to allow her to peek outside and saw a man get out of the car and walk toward the house. Before she could say anything, he rang the doorbell.

Sophie went to open the door and could not believe her eyes. It was the guy from the hospital. Without thinking, she slapped him across the face. "You bastard!"

"Mom!" Michelle ran to the door and pulled her mother away. "Mom, what's going on? Who is this?"

Frank had let himself into the house. From her initial vantage point, Michelle did not get a good look at him, but now she recognized him. She understood why her mom clocked him. She felt the urge to do it herself.

Frank looked at Sophie, then turned his gaze toward Michelle. They were different shades but the same beautiful. "Where's Brianna?" he asked softly. He was not there for a fight. He just wanted to know where his daughter was.

"She was kidnapped, but my boyfriend is looking for her. We're waiting to hear from him."

"Michelle!"

"What, Mom? It's his daughter."

Sophie did not want to tell him anything. He ruined her life. Had he never showed up in the hospital room that day, none of this would have happened. She regretted ever taking his blood money. "She's *my* daughter. *I* gave birth to her."

"I *raised* her, and I deserve to know. I told you she would have the best, and she has."

Sophie hated him. He was still the same smooth-talking, arrogant bastard he had been twenty-three years ago.

"That was a mistake."

"Doesn't matter. The point is, she's just as much mine as she is yours. Deal with it."

Michelle did not know whether she should interfere or let her mother defend herself. She was frustrated with both of them. "Both of you need to go back to your corners. Mom? Frank? Frank, although you have not shown any thus far, please respect my father's house."

Frank simply wanted some answers; he had no intention of getting into it with Sophie. He just wanted Brianna. "I'm sorry, this has all just been a lot to deal with. I didn't mean any disrespect."

"You can wait here with us." Michelle shot a pleading eye to Sophie. "Right, Mom?"

Sophie wanted to say *hell no*. She didn't even want him in her house, but he had been a father to Brianna. "Fine."

"Good. Let's all take a seat. Emotions are running high. Maybe silence would be best."

Everyone seemed to agree, and each took a seat without saying another word. After a few minutes, Sophie broke it up. "How could you take advantage of me like that? I was not in an emotionally healthy place to have made a decision like that."

"Mrs. Lewis, grow up and own your part in this. I needed a child. Just like I told you, I saw an opening, and I took it. I won't apologize for it. You could have said no."

"You bastard, I didn't even know your name! I couldn't look for you. Didn't know where to look."

"Congratulations. I guess you get the prize for being a dumbass."

Frank's insult prompted Michelle to interfere. "Frank!"

He ignored her interjection. "Do you regularly give your children away to complete strangers?"

Michelle insisted on a cease-fire. "Frank, that's my mom! Stop it!" Sophie was too stunned to speak.

Frank finished mounting his defense. "It doesn't matter. Like I said before, I won't apologize for it. It worked out."

Finally, Sophie found her voice. The arrogance of Frank's rationale ushered a rebuttal. "Did it? My daughter was kidnapped!"

Frank was not about to let Sophie blame this on him. Brianna was everything to him. "*My daughter* was kidnapped, and are you saying that it had something to do with me?"

Sophie was at her wit's end realizing that the man she entrusted her daughter to may have gotten her killed. "It must have!"

Frank was done with this frivolous war of words. He was a good father, and he did not need to prove that to anyone. "I'm not doing this with you. I didn't come here to argue."

"I want answers." Sophie was flustered. The mere sight of him nauseated her. She should have never given her child to him.

"Why? It won't change anything."

"How did you even know I was in there? Why didn't I ever see you again? I waited, hoped, but it never happened."

Frank was getting more and more heated. He didn't want to answer her questions. The last thing he felt like sitting through was an interrogation. Lisa had left him. Charlie was missing in action, possibly with his child, and he didn't feel like he owed Sophie an explanation. Their exchange may not have been fair, but it was something they both agreed on, and she was not going to make him out to be the bad guy. "Stop talking to me."

Michelle cut her eyes at him. "Please."

Frank cleared his throat and contemplated leaving. There was too much estrogen in one room for him, not to mention that neither woman cared for him, but at least Michelle was being reasonable.

Sophie was about to say something when another car pulled up. Michelle ran eagerly to the window and peered outside. "Mom, it's Armand!" She ran outside and screamed with glee at the sight of Brianna in the passenger seat. "Brianna! Oh my God! Bria!"

She opened Brianna's door and could see she was in pain. She knelt down by the door and rested her head on Brianna's lap, tears of joy streaming down her face. Frank and Sophie watched from inside. They wanted to run out also but thought it better to let Brianna and Michelle have some time. They had already taken so much time from them.

Brianna rubbed Michelle's hair and took it all in. It was real. She was safe. Michelle stood up and helped Brianna out of the car.

Armand came around to assist, but Michelle waved him off. She wanted to do it alone. She didn't need to thank him. He could see it in her eyes. As Brianna and

Michelle walked slowly into the house, Michelle tried to warn her of what awaited them inside.

"There's a lot I have to tell you, but we can talk later."

"Did you find out who our parents are?"

"Yes, and . . . well . . ."

"What is it?"

"They're inside."

"They are?"

Michelle nodded and gave Brianna a half smile.

They had made it into the den where Frank and Sophie were waiting. Brianna burst into tears and hobbled to Frank. "I thought you were dead!"

Frank wrapped her up in a big hug and held her close. He was so glad Brianna was safe. Nothing else mattered. "No, I'm not dead. I'm here, baby girl. Can't get rid of me that easy. Are you okay?"

Brianna was so happy she couldn't stop smiling. "I am now."

Michelle touched Brianna's arm to get her attention. Brianna let go of her father and looked at her. Michelle walked over to Sophie.

"Brianna, I'd like you to meet your birth mother."

Brianna felt her face warm. She couldn't believe it. Her mother, *her birth mother,* was standing there in the same room. She hobbled to her and lay her head on her shoulder. Sophie held her daughter for only the second time in her life; her heart filled with sadness thinking about all the hugs she missed. She was joyful, knowing that she would not have to miss her anymore. Brianna stood in Sophie's embrace for a good while, basking in her love.

Then Sophie lifted her daughter's face and held it in her hands. "I've always loved you. I held you in my heart, every day. Every night, I sang a song for you. I'm so happy to have you home."

"This is not her home," Frank protested. He was not about to stand by and let Sophie try to take his daughter. "She's coming home with me."

"Dad?" Brianna looked at Michelle posing the question with her eyes.

Michelle shook her head no. "He's gone. I'm sorry, Bria. It was sudden, and the funeral was a week ago."

Brianna's knees gave way as she realized the father Mike was referring to was not Frank but her biological father. Sophie helped her to sit on the couch. Brianna was overcome with sadness. She would never get the chance to meet him. It wasn't fair. The news made her mourn all over again. She had dealt with the loss, had the man she knew as her father returned to her, only to have the other man who was biologically tied to her taken away.

"Brianna, you still have me, okay? I'm your father."

"Shut up." Michelle didn't want to hear Frank say another word.

"Michelle!"

"No, Bria . . . I'm tired."

"Michelle, he's my dad. Relax."

"Frank, are you going to tell her?" Michelle's eyes turned in his direction, causing everyone in the room to follow suit.

Frank grew silent. His mouth went dry, and he strove to find the words.

"Tell me what? Dad?"

"Brianna, I'm not sure how to tell you this but—"

"He bought you, Bria."

"What? What is she talking about, Dad?"

"I did. I went into the hospital room, and I saw you, and I wanted you. I offered, and she accepted."

"She?" Brianna looked at the woman she learned was her mother. Sophie could not meet her gaze. "Mom?"

"It's true, Brianna, and it was a horrible decision. I wasn't thinking clearly. After that, I looked for you, but I couldn't find you. I looked everywhere. You have to believe me."

Brianna was heartbroken. She didn't know what she was expecting, but she had not expected this. She was *sold?* She looked at Michelle with tears in her eyes. Michelle got up and sat beside her on the couch. She wrapped her arm around her sister. "We're in this together."

Sophie was still trying to plead her case. "I have *always* loved you. I just couldn't find you. It was like I had imagined you."

"Get off it. If you wanted her, you would not have sold her to me," Frank snapped.

Michelle felt like she would be sick. "How could you say something like that?"

Armand could see how much distress Michelle was in. He didn't like it. If Michelle had a problem, *he* had a problem. He decided to interject himself into the fray. "There's a reason she couldn't find her, isn't there, Frank? That was not by accident."

Frank looked at Armand. He didn't recognize him. "Who are you?"

"It doesn't matter, but I know what you did."

Michelle stared wide-eyed at Armand, anticipating the answer.

Armand's answer would shock the room. "I worked for the Marx Brothers. Mike told me what you did."

Frank felt the bottom fall out. Now he would need to tell the truth; there was no way around it. He looked at Brianna preparing for the worst.

Armand continued his confession. "Frank hired the Marx Brothers to watch Michelle and this family. He wanted to ensure that you two never ran into each other."

Brianna could not believe it. "Dad, is this true?"

"I just wanted to protect you. I was going to tell you."

"So *you* are the reason they were parked outside my place all this time; you had them watching me?" Michelle felt violated. This was unbelievable. "*You* are the reason they grabbed Brianna!"

Brianna stood and leaped toward Frank, swinging wildly. She was crying hysterically and screaming at the top of her lungs. All of the agony and despair she had amassed over the last few weeks burst forth from her. "How could you do this? I almost died!"

"Bria, there's nothing I could say that would make up for this. I'm sorry. I just didn't want to lose you. I love you so much. One thing led to another, and I was in so deep . . . I couldn't see the way out. I hope you can forgive me."

Brianna cried in Frank's arms. He held her while she hit him. Together, they fell to the floor.

"He *beat* me, Dad," she sobbed. "It's all *your* fault."

Brianna bawled until she lost her voice. Frank rocked her back and forth in his lap just as he did when she was a little girl, hoping to bring some comfort to her. He was truly sorry for what he had done. Brianna was the absolute last person he ever wanted to bring any harm to.

Sophie wished she were deaf. This was all so horrific. Frank could have gotten them killed. The guilt of her decision crept into her mind, and she couldn't say anything. She was no better than Frank. They all could have made better choices.

Different choices.

Brianna and Frank sat on the floor for hours. Sophie, Michelle, and Armand each in a chair. Everyone waited for someone else to speak; to break the dilapidating silence. They needed time to digest it all. Time to celebrate the truth and Brianna's safety. Time to mourn all that they had lost along the way. Things would never be the same for them, but at least they had each other. Starting over will be difficult but not impossible. Each, on their own, had to figure how to adjust to their new reality. To live in the truth. To embrace their new normal.

Epilogue

One month later . . .

Doctor Baxter used his professional contacts to track Brianna down. Fortunately for him, Brianna kept all of her medical information up to date, so it was fairly easy to reach her. It turned out, he didn't need Javan's help after all. She had been home for a few days when she got his call. She was a little bothered by his intrusion into her personal affairs but felt his concern was heartfelt. He expressed the apprehension he had at leaving her with Javan, and she filled him in on the grisly details. He convinced her to seek counseling with a close friend of his. Brianna conceded and agreed to keep in touch.

Doctor Shepherd pushed the thin, ruby-red plastic brim of her glasses farther onto her face, shielding her slightly rose-colored eyes from Brianna's devilishly alluring scowl. Her naturally curly auburn hair was pulled back in a loose ponytail. She hoped this session would go smoothly. "Brianna, shall we begin?"

"Sure."

"Would you like to pick up where we left off?"

"Not really."

Doctor Miya Shepherd, according to Doctor Baxter, was supposed to be one of the best in the area, but Brianna didn't feel like they were getting anywhere in these sessions. She remained calm, despite Brianna's apprehension. "That's fine. You may begin whenever you'd like."

"This isn't working."

"What isn't working, Brianna?"

"I'm not crazy."

"I agree. You are *not* crazy."

"What's your purpose, then?"

Doctor Shepherd ran a successful practice for the past ten years. Most of her clientele were from referrals, and she showed no favoritism. But she had begun to see Doctor Baxter in a different light lately, and since he recommended Brianna, that made her special. If she played her cards right and gave Brianna the proper treatment, perhaps Doctor Baxter would treat her to a little something. She never mixed business with pleasure, but this once she would make an exception. She wanted that man like Mister wanted Shug in *The Color Purple,* and she would have him one way or another.

"My purpose or the purpose of our sessions?"

Brianna stared at her blankly.

"Why did you try to kill yourself, Brianna?"

"I didn't."

"What were you trying to do, then?"

Brianna placed her index finger on her battle scar. The spot above her temple where the bullet grazed her skin. Armand had saved her, again.

"Feel. I wanted to feel something other than fear. I am sick to death of being afraid."

"Let's explore that, Brianna."

Brianna rolled her eyes and checked the time. Forty minutes to go. "Shadows send me into cardiac arrest. I don't feel safe unless I'm in the company of others. If a cat blinks, I'm tempted to swing on it. Do you know what that feels like? It's torture."

"I understand . . . That must be frustrating."

Brianna's frustration rose to the surface. This woman had no clue what she was going through. If she did . . .

She didn't let on. Her entire life had changed. She had gone from being a strong, independent woman to being regulated and managed like a completely dependent child.

"I would rather die than continue to live in fear." Brianna looked out the big bay window overlooking the Big D. "I'm just tired of being afraid."

"Brianna, your fear is natural. You went through a terrible ordeal. Give yourself time."

"Sure."

"Are you still living with Armand and Michelle?"

"Temporarily."

"Yes, temporarily."

"I am. I still have my condo. I like to visit my old life."

Doctor Shepherd made a notation on her legal pad. Brianna was suffering from a clear case of PTSD, post-traumatic stress disorder. She was confident that she could help Brianna to regain her independence by restoring her faith in herself; in her ability to protect herself.

"Good. You need to be around family."

"Family is a loose concept for me, Doctor."

Brianna was still not talking to Frank and trying to adjust to having Sophie in her life. Michelle was all the family she had. Well, the only member she couldn't cut off. She had only spoken with Lisa long enough to let her know she was safe.

"There is a long road ahead of you, Brianna, but eventually, you'll find your footing and accept this new normal."

The doctor's words did little to ease her fears or calm her nerves. In a few minutes, she would have to leave and those eyes, wherever they were, would be on her. She knew it. They always were. It was unnerving.

"You stated that you like to visit your old life. Will you elaborate on that, please?"

Brianna was still grieving the things she lost. Her family . . . the confidence she once had to walk out the door and suspect nothing would happen. It was a false sense of security that she had taken for granted. She would give everything to get it back. "I don't know who I am anymore. I have a mother that I don't know. I love my sister, but she's connected to this change. I don't know if I want to accept it. My life has been in a downward spiral ever since I walked into that restaurant."

"You mean, the day you met Michelle."

Brianna wiped the tear from her eye. She hated that she blamed Michelle, but she couldn't help it. Everything changed for her that day. "No . . . yes . . . I don't know. I just don't know."

"I think you do know, Brianna." Doctor Shepherd decided to push her a little further. "Michelle is just as much a victim as you. The tendency to blame someone for this unspeakable turn of events is completely normal. I know this might sound off base, but out of all those who deserve the responsibility, Michelle deserves the least."

"What are you talking about, Doctor Shepherd?"

"Your parents. Not talking to your dad is not helpful and this happy façade you have with your mom is going to ensure your place here."

Brianna took a deep breath. She knew what Doctor Shepherd was doing. It was the same thing she had been trying to do since Brianna started seeing her. She wanted her to blame her mother, to be angry with Sophie, but Brianna couldn't do that. "I just got her. I hardly even know her, but I'm a part of her. It's the strangest feeling. I have her eyes, nose, and even a few habits, but I don't know anything about her."

"Are you afraid she'll leave again?"

"Maybe."

Doctor Shepherd noted the time. "For our last ten minutes, I thought we should discuss your expectations for this meeting at her home. I want to make sure you're up for it."

It was not the possibility of what may transpire at her mother's that Brianna was worried about. Getting there was the bigger issue. "I'll be fine."

"Are you sure certain? What is this meeting about?"

Brianna shrugged her shoulders. "I don't know."

Doctor Shepherd was concerned that Brianna was not giving the situation the proper attention. "Considering what happened during your previous visit, are you truly certain about this?"

"If you are referring to my hitting her with the frying pan, I explained that it was an accident. I thought she was a burglar. She was not supposed to be home."

"She wanted to surprise you."

"I don't like surprises!"

Doctor Shepherd remained expressionless, unmoved by Brianna's outburst.

"Not anymore."

Two minutes.

"I'll be fine."

Brianna felt her phone vibrating. Their time was up.

Michelle was shaking with excitement. She couldn't believe it was happening. Armand stood before her on one knee with the most beautiful ring in his hand that she'd ever laid eyes on.

"Michelle Kaye Lewis . . . I love you. There is no other woman for me. You have given more than I can express in this way. If you'll have me . . . I'd like to try to be the man you need and deserve for the rest of my life. Will you marry me, MK?"

"Yes! Yes, Armand!" She didn't need to think about it. She loved Armand and knew that her heart was safe in his capable hands.

He slid the ring on her finger and scooped her up into his arms. He showered her with kisses and cried tears of pure joy. Michelle would one day be Mrs. Armand LaCroix, and he couldn't be happier.

"I was not expecting this, Armand! It's marvelous."

"That's kinda the point, MK." he laughed. "I know the timing seems off, but I wanted to do it before we got to your mom's for the reading. I don't know what we will find out. I wanted you to be assured that regardless of whatever may come . . . I'm yours."

Michelle grabbed his face with her hands and planted a wet one on him. "You are so incredibly thoughtful. I love you."

"Love you too."

"Well, we need to get out of here. Mom will not be happy if we're late."

"You need to be nice, Michelle."

"Thanks for ruining the mood."

"Listen," Armand began, taking her hands into his, "I just want things to go smoothly. Brianna has been having a rough time."

Michelle opened her mouth to interrupt, but he placed a finger over her mouth to silence her. "I know you have too, but Brianna has not adjusted as well as you have."

Michelle conceded.

"I am simply suggesting that you put your issues with your mother to the side for her sake."

This is why she loved this man.

"Of course. For Brianna, I'll be cordial."

"That's my girl."

They shared a brief kiss, grabbed their things, and left their townhome for Sophie's humble abode.

***

It did not take Frank very long to locate Lisa. He may not have known a lot about his wife's past, but he knew her habits and how much she loved Saint Maarten. He flew out of DFW airport, caught a connecting flight in New York, spent a few days there, and then took the first flight out of LaGuardia. He had been on the island for about four days or so, watching Lisa and waiting for the right time to approach her.

He was walking along the beach enjoying the breeze when he heard it. The wind carried it gently and tucked it away in his ear. His mind's eye replayed it over and over again. The beautiful wave showing its dominion over the Caribbean, the sun's rays kissing the sea's surface, a child's hearty laugh at the expense of a younger sibling . . . then that word.

"*Franklin.*"

Frank turned around to face his wife. She was gorgeous in her white bikini. To be so near to forty, it was obvious that Father Time had been kind to her. He stood gawking for a moment, completely captivated by her.

"Franklin."

"Lisa. Surprised to find you here."

Lisa laughed, adjusting her white, wide-brimmed straw hat to give her some protection from the relentless shine of the earth's brightest star. "What are you doing here, Mr. Mason?"

"Well, I have come to get my wife. Have you seen her?"

"Nope. What made you think she was here?"

"I know a few things about her. Maybe not everything I should but the important things." Frank pointed to his temple. "The important things I have sealed for emergencies."

"I see. What else do you know? Maybe I could help you look."

Lisa was shocked when she saw Frank walking around two days ago. She expected that he would look for her, but she didn't expect him to find her. She didn't think he knew enough about her, but apparently, she was wrong . . . and was kind of glad she was.

"I know she likes to dance, and she has a pretty awesome singing voice too."

"Oh really?"

"Yea . . . She has like an Anita Baker meets Karyn White thing going on."

"You're a mess."

"I miss you, Lisa. Can we go somewhere and talk?"

Frank felt his phone vibrating. It was probably Charlie calling again. She had been calling nonstop since he told her where he was headed. He didn't feel like talking to her at the moment. She could leave a voice mail. There was a chance he could get his money back . . . and his wife too. He was not going to let Charlie ruin it.

"Come on, Lisa."

Lisa weighed her options. She had been in Saint Maarten for nearly a month and had loved every minute, but she had missed Frank. She missed Brianna. On some level, she even missed Charlie. One conversation couldn't hurt, and if it did open a door for them to repair their marriage . . . Maybe that wouldn't be such a bad thing. "Sure, we can go to my room. Follow me."

Lisa entered her suite with Frank just a few steps behind her. "Can I get you anything to drink?"

"No, I'm fine, thank you."

His phone vibrated again. Charlie was getting on his last nerve.

"May I use your restroom?"

"Down the hall to the right." After noticing the flashing red light on the suite's courtesy phone blinking, she added, "I have a few messages anyway. I'll check those while you're in there."

"Great, thanks. I'll just be a moment."

Frank closed the bathroom door behind him and turned on the faucet so that the water would run as loud as possible. He also turned on the fan to help drown out his voice while he made the phone call. "Charlie, what is it?"

"Did you find her?"

"Stop calling me."

"We have a child, Frank!"

"*You* have a child. I don't know if that kid is mine or not."

"Did you find her?"

"That is none of your business." Frank tried to stay calm, but he was losing his patience.

"It doesn't matter anyway." Charlie sounded cryptic.

"Right. What was your endgame, huh? Hit me up for eighteen years for someone else's mistake? Leave me alone, Charlie."

"Whatever. If you did find her, I suggest you not let her listen to any messages."

"What in the hell are you talking about, Charlie?"

"I may have let our little secret out."

Frank dropped his phone and ran out of the bathroom without even turning the water off. He struggled to breathe as his lungs filled with regret. His eyes filled with horror at the view before him once he reached the living area of the suite. Blood was everywhere. He dropped to his knees as tears streamed down his face. He cried so hard his eyes hurt, and he wished with all his heart he could un-see what he saw. If he could have just one more chance, he would take it all back. He swore he would take it all back.

Brianna could have sworn she smelled a familiar cologne as she left Doctor Shepherd's office, the same scent that Javan always wore, but she tried to convince herself she was imagining things. Doctor Shepherd advised her that paranoia was completely normal given everything she had gone through. It seemed like every problem she had was completely normal. She didn't want to be normal anymore. Despite her reservations, she made it to her mom's home without incident. Sophie had been a damn chatterbox the whole fifteen minutes she had been there. It was like she was constantly trying to make up for lost time, but Brianna didn't need that. That part of her life was gone as far as she was concerned. She was never getting it back.

"Mom, please," Brianna forced a laugh. "Give your lips a rest."

"I know, I'm talking a lot. I just . . . It's always good to see you, Brianna."

While Sophie was pleased with the speed at which their relationship progressed, she was equally devastated by the rate that her relationship with Michelle was deteriorating. She had no apologies left. It was up to Michelle at this point, and that girl was as stubborn as a mule. Sophie was adjusting to her life without Lewis. It was not what she expected it would be, but she was still trying to enjoy her freedom. Lewis's lawyer called and notified her that Lewis had drafted a will shortly before he died. Naturally, she was surprised because Lewis had not said a word to her about it, but then, that was his MO. She called the girls immediately to let them know about it. This was the day when everyone would be available for the reading, so they had arranged for the lawyer to come to the house.

"Mrs. Lewis, hello."

Sophie looked up to see Armand strolling in with Michelle on his arm.

"Hi, Armand."

Armand gave Michelle a little nudge. Michelle huffed briefly before speaking. "Hi, Bria . . . Mom."

"Hi, Michelle."

Brianna started to speak, but the lawyer walked in before she could. She mouthed a hello to Michelle and her beau before turning her attention to the lawyer, a partner at her Uncle J's firm. She really hated surprises. He had stepped in for Jacob since he was still in recovery and unable to attend. Jacob had been Lewis's lawyer. She was certain she didn't want to know how or why her uncle had kept Lewis a secret from her all these years. Brianna sat through another round of uncomfortable introductions before the lawyer got down to business. He read the will, and for the most part, it was pretty standard. Then he read the following:

"And to my children, I leave $15 million in bonds, to be divided equally."

The girls looked at Sophie, who was as shocked as they were. Lewis did not know about Brianna. Sophie had only told him minutes before he passed. Suddenly, they heard a knock at the door, and Armand got up to answer it. Brianna, Michelle, and Sophie were discussing how he could have possibly known when Michelle heard a familiar voice say hello. She looked up to see Charlie waddling into the room, holding her very round belly.

"I heard Lewis left a will. I thought that *we* should be present for the reading."

They each looked at one another with their mouths agape. Brianna looked at Charlie and rolled her eyes. "That child is the only thing keeping me from chunking something at your face. In fact, I still might."

Then Brianna looked at Sophie and wondered if she was breathing. It didn't look like it. She really hated surprises. What would Doctor Shepherd have to say about *this* mess? Surely, this wasn't completely normal—or was it? Nah. Brianna took a seat beside Sophie on the couch. She still hadn't seen her breathe.

"Mom. Mom, are you all right?"

Sophie looked at her and realized her mouth was dry. She closed it but remained silent for a moment. "I don't know, Brianna. I'm not sure what to do or how to feel."

"Well . . . You still have that frying pan?"

Sophie laughed a little at the joke, but she kept her eyes on Charlie's belly. She didn't know whether Lewis fathered that child, but she knew one thing for certain: that bastard would not get any part of her girls' money. She didn't know who this woman was or what her plans were, but she should not have come to her home. Sophie would do *anything* to protect her daughters. If she made love to her husband and still had enough steel in her veins to watch him die by her hand, she knew getting rid of this trick would be easy.

Sophie smiled, rose to her feet, and extended her hand to Charlie. "Hi, I'm Sophie Lewis, and you are . . . ?"